UNUSUAL EFFUSION

100 Short Stories

DANIEL L. CINELLI

ISBN-13: 9780692538678
ISBN-10: 0692538674
Library of Congress Control Number: 2015915608
Daniel Cinelli, Port Charlotte, Florida

INTRODUCTION

The following short stories represent the author's unfettered works inspired by a lifetime of diverse experiences; however, they should in no way be construed as anything other than fiction. Having said that, I must continue my admission that many of the more poignant aspects have been stimulated into the written word by myriad pinpricks endured during real-life experiences.

If at times a portrayal seems irreverent, you are not mistaken. It is my belief that many of the political causes—so prevalent in our society today and that manifest themselves as political correctness while attaining their agendas— tend to repress the written art form, and it is with this conviction that I strike a blow for freedom.

If there is any group or cause that I have omitted and thus failed to offend, it is not intentional. Close proximity to liberal causes has left me with the belief that the abused, when given the opportunity, soon become the abusers. It is through this lens that I have woven many of these stories.

THE MOLE RUNS

It was 1867, two years after the end of the American Civil War, and the widow of a mortally wounded Confederate soldier, who lived only briefly after returning home, struggled to feed her three small children on a small mortgaged Virginia farmstead. She had been reduced to growing yams and corn for sustenance. Just over the property line were the remains of a once-magnificent plantation house. Large marble columns were now strewn at odd angles, and piles of what had been ornate woodwork lay about in various stages of decay—stark reminders of a lost world.

Now a widow with three children—a boy of ten and two girls, two and three years of age—she wondered how they would survive, when the boy came rushing into the house clutching a gold coin. He had unearthed it while tilling the soil in preparation for the planting of pole beans. She knew it to be a $20 double-eagle gold piece minted in 1850. In today's money, it has the buying power of $1,200. The mother was ecstatic. It was 90 percent gold with a 10 percent copper alloy. It was twice the value of the eagle coin, hence the designation *double-eagle* and was first minted in 1849.

The boy led her to the point of origin. She inquired about the depth, and the boy indicated it was just below the surface. She wondered whether someone had dropped a single coin at random or if it was a token of a larger cache hidden somewhere beneath the surface. Reasoning that there could be more, she began to turn over the soil in an ever-increasing circle, with the origin of the coin as its center. After several hours and a circle that was now thirty feet in diameter, she had unearthed two more double-eagle coins. She carefully marked the locations with stakes. It was too little to establish a pattern. With the coming of darkness, thinking it unwise to work by the light of a lantern, she retired to her cabin to feed her children. They had subsisted at near-poverty levels, and their fare that evening was typical of their diet. It consisted of bacon, corn bread dipped in bacon grease, seed potatoes, and fallen, runt apples from an old decrepit tree. She pondered how her new wealth would change all that, and then in fit of realization, she admonished her little boy to maintain secrecy lest hordes of treasure seekers descend on her property like locusts.

The next morning found her hard at work, and at midmorning she was near giddy when a fourth coin sparkled in the daylight for the first time in only providence knew when. She marked the location with a fourth stake and stepped back to gaze at the pattern from all angles. Still, she could discern nothing, but by the end of the day, a fifth coin presented itself. A fifth stake was driven in, and now with the sun casting longer shadows, something began to stand out in sharp relief. The last coin was found in the midst of a freshly dug mole tunnel. The tunnels, called mole runs, were just below the surface so that a distinct ridge existed along its track if freshly dug.

She followed this mole run, first in one direction, and placed a rock at its terminus and then going back in the other direction, where she found it disappeared beneath a granite boulder approximately eight feet in diameter and five feet high. Circumnavigating the boulder, she found other mole runs radiating from it and began to unearth each tunnel in turn. Her heart began to race as she unearthed a sixth coin in one run and then a seventh in another. She stood up slowly, gazed at the boulder, and then with wobbling legs entered the cabin, where she dusted off a long-since-neglected jug of corn liquor and took a deep draft. Thus fortified, she took a long-handled shovel and began to dig a pit alongside the boulder, and from it, to tunnel beneath it.

Soon the shovel caved in the side of a well-rotted wooden box, and in the same instant a cascade of brightly colored double-eagle gold coins showered down, nearly covering her boots. It was too much excitement at once, and she involuntarily soiled herself. She thought about the ruins of the plantation house only a stone's throw away and how the owner, a colonel Nathaniel Oglethorpe, may have hidden the cache by the light of a lantern. With his death, it lay long forgotten. She thought about the moles, who for whatever the reason, had found these brightly colored coins irresistible, and clenching them tightly in their jaws, had transported them to and fro.

She climbed out from the pit, sat down, and descended into deep thought. She was a lone widow with three young children and possessed not a single firearm. Between the greedy carpetbaggers and the bands of marauders who still roamed the countryside, she would be cheated of everything and left bereft. She determined that secrecy was her only recourse. She swore the boy to such, and in the years that followed, various improvements in their diet and to the property took place ever so slowly.

Eventually she acquired shares in a lumber business and then its complete ownership. Last, she sent all three children to eastern colleges. To the occasional query about how she managed to do so well, she would always wink and attribute it to frugality and the sale of homemade jams and jellies early on.

KALLEN STREET

I t is 1980, and I am recently divorced—a month to be exact. I have two dependent daughters who live with their mother here in Buffalo, New York. A lady
friend of mine has provided me with a third-floor apartment at a very favorable
rent. It is in a nineteenth-century mansion on fashionable Delaware Avenue and
is paneled in mahogany throughout. It is stately but quiet and lonely.

Two blocks away is Kallentown, a district in Buffalo similar in freestyle living to Greenwich Village in Manhattan. It is everything the mansion district is
not, and I soon gravitate there. A sprawling Greek café on the corner of Kallen
and Ashland streets is a hub of activity, and I have been there numerous times.
Many of the regulars I know by name now, and I move freely among them.

Being open all night on Christmas Eve, it is the last refuge of warmth and
conviviality in a world otherwise cold and heartless. As I enter, I look to my
left to see Fred—an elderly man, neatly dressed, of quiet dignity, long since
forgotten by relatives—seated at the counter. He is communing with a bowl of
macaroni and cheese, and it is probably his only hot meal today. I put a hand on
his shoulder, and he looks up and smiles.

Coming up on my right is Evelyn—a retired artist of some sort—seated at
a small table by herself in quiet dignity, still possessed of her physical charms.
She looks up at me and in motherly fashion admonishes, "A dollar and a cup of
coffee are your only friends in this world." I answer, "I gotta agree with ya," and
we smile.

I turn to see Frank—a highly intelligent retired court stenographer, always dressed immaculately in a business suit—seated at the counter. He has battled paranoia all his life, but if you can overlook that, he has excellent tips on the stock market, and he helps me to prosper.

Continuing on, I pass Larry, also seated at the counter. Waitresses are visibly nervous in his presence. The dead body of a nude woman was found in his bathtub with a cross carved into her chest. The apartment had been broken into, and he is released for lack of evidence. I smile as I pass.

Moving farther down, I seat myself at a stool and order coffee, a seafood dinner for myself, and a shrimp salad to be served anonymously to Evelyn, the dollar-and-a-cup-of-coffee lady. In less than a minute, an attractive lady in her midtwenties, with short black hair, seats herself beside me and strikes up a conversation. I am enthralled and can't believe my good luck. At a point where I feel I have taken the hook and it has firmly set, she excuses herself saying she will be back and for me to save her stool. She leaves the café, and through the plate glass windows I see her stride to the middle of the intersection, pull down her slacks, squat down, and urinate. Strangely, though she has stopped traffic, there is not a single horn blown in protest, and true to her word, she returns to claim her stool. Having finished my seafood dinner, though it is all-you-can-eat fish night, I refrain from ordering more knowing that the second helping will be the envy of the Goodyear Tire and Rubber Company, having been overcooked. Opposite my seat at the counter is the stairway down to the cellar kitchen. The Greek American owner's wife passes me and descends halfway down the stairs. She is a lusty American lady sporting a lot of meat on the hoof, a preference among Greek men. In the sheltered stairwell she hikes up her skirt and looks up at me. Because she has my attention, I stare back and blow her a kiss, being careful that she does not feel jilted. Not wanting to wind up in the lamb stew, I do not pursue the invitation.

A hush falls over the congregation as Rodney enters, a black American charged with running a boys' prostitution ring. He is out on bail and takes a seat at the counter. As I am finishing my last cup of coffee, Elizabeth walks in, asks a patron to move down a stool, and sits down beside me. Elizabeth resembles a fifty-five-year-old Rita Hayworth. She had been a fashion designer in New York, is well off, divorced, and lives in a high-rise condominium half a block away.

She has long auburn hair that hangs down to her waist, and after locking eyes with you—which I always equated with the tractor beam on *Star Trek*—would proceed to stroke those long strands of hair much the way a musician strokes the strings on a harp. Thoroughly enchanted and able to identify with a fly caught in a web, I find myself escorting her to her condominium where I am served liberal helpings of carnal delight. A dish, that I understand has been in the family for aeons. The next day, I find a long-stemmed rose tucked under my windshield wiper with a thank-you card signed Elizabeth.

Years later, as I now sit in the food court of the Town Center Mall, sipping a Starbucks coffee, I can't help thinking that things are no longer as biotic as they once were in those days.

MY DOG FLAG

It was with great anticipation that I headed for the dog shelter one crisp winter morning. I had finally decided that I was ready for a dog, not just any dog. I wanted to experience the wolf. He was not to be my robot cloaked in fur. I wanted to savor every whim, quirk, and fury within reason. Soon the matron was escorting me down the row of cages. As we passed, she rattled the wire screen with her knout. I found a more motley-looking collection of hounds than I had ever seen until I came to one cage that contained an extraordinarily beautiful golden retriever. He was snarling furiously, left and right, at whatever dog caught his attention. The matron exclaimed, "He don't like other dogs," and then spit a wad of tobacco juice over her shoulder as if to emphasize her point. It was readily apparent that he was a male, one year of age, house trained, and with a soft long-haired reddish coat complete with recurving tail. The color reminded me of an Irish setter. The face was nothing less than handsome with large intelligent eyes and a wolf-like regal bearing. Indulging his aggression against the other dogs, he took no notice of me. The matron allowed me to take him out on a leash. As we threaded our way through the tobacco juice, I felt like the caboose on the end of a locomotive. He could easily have found employment as a sled dog. Alone together, outside the shelter, I could not get him to look at me. No matter how I maneuvered, he would further turn his head to avoid my gaze. An inner voice told me I had to have a hole in my head to adopt this dog; so with that little bit of insight in mind, I realized we would be a perfect match.

He proved to be everything I wanted and everything I had never imagined. Despite his retriever-like appearance, his idea of retrieving imparted a new twist to the game, which usually left me befuddled. Upon returning the rag doll, he would accept his treat and in the same instant, with lightning speed, repossess the doll. Confused and embarrassed and not willing to admit I had been taken to the cleaners, I would find myself feigning ignorance of his little confidence game.

During walks on the street, when in the presence of a lady, he would always ignore my commands, as if to show her he was his own dog.

At night he was free to roam the entire house. His favorite thing—and this would happen three or four times a night—was to jump on the bed and with great force slam his body into mine, back to back. I'd turn my head to face him; we'd lock eyes—he with his tongue hanging half out—and stare at each other for thirty seconds. I'd think to myself, "OK, he likes to throw his weight around," and go back to sleep.

Now lest the reader thinks that Flag was just another gay blade, let me tell you that he was a working dog. I was sole owner-operator of an upscale lawn maintenance business, and Flag would accompany me on my rounds six days a week. It was Flag's duty to guard the truck, trailer, and equipment from theft and harm. We never lost a single piece of equipment. Oftentimes a gaggle of housewives would gather at the trailer and Flag would play them for all they were worth. His favorite ploy was to abruptly snub a housewife's palm. This would startle her, and in a minute she would disappear and return with an assortment of chopped meat gleaned from her refrigerator. I saw him use this tactic time and time again.

At the end of the route, Flag would ride with me in the cab with his head and neck out the side window, looking straight ahead. He was not your typical kid in a fire engine. He had the demeanor of a naval PT boat commander. As we flew by other dogs, he would deliver a salvo of barks designed to startle both dog and owner. He exuded both nerve and courage, and many times I ran a red light after looking into his steely eyes.

Then there was the habit of his of looking up at me, locking eyes after I had given him a command. It was as if to say, "You gotta be joking" or "Are you sure you wanna do this?" It always made me think twice.

There was the time he ran off into the densely wooded lots next door to disappear for four hours. I was highly distraught and kept circling, calling out his name. Eventually I dozed off on a lawn chair to be awakened by a hot moist tongue. Sure enough, it was Romeo, and he was covered from nose to tail in burrs.

The time in the late evening when I secured the garage and Flag and I were alone in the brightly lit interior—Flag began to give off a low menacing growl. His attention was focused at the base of a low-slung cabinet. Try as I might, I could not see what it was without getting on all fours and lowering my head to the floor. As I did so, a large black snake, five feet in length, sprung out at my head. As I tensed up expecting my face to be punctured, I felt a furry jaw shoot across the top of my head intercepting the snake. He pulled the entire snake out, bodily snapping its neck, and followed it up with powerful lightning-like bites. Still shaking, I rose, dusted myself off, and thanked him profusely.

Regarding his appearance, it was soon apparent that women were enchanted by his looks. His favorite lady was my good friend Peg. He would pose himself dutifully in front of her with one paw resting on her lap while she petted him. Yes, he had an eye for women, and so it was that Peg and I took him to the environmental center to hike along the numerous trails. I packed a liter of ice water and a water bowl for Flag's consumption. The day was exceptionally beautiful with plenty of sunshine and reasonable temperature. I could feel by his tug that he was enjoying himself immensely. But on this particular hike, it became very apparent that something had gone very wrong with Flag. His breathing became very audible and abruptly turned into a hoarse rapid cadence at which point he collapsed onto his side. He was able to lift his head and vocalize small incoherent barks. I filled his bowl with ice water and put his head over it; his tongue hung down into the water, but he was never able to drink. A wave of anguish, despair, and hopelessness swept over me. I dragged him into the shade, left Peg there to watch him, and ran back down the trail to the visitor's center. "I need a wheelbarrow!" I blurted out to the clerk. She opened the maintenance shed and I yanked out a two-wheeled cart. Swarms of birds rose along the trail as I galloped along. The cart at times bounced high in the air, which was heavy with the fragrance of blossoms, but I could smell only death. On my arrival I could see that he was in worse condition. I loaded him onto the cart and proceeded to the car as gently as possible. With the air conditioner on full blast, I dropped off Peg and sped to the animal hospital. From the veterinarian, the only tangible piece of information I got was "Flag's in a bad way." He did let slip one pertinent fact, which enabled me to render a prognosis of what was to come. As I left Flag there for overnight intravenous fluids and pain killers, he mentioned that the dog's temperature was 107 degrees. When I got home I referred to my reference library and found that at 107 degrees a dog's brain will cook.

At about eight o'clock that evening, the vet called to say that Flag had died. Having anticipated the outcome, I was already in a state of shock. Peg and I arrived the next morning for a final farewell. He was laid out on a blanket and was all shampooed and fluffed up. His eyes were open and bright, and aside from having absolutely no movement it was impossible to tell that he had left us. I brushed the side of my cheek back and forth across his jowl, and my tears began to flow copiously. "Good-bye, my child, my buddy, my cohort, my faithful companion." When I walked out of the room, I left my heart on that gurney.

For the next week, I cried numerous times a day. Relief came only when I rescued, from the pound, another young dog who was five months of age. His name is Tony, and I often speak to him about the legacy of his predecessor. Tony has filled all expectations and more, but that's another story

THE SNOWPLOW

I f you have ever tried to rebuild your life after a divorce, you know how agonizing it can be. I was thirty-eight years of age with two dependent daughters
living with their mother. After twelve years of marriage—the first ten of which
were the happiest of my life and the last two the worst—I was steadily building
up a clientele of upscale property owners interested in superb landscape maintenance and dependable snowplowing during the winter months. My reputation
for excellence was spreading rapidly by word of mouth through the professional
community. In the spirit of optimism, I purchased a large and powerful F-350
pickup truck complete with snowplow assembly. It was winter, and I put it to
immediate use, developing my skill from one driveway to the next.

One Friday, with a winter storm approaching that night, I pulled up in front
of Howard Johnson intending to wolf down their fish fry and follow it up with
a torrent of coffee. As I sidled up onto the stool, I was treated to the customary
practice whereby the miniskirted waitress bends over to pick up a piece of fallen
silverware. With that panorama in full view, my mind went completely blank.
As I stuttered the words "fish fry and coffee," I noticed a certain gratification in
her eyes as though a sexual prowess had been validated. Frequent coffee refills
indicated she was trying to fill a five-gallon gas can.

As I was finishing up, I felt a tug at my elbow. I turned to see an attractive
woman in her midfifties, stylishly dressed. It was apparent that she did not shop
at Good Will. Seeing my truck outside, she took the opportunity to request

an estimate, saying she had a home on Willow Run Drive where some of her neighbors, my customers, had recommended me. I took down the address and specified a time later that afternoon for an estimate. During this interchange, it occurred to me that at no time did we avert our eyes from each other. Though our conversation was limited to business, the eyes had spoken volumes. It was all I could do to keep my eyes from looking down at the rest of her. Finally on parting, as she walked away, I was able to feast my eyes. "Marvelous," I thought to myself.

At the agreed-upon time, I pulled into her driveway. Typical of most homes on this street, it was gracious, spacious, and well appointed. She rushed out to accompany me on my rounds, clad only in a miniskirt and halter top. I abbreviated the inspection when I hopelessly lost count of her goose bumps. Once inside, I learned that she was recently divorced. Speaking softly, she said, "I am very independent and unconventional, and when I see something I want, I take it," all the while her eyes were locked on mine. Having accepted my bid, I told her that with the storm coming, I would plow her for the first time tonight. Her eyes lit up, and we both began to laugh. She said, "Well, in that case, make mine the last stop. I'll wait up for you." "That might be as late as four in the morning," I said. "That's fine," she said. "Do you like bacon and eggs?" "I never refuse," I said. "And hot coffee?" "I have been known to slosh down a few cups," I said. "You had better bring a fresh change of clothing for after the hot shower." "Terry"—her name was Terry—"I can hardly wait for the snow." ·

It was near 4:30 a.m. when I arrived at her drive, and true to her word, the house was lit up like the Taj Mahal. The storm had been raging for five hours. Two and a half feet of blowing, drifting snow formed numerous deep drifts across the driveway.

Now, there is a certain sense of power that only the operator of a snowplow experiences. It is the powerful drone of the engine, the grating of the massive blade against the concrete, the resultant flurry of displaced snow, and the before-and-after effect on the driveway, now clean as a whistle.

Imagining the smell of bacon and eggs, I gunned the engine, and the beast surged forward. Midway down the drive, as I plowed through a drift, a sickening thud reverberated through the frame. In a blinding instant, a large object, having ricocheted off a nearby garage wall, crashed through the windshield striking me in the right forehead. Shattered glass was everywhere. As my eyes began to focus, I realized the object was Terry frozen solid. Shutting off the engine, I staggered down the drive, intercepting a city snowplow. With his radio, he called for EMS and the police. I then staggered back to the cab to get out of the biting wind. With Terry's head barely eight inches away from mine, I poured myself a hot coffee from my thermos. This was to be the first and last time I had coffee with Terry. I lifted my cup and said, "Here's to you, kid," and the tears began to flow. I had been smitten by Terry in more ways than one.

The autopsy determined that Terry had suffered a massive heart attack. Returning home late that night, she was apparently on her way to the mailbox with two letters when she was overcome. By the time I had arrived, the blowing, drifting snow had masked her location. After that incident, snowplowing was never quite the same.

IS ANYBODY HOME?

It was the domain of the bighorn sheep, the Sierra Nevada Mountains of California, and Judith Butinski, my live-in partner, and I were preparing for the annual hunt. The flesh of the sheep was a culinary delight, and the males equipped with massive recurving horns were highly prized as hunting trophies. The horns were cored with solid bone covered with a thick layer of keratin, the protein found in hair and nails and was once used by the Shoshone Indians to make powerful compound bows.

I was forty-five years of age and employed as a structural engineer, as was Judith. She was thirty-two, an avid survivalist, hunter, and from the male perspective, an eyeful. We intended to spend four days on the hunt ascending to altitudes in excess of five thousand feet. Here, at night, we would encounter winter-like temperatures in addition to accumulations of snow. We carried arctic sleeping bags, hooded parkas, mittens, snowshoes, and warm underwear. Our food stuffs included hearty canned soups, powdered eggs, bacon, cornmeal, flour, ground coffee, and a bottle of Southern Comfort. I was armed with a Remington .270 high-powered rifle with telescopic sight, a Smith & Wesson .44 caliber magnum revolver, and a bowie knife. Judith was similarly equipped. Ammunition, a not inconsiderable weight, was also included.

To haul this traveling circus, I had rented a mule and its trailer. The mule required a large pouch of feed in addition to our baggage. The trailer we would leave at the base of the ascent. Now prepared for arctic conditions, we gazed ever upward in our quest for the bighorn. The main source of predation for big-horn sheep was the mountain lion, which was not above attacking an occasional human so that its diet could be considered varied. It was for this possibility that we kept our revolvers on a waist belt ready for mayhem.

Because gold has been a by-product of the Sierra Nevada since its exploitation in the nineteenth century, I kept a sharp eye out for shiny yellow pebbles when crossing streams; these are known in mineralogy as a placer deposit. As such, we were more likely to run into an old prospector than we were a young hunter. Now equipped with a strong mule, I indulged my thirst for adventure by leaving the well-worn trail and mindful of my lensatic compass, struck out on paths unknown. Traversing ravines and rocky wind-swept open areas, we came upon a remote canyon, the center of which was scoured by a swift-moving stream. At the far end, I saw the outlines of a log cabin. It was at this point that we heard the barking of a dog. As he got closer, I could see it was a border collie, a highly intelligent sheep herder. Though most likely a pedigree, he was emaciated but managed enough protest to make it clear we were infringing on its territory. As we approached the cabin, I called out a salutation. There was no reply from within, save for the dog who was now more agitated. When I approached the front entry, the dog placed himself in front of the door and bared his teeth in an intense menacing snarl. I knew many men who would have shot him outright then and there, but I could not. There was something inside that he intended to protect with every fiber of his being and by no means could I be the one to thwart his noble instinct. But our curiosity was now overwhelming, and I had Judith open a can of soup, lace it with cornmeal, and proffer it to the dog. Half-starved in a harsh climate, it was far too much temptation for the dog, and in his distraction, he allowed my passage. The door was latched; the dog had free entry through a canvas portal. The interior was dank and musty, and by the light shining through the door, I could see the skeletal remains of what had once been an old prospector, now lying on his bed. It was the dog's master, the source of his noble compulsion. He was his master's guardian no less in death than in life, a role he did not take lightly.

In time I was able to touch the dog, stroke it, and was able to tie it to a small tree with a length of rope. Because there seemed to be no sign of violence or foul play, I determined to simply conduct a Christian burial. Though tied up, the dog was greatly agitated. Above the buried body, I erected a round stone cairn, surmounted with a wooden cross. Prayers were intoned, and because we had lost all mood for hunting, we decided to head for home. I was determined not to abandon the dog but to make him my own, deeming such nobility worthy of survival. But alas, as we prepared to leave this remote canyon, not knowing if I could ever find it again, the dog would not leave the grave. With a tear streaming down my face, I told him that he had done all that he could and that his master was now in a better place. But to no avail and as our little caravan was about to exit the canyon, for all eternity, I looked back to see him still laying at the foot of the cairn. Then at the instant our eyes met, he leaped up and ran after me. With his obligation now fulfilled, he became truly mine. Years later, long after Judith and I had parted, he was still with me.

THE FLOTATION DEVICE

I was a US Army Air Corps pilot, a captain newly arrived in Dutch New Guinea from the China-Burma-India theater, where I flew numerous supply missions to China over the Himalayan Mountains. It was late 1943, and we were still mopping up Japanese resistance here in New Guinea. I flew a Curtiss C-46 Commando, twin engined transport plane, having taken possession of it when it was new. We lifted off from Sentani Air Field heading for a newly constructed airfield in the interior. There were five personnel on board: a copilot who was a lieutenant; a flight engineer who was a sergeant; and two army nurses, both lieutenants, one of whom I found totally captivating, a Danish American girl by the name of Margrethe Ingeman. The intense attraction seemed mutual. Our cargo consisted of c-rations, canned water, and small arms ammunition.

We flew over terrain considered even impassable on foot—a dense jungle canopy of hardwood trees reaching to a height of one hundred and fifty feet. Below, the ground was crisscrossed with ravines and numerous water courses choked with vines. In this "Alice in Wonderland" resided aboriginal tribes, half of whom were headhunters and the other half cannibals. In midflight, we were jumped by two Japanese zero carrier-borne fighters. Their 7.7 mm machine guns raked the fuselage, killing the copilot and the flight engineer. With both engines now set aflame, in a powerless glide, I lined the plane up with a creek bed visible through the jungle canopy. Upon impact, a spray of minute particles of aviation gasoline ignited in a roaring inferno. The other nurse was consumed in the flames. Unhurt, I put my arm around Margrethe's waist and dragged her through a jagged opening in the fuselage. It was in this embrace that our eyes met; it was a look that spoke volumes. I found a nook away from the inferno and found on my person a hunting knife, cigarettes, and a Ronson lighter. Scattered beyond the inferno, dispersed on impact, I found cans of water, c-rations, and a survival kit containing a compass and a crude map of New Guinea. I clutched the compass and began to feel in control. Estimating our position on the map, I determined an azimuth for a general line of march. We packed up a kit of rations and began our trek, which I estimated to be no less than eighty miles.

It soon became apparent that we were not alone. We were being stalked by numerous figures. Abruptly, an arrow buried itself in a tree trunk with such resounding force that the shaft vibrated back and forth. I told Margrethe it was their way of asking "Can we be of service?" She could not decide whether to laugh or cry. Sensing their numbers were great, I determined our only recourse was to parley, and in bargaining, to somehow effect our salvation. It was with great trepidation that I stepped into the open knowing that within an instant I could become a human pin cushion for a volley of arrows. In an icy sweat, I raised my arms upward and beckoned them forward. Within seconds, figures too numerous to count emerged from the surrounding foliage. A chieftain appeared in the forefront. They were aboriginal, of a complexion nearly black, almost naked save for a penis gourd enveloping the genitalia. A horizontal bone adorned their lower nose, and all were armed with bows, arrows, and spears. The chieftain, together with a young warrior who understood a passable form of pidgin English, approached to within speaking distance. In emphatic tones, we were informed that we were their prisoners. We were stripped naked. Our hands were bound behind our back, and we were tethered to each other by the neck. At the village, it was apparent that they had never seen a white man or woman. We were thrown into separate cages. These, although of a somewhat better accommodation than the adjacent pig sties, were inescapable and used for the fattening up of prisoners prior to their being butchered and consumed after being slowly roasted on a massive revolving spit. The human roast consisted of an entire leg, with foot and buttock still attached, portions of which were served piping hot on a banana leaf. There were no potato salad and corn on the cob here. These feasts were held in homage to the god of war, a fate befitting prisoners taken in battle.

From my cage, I could see the Baliem River, which swept through the center of the village in a high-speed torrent. Anything falling into the river was mercilessly swept down river and out of sight. Knowing that the Baliem River coursed its way toward coastal New Guinea and civilization, a plan began to take root in my mind. But without a flotation device of some kind, drowning was the most likely probability after plunging in. Given the limitations of our captivity, I determined that the swiftly moving current was our only means of escape. Access to a boat or raft was not an option, and in any event, they would most certainly capsize. I thought of my beloved Margrethe, who being fed an all-you-can-eat diet of pork and yams was now approaching the size of a small jeep, and then it hit me. Margrethe would be our flotation device. Her high body-fat content together with an increased proportion of body volume to surface area meant that she had an exaggerated inherent buoyancy. All that was needed was a length of palm fiber rope to lash us together bosom to bosom. Not quite like a ride on the *Queen Mary*, but given the circumstances, the accommodations were no less appealing.

It was day two before the feast, and Margrethe was subjected to a physical inspection. Fondling hands knew no bounds. It was the butcher, and he was responsible for butchering, cleaning, and dressing Margrethe. She met with his approval and was left hog-tied on a bed of soft grass. She wallowed on her stomach like a stranded whale. Tomorrow morning he would slit her throat with an obsidian knife made from a type of natural glass. In preparation, I had squirreled away my own obsidian knife, and in the now-darkened village I cut through the fastenings that secured the cage doors. In few deft strokes, a big girl could stretch her legs. We embraced with a deep kiss, and I slapped a massive fanny for good luck. Hand in hand, we bound for the raging torrent. At the top of a twenty-foot bank, we lashed ourselves together. One more kiss and then the plunge. We hit the water with great force, sank below the surface, and upon rising found that we were bobbing along at great speed. Margrethe rode high in the water, and I found that by extending one leg, not to mention another appendage, I could mimic a rudimentary rudder, steering around obstacles. In all fairness, I must admit that Margrethe was the perfect hostess, seeing to my every comfort within reason.

We were making such rapid progress, and not knowing what awaited us on shore, we kept to midstream. After dozing in each other's arms, we found that we were still bobbing along well into darkness. At dawn the next day, we were spotted by a US Navy patrol boat. I would never forget the expression on the faces of the young sailors as we were winched out of the water within the confines of a cargo net. The provision of clothing for me was no problem, but for Margrethe, a sarong fashioned from a blanket was required, and it was not unlike a small tent. We were both sent to the US naval hospital in Brisbane, Australia, for an extended recuperation and weight reduction. So attached had I become to Margrethe that at war's end, I married her. In return, she bore me four children and provided a lifetime of love and devotion. and always she was affectionately known to me as my Great Dane.

THE RESTORATION

It was October 1942, and a newly inducted soldier in the US Army emerged from a Greyhound bus in Elmira, New York. He was home on a ninety-six-hour pass, and because his unit was shipping out on his return, for he knew not where, his visit to his beloved was fraught with a fatalism that he could not shake. Her name was Margo, a classic beauty, three years his junior. She greeted him with a tearful embrace possessed with an overwhelming sadness that she could not explain. In the few days that they had remaining to them, he had a jeweler cut an American silver dollar in half, forming a unique pattern. The two halves now meshed like two pieces of a puzzle. Each half was mounted on a solid sterling silver chain. He put the chain with a half coin around her neck and told her that these two halves when united represented their love bond, and like the coin, one of them without the other was incomplete. In a mood of deep reflection, he added that should he not survive, it was his fervent hope that his half would be returned to her, and like the coin, now united, they would always be together in spirit. The half he would carry into battle was engraved "To my beloved Anthony—Margo A. Fontaine, Elmira, NY, 1942," and hers the reverse.

Within a month, he and his infantry unit were loaded aboard a ship for what would be an essentially unopposed amphibious landing in North Africa. It was a green army, untested in battle, that had not yet developed the psychological case hardening required of a fighting force. Their officers, in most cases equally inexperienced, along with a weaponry that was in many ways inferior to the equipage of the German Wehrmacht, resulted in many bloody repulses. It was a teething period. But these analytical musings provided little comfort to Anthony who at that moment was locked in combat with a German armored brigade. He was torn from the cover of a small hillock by an 88 mm shell, and thus exposed, his chest was riddled with German machine-gun fire. Now mortally wounded, he instinctively clutched his buttoned breast pocket and sensed that the half coin within was unscathed. Strangely, his last sensation on earth was a sense of relief, and with that, he transcended this world for the next.

All was dark now. Both opposing forces had retired in haste, leaving their dead in silence. In the moonlight, Arabs scavenged among the dead, removing all clothing save for underwear. His shirt with the engraved coin within was stuffed in a sack mounted on a donkey. The coin within escaped notice. The Arab, no more than a boy, returned home with his treasure. It was his mother, rifling through the pockets, who discovered the half coin. She could neither read nor write in any language and could only wonder at the engraving. But no matter, her husband was traveling to Algiers in a few days. There would be plenty of opportunity for an appraisal in the many shops and bazaars.

The husband, as one might expect, was told it was of little value, and on the fourth estimate, he accepted a trifling sum in exchange. It languished for some fourteen years in a pail of trinkets, part of an inventory, long forgotten, in a musty bazaar in a back alley. Upon the death of the merchant, his entire stock was purchased by a Parisian pawn broker and now resided in a glass case for estate jewelry—a curiosity among hundreds of baubles. Ten years later, it was purchased in a bulk sale by an English pawn broker, an oddity among other estate jewelry now displayed in a glass case in his London shop. Two years later, it was purchased by a British eccentric, who for whatever the reason was fascinated and yet pursued his curiosity no further. It languished in his collection for decades, and it was only upon his death that his daughter, who was now holding the half coin in her hand, became intrigued by the inscription. A highly intuitive woman, she suspected that the date 1942 indicated he was an American serviceman caught up in a wartime separation from his beloved. Surely the other half coin was in Elmira, New York.

A persistent flurry of long-distance calls to the Elmira information operator allowed her to speak directly to Margo's adopted daughter. Yes, Margo had her half coin, and the daughter, having heard the story a thousand times, cried unashamedly. Margo, still among the living but now in her eighties, was dying of cancer. The woman sent the half coin by air mail to the Elmira address, refusing reimbursement. It arrived while Margo lay on her death bed. She wore her chain with her half coin around her neck as she often did. She had been a head librarian and had never married. Anthony truly had been the love of her life. As Margo began to fade, the daughter opened the box, and Margo's eyes became as big as saucers. She fingered both half coins and meshed them together in a perfect embrace. She remembered his words—"And like the coin, now united, we will be forever together in spirit." The daughter remembered Margo's look of utter tranquility and fulfillment, and with that, she left us to join her beloved Anthony.

THE BOLO KNIFE

As a newly minted US Marine, I arrived in the Philippine Islands in 1961 to find that one of my duties would be to conduct jungle patrols of the US naval reservation to thwart timber thieves illegally trafficking in mahogany trees.

It was common for patrol leaders to have custom-made machetes. A meeting was arranged in a small jungle clearing into which a Negrito family emerged. Negritos were pygmy-like in stature and were the original inhabitants of the Philippines. The man carried a bow with a quiver of arrows and a bolo knife; the woman carried a small infant. This Negrito was a superb blacksmith whose blades were renowned for holding an edge. He made them by forging leaf springs from derelict Japanese ordnance. I gave him the equivalent of five dollars and my specifications for the blade.

Weeks passed and I had almost forgotten about it when one afternoon as I was emerging from the shower room, clad only in a towel, he appeared in the corridor complete with bow, arrows, and my machete. He had a smile beaming from one ear to the other. I expressed my awe and appreciation and gave him a large packet of cookies my mother had sent me.

He disappeared as quickly as he came. None of the sentries had seen him come in nor did anybody witness his leaving, but I knew he had been there because I was holding the blade. A mild chill ran up my spine as I thought to myself, "Not everything was beaten into plowshares." The fact that my towel had mysteriously disappeared may also have contributed to the chill. However, it was a small price to pay, for in the months to come, cookies would be the key to obtaining timely information. Although my mother had long since passed away, I sometimes regretted not having told her of the significant role she had played in those operations.

MY KNIGHT IN ARMOR

It was 1951, and I was eight years old. We lived in a working-class neighborhood in Buffalo, New York, and I was the oldest of four boys. To help augment family expenses, I had a small paper route, the highlight of which was delivering Tony Federico's newspaper every evening. Tony was an Italian American in his late twenties and the idol of every little boy in the neighborhood.

You see, Tony owned a massive dump truck with a candy apple–red finish, crowned with a huge chrome grill. Every night, this Goliath was parked in his driveway. To me, it was the eighth wonder of the world, and when the engine turned over, it was like hearing the sound of God.

My mother said he looked like Robert Mitchum, whoever that was. To me, he was just Tony Federico. What more needed to be said? We even chased after the truck just so we could smell the fumes, but Tony discouraged us. He said it wasn't dignified. Every once in a while, Tony would cram four of us into the front seat and take us around the block. To us little guys, it was the equivalent of orgasm. I remembered looking over at Franky. His mouth was wide open, and a fly kept going in and out, but Franky never noticed.

Then there was the time Joey got cracked in the head with a baseball bat. When Tony heard the screams, he wrapped Joey's head in a towel and took him in the truck to the hospital. Joey said it was worth getting cracked in the head just to ride in the truck, though he was careful never to repeat the experience.

Then there was the time when Tony raised the huge bed of the truck, causing little Jerry to load his pants and having to run home. Looking back, though, Jerry said it was a whole lot better than taking castor oil.

One time, Tony demonstrated the horn and blew the scoop of ice cream off Arty's ice-cream cone. Arty was not amused, and it was the only time I ever saw Tony lost for words.

Tony made his living trucking huge loads of gravel and concrete slabs constructing seawalls. He owned the two-and-a-half-story clapboard house he lived in, had a petite pretty wife, an infant daughter and a two-year-old boy. His elderly parents, who looked as though they had stepped out of a Norman Rockwell painting, occupied the upper floor.

He was the apex of our little boys' world until one day I walked into the kitchen and my mother and father sat me down and told me that Tony went to heaven. I said, "What? He just left without saying anything?" "He died, Danny. There was a terrible accident." Tony had backed up his truck to the edge of a seawall on Lake Erie with a load of concrete slabs. The truck backslid and careened backward end over end. Tony was pinned in the cab and drowned.

Try as I might, I could not wrap my mind around it. I ran out the door and raced down the street to Tony's house. The driveway was empty save for people carrying flowers and baskets of fruit. I thought about myself, his parents, his wife, his toddler, and his infant. Tony was big and strong and yet he couldn't save himself. What chance did we have? It made a deep and searing impression on me and was my first introduction to our mortality.

THE VOYEUR

I was thirty-five years old, a consulting engineer, single, and frequently dated women though I was not attached to any. I lived in a fourth-floor condominium, directly across and three hundred feet away from another condominium occupied by a very attractive female, who was probably between thirty and thirty-five years of age. She was apparently single and not attached to any one male. Her bedroom, living room, and bathroom windows, all facing me, were never veiled. Sheer linen curtains hung along the sides of each window, affording a clear expansive view through each. She was voluptuous with long auburn hair that hung down almost to her waist when not done up. Her grooming was meticulous, and hours were spent in front of the mirror. I watched her paint her toenails as fascinated as if she were doing the ceiling of the Sistine Chapel. I found the way she bent over to test her bathwater very unsettling. She pranced from one room to another, in the nude, in what was almost certainly a cardio-vascular regimen. Even though my body temperature was clearly elevated, I convinced myself that I was still in control.

She regularly dated men once or twice a week. Shortly after entering with her date, the condo was plunged into darkness. On parting, it was fully lit, and her partner displayed great affection. I never saw an exchange of money. Before long, we began waving to each other. Although she must have known that I watched her, it did not seem to annoy her. I soon became addicted and found that I was rearranging my schedule around her exhibitions. Exasperated,

I left a note on her door complaining about the times she had chosen to perform her toilet and suggested an alternative schedule. To my surprise, she wrote in return that I was not the only one watching, but that she would make an effort to accommodate me. Having now heard that I was not the only one watching, in a fit of nonsensical jealousy, I admonished her for not pulling her drapes, to which she responded that being watched and coveted conferred on her a womanly fulfillment not otherwise attainable. Because it sounded plausible to me and having returned to my senses, I allowed her dominance and her view to prevail, becoming accustomed to my perpetual state of heat.

Though greatly enthralled by her theater, I decided not to establish physical contact and contented myself with sitting on the sidelines even as some of the males in my building became frequent daters. Week after week, at a pivotal point the apartment was plunged into darkness, and I was left bemused with an endless list of scenarios. Because there was not enough light, I immediately ruled out poetry reading and shadow boxing. But the process of elimination was a poor vehicle for obtaining carnal knowledge. Eventually, I employed a pair of binoculars, but that only elevated my body temperature another degree.

Months passed, and I began to notice a change in her figure. It was apparent that she had stumbled along the way, the proverbial water melon seed having taken root in her belly. Her frequency of dating dropped off drastically, and I began to sense the onset of a mild depression. It was a cold, dark, moonless winter night when I saw her affix herself to an appendage by the neck. She allowed herself to collapse, and under her own weight, the noose drew tight. I jumped to my feet, raised the binoculars to my eyes, and then allowed them to sink to the floor. I raced down eight flights of stairs to her building and raced up another eight flights to her floor. I battered in her door only to discover it was the wrong condo. The terrified woman pointed out the correct door. I attributed the error to a lack of practice. As I battered in the correct door, the woman phoned for EMS, not to mention the police. I found my diva collapsed, suspended by a cord around her neck. I cut the cord with a pocket knife and began CPR. The color contrast between her auburn hair and the bluish cast of her complexion suggested a comic-book heroine. She was more beautiful than I had conceived, and I gave her a deep kiss for good measure. Her eyes flickered, and my heart fluttered.

In the weeks that passed, we fell into a deep love so that within two months we were married. Because I had a hole in my head, people readily understood why I would marry her. Her baby, now our daughter, I raised as my own along with four others of our own. In the end, I beat the odds, and the drapes always remained drawn at night.

WE NEED SALVATION

It was 1964, the year the Beatles invaded America, and I was a US Marine sergeant stationed at the American embassy in London, England. As a marine security guard, a "spit and polish" image played a vital role in our mission. I was in the marine apartment adjusting my white grommet cap in front of a full-length mirror. It was the frosting atop my dress blue uniform. As I peered into the mirror, I exclaimed, "Marvelous, marvelous," to which Corporal Mailer behind me added, "And invincible, too." "And that, too," I affirmed. Last, I donned white gloves, gathered up my two sentries, and descended the stairs to a waiting black embassy sedan. We were on our way to the embassy to relieve the three marines who had been on duty all night. Even though the glass on the sedan looked to be bulletproof, in reality it was not, the marines being expected to dodge incoming fire.

As we approached the embassy, by dint of habit our British chauffeur entered Grosvenor Square, the embassy being at the far end. The number of pedestrians in the square began to thicken, and we soon found ourselves besieged by a small army of demonstrators. Placards came out of nowhere admonishing us to keep our hands off Cuba. We became the focal point of their wrath, and they were not unlike ants swarming on a wounded grasshopper. All forward movement of the sedan came to a halt. Fists began pounding on the windshield, and we were now isolated in a sea of anger. Had we prepared for this event? Only to the extent that we had on clean underwear. From the back seat, our marine diplomat, Corporal DiMaggio asked, "Boss, do you want me to get out and crack a few heads?" "No," I replied. "Stay in the car. Do not get out. The bobbies will come and get us," I intoned. Our tormentors began rocking the car, and I envisioned being tipped over in the midst of a gasoline fire.

But soon enough, a rescue party was mounted. What I had not foreseen was who would do the rescuing. Unbeknownst to me, there were not enough police at the scene to attempt a rescue, though reinforcements were on the way. Above the din, I began to hear the strains of "When Johnny Comes Marching Home." It was the Salvation Army Band who had been performing on one side of the square. There were seven women in the band, each one about five foot five inches and weighing no less than two hundred and thirty pounds. Three of them played the tuba, two played the trumpet, and one—who looked like she could have withstood machine-gun fire at the Somme—played the drum. The demonstrators' resolve proved no match for the relentless blasts from the tubas, and the throng parted the way to avoid being trampled, with the drum major's baton catching many a reluctant straggler.

I peered through the windshield and watched as the small platoon of brass instruments surrounded our car and formed a protective wedge with the drum major at its apex. She alerted the chauffeur, and the car lurched forward to the ever-more-vibrant strains of "When Johnny Comes Marching Home." My goose bumps were now so large that I felt as though my tunic was one size too small. As we approached the embassy's front entrance, the doors of the sedan flung open, and as we emerged, it seemed only fitting for each of us in turn to wave to the crowd. Resounding boos grounded us back to reality, and we raced up the steps to safety.

Weeks afterward, a fund-raising dinner was held in the embassy banquet hall with the seven musicians as honorary guests. They performed "When Johnny Comes Marching Home," and it was apparent that the audience was emotionally moved. They each received a plaque from the City of London commemorating their act of bravery and civic duty. Even though I could just barely get my arms around each of them, I managed to show my deep appreciation for their selfless valor.

Weeks later, our detachment received a letter from Headquarters Europe pointing out that this was the only instance in the history of the corps of a marine unit being rescued by a unit from the Salvation Army. In response, one of our wags shook his head and piped up, "Well, you know, pride always goeth before a fall," to which our noncommissioned officer-in-charge threw his arms up into the air and walked out of the room. As for me, I never passed one of their kettles without throwing something in.

THE SONIA INCIDENT

My name is of no importance, suffice it to say that I was a US Marine security guard at our embassy in Moscow, USSR, during and after the Cuban Missile Crisis of October 1962. The detachment then was an elite force of eight marines responsible for internal security. It was apparent that all had distinguished themselves in some act of bravado, and if there was one characteristic they all shared, it was tenacity.

To either side of the two portals to the embassy compound stood two pairs of gargantuan Soviet policemen who we referred to as "wood sheds." It became our time-honored tradition to irritate them and occupy their time. Corporal Burns would initiate a game in which he would allow the wood shed to punch him with all his might in the upper chest and then, not wanting to ignore him, would return the blow. This typically went on for ten minutes during which time I would watch from an upper-floor window ready to spring into action at the first sign of cardiac arrest.

A favorite antic of mine was to sashay through the portal with a head of cabbage and proceed to devour it in much the same fashion you would an apple while intensely eyeballing the wood shed. It soon became apparent that this was being misconstrued. Subsequently, we were apprised that not only weren't they irritated, but they thought the practice quite wholesome and that I was the only marine who had any breeding. I was crestfallen!

To get to and from the American House Club (our USO), two miles down the road, embassy cars with chauffeurs were available. However, most marines considered this too mundane. Hitchhiking on a Soviet garbage truck clanging its way to the city dump with a female driver in a triple-wide snow suit was the preferred method of conveyance. The thought of the KGB having to trail along in the midst of the noise and vapor trail was always a source of great satisfaction.

All was a blur of comedic situations until one day an old rickety yellow bus barreled its way through those portals and lurched to an abrupt stop in the courtyard and into my life. It would sear the image of a wailing little girl forever in my mind's eye. A scar that was still with me at seventy years of age.

Within minutes of the bus intrusion, six marines materialized at the portal like white corpuscles on an infection. A phalanx formed of its own accord. The last mile of the bus route had involved a high-speed pursuit, and the Soviet militia in three cars were highly agitated. Emotion got the better of reason, and they surged forward. In the clash, the marines suffered a split lip, a bloody nose, an assortment of black-and-blue marks, sprained fingers, and torn blouses, but threw them back, giving as good as we got.

I was one of two marines together with two US Foreign Service officers to enter the bus. A weapons search was conducted as the Foreign Service officers queried the passengers. There were men, women, and children as young as toddlers. The din of wailing made for a highly charged atmosphere. My fluency in pidgin Russian together with a box of chocolate bars and a case of apple-juice containers—thanks to the secretaries—had a calming effect.

I soon found myself holding a little girl in my arms, her mother telling me her name was Sonia. She was about four or five years of age, and when her tears dried, it was like the sun coming out after a morning rain. We learned that they were a religious sect, had traveled from a town in Siberia, and were being relentlessly persecuted. In desperation they sought political asylum.

Things now began to move with kaleidoscopic speed. All American personnel were instructed to leave the bus. Apprehensively, I gave Sonia back to her mother and made a feeble attempt at reassurance. I remembered a sickening feeling in the pit of my stomach. No sooner had I left the bus than five Soviet security personnel tramped aboard, one of whom got behind the steering wheel. The doors abruptly closed, and a sickening wail rose from inside the bus. I stood transfixed no more than four feet from the bus, when in the window in front of my face, Sonia appeared. Her face and beseeching hands pressed against the glass, droplets, her tears, wending their way downward. In a matter of seconds, what had been a bus became a cloud of diesel exhaust. The bus forever gone.

The marines dispersed, and I remembered putting one foot in front of the other as I sought the sanctuary of my room. I locked the door behind me, sat down, cupped my head in my hands, and sobbed uncontrollably. Nausea intervened, and I found myself retching into a commode.

That evening in the marine apartment, the dinner table was set as usual, but no one came to eat. It soon became apparent that the marines had undergone a profound change, and a conference was arranged with the political officer. We were told that very delicate negotiations were under way and that accepting these refugees would have angered the Soviets at a critical juncture.

I am seventy years of age now but can still remember the image of that little girl huddled against the glass. Naming my firstborn daughter Sonia has helped me to atone. The occurrence stoked an empathy and compassion for all humankind that I carry with me to this day.

———— ⊖⊜⊖ ————

THE MAHOGANY MAIDEN

It was 1961, and I am a sergeant in the US Marine Corps stationed at Subic Bay US Naval Supply Depot in the Philippine Islands. In addition to intercepting contraband goods and stolen property at the gates, I was responsible for conducting jungle patrols of the US naval reservation—a considerable expanse, forested with valuable mahogany trees whose loss would entail erosion of topsoil into the harbor.

A Wednesday morning dawned hot and humid, and I washed down a breakfast that would have choked a python with two cups of black coffee. For the patrol, I mustered three pfcs and one lance corporal, and we marched to the armory. We each were issued a Garand 30/06 M1 semiautomatic rifle containing an eight-round clip and a bandolier with eight clips; this was augmented with a Colt 1911M .45 caliber handgun with two extra clips. There were no automatic weapons, but all marines were deadly shots. We would have no radio equipment, and once we left, we were entirely on our own. No matter what befell us, each marine was expected to give above and beyond. The fact that in the event that he was wounded, he might bleed to death, notwithstanding.

At the gateway to the jungle reservation, we picked up our Filipino constable, essentially a state trooper, who would accompany us and act as our interpreter. Armed with a 30/06 carbine that would fire automatic, he was cocky and ill-disciplined and required a tight rein.

Five hours out on the trail, we were jolted by a burst of carbine fire and watched in astonishment as parrot feathers rained down from the jungle canopy—the target having been irresistible to our constable. I flew off the handle just enough to make an impression on him for giving away our presence.

I halted for chow, hoping things would settle down in the interval. Our constable uncovered his mess kit to reveal about a dozen small fish heads on a bed of boiled rice. The aroma hit me like a wooden mallet, and I braced myself as I turned down his offer to share.

After resuming the patrol, we heard the loud dull thudding of a bolo knife hacking away at a tree trunk and realized that an engagement with timber thieves was now imminent. I glared at the constable implying restraint, and we fanned out to either flank. Without firing a shot and using brute force, we apprehended two Filipinos. The one I felled and lifted from the ground gave me a mild shock when I quickly realized it was a young female, probably eighteen to twenty-two years of age and of extraordinary beauty. Her large almond eyes were framed by an abundance of glossy black hair and beautifully shaped pouting lips. Her bewitching expression was a mixture of fear and anger.

The constable explained to whom we believed to be the father that he and his daughter were under arrest. Hearing this, he babbled hysterically, grabbed his daughter by the neck, ripped her blouse down, and thrusted her to me. I locked eyes with her, and I could feel my Adam's apple bob around like a cork in a gale. It was clear that he was proffering his daughter to avoid prosecution. I knew that I could only refuse, but the look in her eyes told me it must be done tenderly. Through our interpreter, I expressed great sadness in having to decline but must adhere to military decorum. The constable volunteered his services, but I waved him off with a smile.

We insisted on eliminating his campsite, and reluctantly he took us there. We were greeted by a scene of abject poverty and deprivation, and we were there in the nick of time. His wife had just been bitten by a Philippine cobra and had only a few hours to live. The girl became hysterical, and the father was overcome with anguish. Time was of the essence, and distance was our greatest enemy. A hurried conference ensued, and I changed the mission to one of emergency medical evacuation. Discarding the evidence and hastily fashioning a litter for the mother who was now incapacitated, we began our trek to the naval hospital at Cubi Point at a brisk trot, maintaining this pace as long as possible.

As the mother's condition worsened and we began to despair, we were overtaken by a swarm of Filipinos, whom I estimated at over one hundred, all brandishing razor-sharp bolo knives. They pointed to a jungle-covered mountain so densely covered with undergrowth that a snake would have complained. We learned that the hospital was directly opposite that mountain, and they intended to hack a trail up and over. These men were the sons of fathers who had fought the Japanese in the Battle of Bataan in 1942. We were in dedicated hands. The swarm came to life like a cloud of locusts and began to tunnel through the undergrowth as fast as we could walk. I remembered the flashing of blades and the cacophony of thuds as the blades bit into the wood. A chant soon arose of its own accord: ON-DA-DEE-YEH, BITY-BITY-BITY-BEE/ON-DA-DEE-YEH, BITY-BITY-BITY-BEE/ON-DA-DEE-YEH. Once over the crest, they melted away. The other side being relatively clear, we raced down to the hospital.

I barged into the emergency room and yelled, "Let's go! We got a snake bite here—Philippine cobra." This produced a flurry of activity involving anti-venom, a respirator, and kidney dialysis. I charged all three with trespassing and arrest, thereby necessitating our responsibility for the mother's medical treatment. She recovered nicely, was let off with a slap on the wrist, and I never saw them again until a year later when I saw the daughter in Manila. There was no mistaking her when our eyes locked once again. She was stunning and was dressed in finery. Her name was Luling, and she was the mistress of a wealthy Filipino businessman. Accompanied by her maid, she said little, but her longing look spoke volumes. She wrote an address and time on a business card and crumpled it into my hand.

Having been totally captivated I appeared at the time and place. I knocked on the door. It swung open. She was standing there in a silk nightgown, and in the blink of an eye, it dropped to the floor. I tried not to notice, and having failed at that, I stepped into the room. She began to remove my shirt, and I came to her assistance. In no time at all, we fused into what seemed to me a seamless meld. It was one of the ten greatest raptures of my life.

I never saw her again after that, and soon after I was transferred to Embassy School in Washington, DC. Some said she still lived in Manila in a lavish villa; others said her businessman benefactor whisked her off to Hong Kong where she lived in equally lavish surroundings.

To this day, when told something is made of mahogany, I never fail to think of her, and my reverie is always bathed in a thousand-yard stare.

TOTAL IMMERSION

Becoming a member of a Russian Orthodox religious congregation required the convert to be totally submerged in water three times during the course of the ceremony. Having been a marine who was required to retrieve a 9.5 pound semiautomatic rifle from the bottom of a twelve-foot tank, I thought to myself that this was well within the capabilities of my endurance. What I was not prepared for was the comedy of errors that would result.

I, am Italian American, was raised Roman Catholic. But having a beautiful Russian Orthodox wife and two daughters, I decided for the sake of family unity to convert to her faith. She was an avid religioso; I was a half-baked Catholic— the other half being atheist.

For my godfather, they selected a six foot two barrel-chested Welshman, who had also married into the faith, believing that he would best be able to keep me in bounds. The instrument of torture, as I liked to say, was a fifty-five-gallon oil drum spray painted blue on the inside and gold on the outside. This was situated in the middle of a gleaming hardwood floor. There were no pews. Along all four walls stood a veritable forest of candles whose collective gleam was reflected off the highly polished hardwood floor. Soon, altar boys were scurrying to and fro lighting incense burners that resembled the smudge pots in an orchard. An asthmatic would have been hard pressed. I began to think of submersion as a means of temporary escape. Superintending the ceremony was a ninety-six-year-old venerated cleric who was well on his way to senescence.

He was ensconced behind a long flowing beard and a golden robe. Perched squarely on his head was a jewel-encrusted cap that would have made Carmen Miranda wistful.

Anticipation heightened as crowds of worshippers closed in on my water tank. Clad only in bathing trunks, I was led from a rear chamber to the tank. Along the edge stood the cleric and my godfather who helped me onto a foot ladder and into the tank where I stood half submerged in water. The cleric began chanting and reading in loud sonorous tones punctuated by unduly long pauses, at which point, an altar boy would prod him with a crucifix, startling him into continuance. It was apparent that where he started was not always where he left off.

As he finished, I felt my godfather's large hand on the top of my head. Soon, I was compressed into the tank. But pressing with all his strength, he could not depress my head below the waterline. Godfather panicked and let go, at which point, the cleric peered over the edge of the drum. As he looked down in disbelief, his large jewel-encrusted cap fell off into the tank. In with me in the tank, I now had a large hat and two pairs of groping altar boy hands. As the cleric declared the attempt null and void, an altar boy placed the hat, which had not been emptied completely, back on his head. A torrent of water streamed down his face. An immense roar of laughter rose from the onlookers. The cleric, godfather, and altar boys formed a huddle after which they returned and poured two additional buckets of water into the tank. Again I was pressed down, this time achieving total immersion. My relief was short lived as I realized that I had displaced a significant amount of water onto the hardwood floor. The cleric having borne the brunt of it now looked like a drowned rat. Twice more was I compressed. The altar boys and the cleric then retreated to a back chamber where he collapsed into a chair with a goblet of altar wine. God knew that he had earned it.

In the meantime, I was swept off my feet and carried on their shoulders in a procession around the church. I highly recommend it as an ego booster. My wife told me afterward that I had narrowly escaped being proclaimed a saint because there was no ring on the inside of the drum.

The baptism ceremony would turn out to be prophetic in that in the end, I was officially excommunicated. This distinction I now wear with pride, and I am now an avid atheist with credentials.

THE FIXATION

Purchasing a set of front tires for a car was essentially a mundane, modern-day activity, or so one thought, but it was what I did while awaiting installation that had a profound spiritual effect. Because the wait was upward of half an hour, I decided to take a walk around the block. This area of town was the oldest and had a Florida cracker-like atmosphere. A quaint little cemetery, clearly from another age, caught my eye. I walked slowly through the open gate as if drawn by an invisible hand. Glancing to my right and left, tombstones etched with dates as early as 1883 presented themselves. The grounds were decidedly unkempt; being a landscaper, it was painfully apparent to me. Many of the tombstones had settled at odd angles, contributing greatly to the image of a long-since-forgotten age, and I wondered whether anybody at all ever came here anymore. At one point, I was gripped by an icy chill causing me to look backward to see if I could still see the gate. But still, I was drawn ever onward toward the rear left corner of the cemetery. At the foot of a massive gnarled oak, my line of sight fixated on a tiny tombstone, now settled at an odd angle. The unmistakable sensation of having arrived swept over me, and I looked down to read the inscription. It was dated 1942–1948. We were both born in the same year. It read, "Here lies our beloved Sarah—aged 6 years—who now lives with the angels." It seemed as though from that point on I had entered into a deep communion with this spirit child. A thousand questions flooded my mind. Where were her parents now? Were they still here or had they moved away or died? Did anyone at all visit her grave? Indeed, did she still occupy the memory of any living being? Lacking this, had her spirit beckoned me here? Was she that desperate to be remembered, that she would captivate a passerby to simply have someone, anyone, to remember her? To my astonishment, I found myself saying out loud, "I will remember you, Sarah, from now on. My name is Daniel. I live here and will visit you from time to time." And so it was that every time I visited my parents' graveside, I would also visit with little Sarah, and talking out loud, I would tell her things that were for her ears only.

Though I had never seen her, we had a special bond in that of all the people who passed by that cemetery, she chose me.

THE BIG TRUCKS

It was 1950, and I was eight years old. Our next-door neighbor was a lady by the name of Pamela Hurst. She was single, highly intelligent, vivacious, possessed of a singular beauty, and in many respects was light-years ahead of her time. My mother was always fascinated by Pamela and awed by her audacity. Both my mother's parents were Italian immigrants who provided a strict Catholic upbringing so that the contrast in lifestyles was all the more stark. My mother's reaction to Pamela's antics was always one of comic relief short of condemnation.

As for me, I was fascinated with the way Pamela could attract the attention of truckers. Our homes were situated, side by side, on a truck route. Pamela, who always donned a ponytail, did her gardening in slacks and high heels and usually wound up on the front lawn with a garden hose in hand. As large tractor trailers passed the house, groaning through the gears, Pamela would wave to each one as if waving to a long-lost brother. I usually found myself sitting on the front stoop, watching in fascination. Pamela almost always got a wave, and in one instance I thought the driver was going to fall out of the cab. Sometimes they would turn off, go around the block, and come by again repeating their passage two or three times. All this was accompanied by a cacophony of blasts from the air horn. My father, a veteran of World War II, said it reminded him of the passage of the Red Ball Express.

To me, these trucks were awesome, some even painted candy apple red with external chrome-plated air horns and some had a rear compartment for sleeping accommodations. Once in a while, one of the rigs would pull over and park neatly at her curb, the door would fly open, disgorging the driver who would then walk over and introduce himself to Pamela. They'd chat for a while, and oftentimes they'd disappear together into the house or for what I presumed was a guided tour of his sleeping compartment. How envious I was. Her prowess to me became larger than life. Because my perception of Pamela was now greatly inflated and because imitation was the sincerest form of flattery, I began to stand on the front lawn with hose in hand waving vigorously to passing rigs, thinking that in no time at all I, too, would be the object of their attention. But for some reason, unbeknownst to me at the time, they seemed to pay me very little heed. Once in a while, a trucker would smile and wave, but for the most part, there was something missing, and I soon despaired of having a rig parked at my disposal. At eight years of age, it seemed beyond my comprehension, but it ignited in me a burning curiosity. I knew that Pamela played the harmonica. Could that be the attraction? I had heard her play, and I didn't think she was that good. Pamela could also do an assortment of birdcalls, but even in close proximity to the cab, I had never heard any of these sounds. She had been a Girl Scout and was forever showing us different knots. There was a knot for this and a knot for that. Could it be that the truckers had a grudging admiration for her practicality. Because all this seemed beyond me, I became determined to investigate on my own. Perhaps I could sneak into the cab and peak into the sleeping compartment when they were thus occupied.

My opportunity came two days later when she disappeared along with a trucker into what looked like from the outside a very luxuriant sleeping compartment. I waited five minutes before entering the cab from the passenger side. It took another minute to work up the courage to slightly part the folds of the privacy curtain. Incredibly, they both appeared to be naked. So that was it, I thought. They were showing each other their tattoos. He appeared to be near-sighted and was very up close and personal. This was out of my league, I thought. I didn't have a single tattoo and there was no prospect of getting one in the foreseeable future.

About a week later, being unable to drop my preoccupation with this matter, I asked Pamela if I could see her tattoos. She seemed very taken aback by my presumption and told me in no uncertain terms that she had no tattoos. From this little rebuff, I surmised that this was how the belief got started that women would never be interested in you unless you had a big truck.

THE DISPATCH RIDER

It was July 1863, and I was a major in the Union army attached to the staff of General Ulysses S. Grant. A dispatch of great import was entrusted to my care to be delivered to General William Tecumseh Sherman, who was encamped seventy-five miles to our south. Upon delivery, I was expected to clarify any questions General Sherman may have regarding these crucial instructions. The journey sometimes required two days and as such I carried rations, water, a new repeating rifle, and a revolver, and trail a tethered, second horse for a fresh mount.

My route was highly dangerous in that the area was heavily infested with Confederate guerrillas and many atrocities against isolated Union troops had been committed. I was given the chance to pass up the assignment but decline. It was a full moon when I slipped off into the night. I kept up a brisk pace for several hours when suddenly I was grazed on the head by a rifle shot. I broke into a gallop and now had upward of twenty desperadoes in pursuit. My second horse was shot dead and tumbled to earth. It was my turn now, and I was hit three times, suffering painful flesh wounds. In desperation, I wheeled my horse into a large expanse of densely wooded area. Knowing they would follow my blood trail, I was relieved when I crossed a shallow swiftly moving stream and plunge in, following it for three quarters of a mile before slipping back into the woods. Now suffering weakness and bouts of delirium, I broke into a clearing and glimpsed a large white mansion to my front. I passed out in the saddle and upon hearing a human voice, bolted upright with revolver in hand. Fortunately, for what might have happened, its cartridges were expended, and the beautiful woman to whom the voice belonged, stood before me unfazed. Her countenance was more of pity than of shock. With that vision, I drifted into unconsciousness. Helped from the saddle by two faithful house slaves, I was ensconced in a room on the third floor. Thrilled to be helping Billy Yank, they took care to conceal my horse and belongings. The mistress of the house was a beautiful, young, newly widowed wife of a Confederate colonel. She was originally from Philadelphia. Her sentiments had always been with the North, against secession. She took care to hide the dispatch in a secure place.

Having been a volunteer nurse assisting in surgery, she cleansed and dressed all four wounds. I was captivated with her visage and my gratitude knew no bounds. I had lost a great deal of blood, and it would be two weeks before I could take to the saddle. It quickly became apparent that our attraction was mutual. Over the next several days, we became intimate, but there was a serious problem in that she was the object of unwanted attention from the guerrilla leader. It was the same murderous band to which I succumbed. With this realization, I loaded and kept my revolver beneath my pillow.

She was as willful as she was beautiful and became very possessive. As it happened I was married and had three beautiful young daughters, but this seemed not to deter her in the least. This dilemma was superseded when the guerrilla leader paid her an unexpected visit. He was forceful, loud, and raucous, and she was hard pressed to constrain his advances. Things took an ugly turn when he beat and kicked the two house slaves, ejecting them from the house. I began to descend from the third floor with revolver in hand, still bandaged, and with my strength not yet fully recovered, knowing full well I would shortly be engaged in combat. He was a large powerfully built man and was already on top of her. Faltering as I entered the room, I knocked over a vase. With its shattering, he bolted upright and faced me. It was at that very instant that my revolver erupted, hitting him squarely in the face. When his head jerked backward, he was already dead—a great deal more merciful than the torturous deaths he had inflicted on many of his victims. No sooner had the shot been fired than the front door began to pulse under the blows from a battering ram.

In a tearful embrace, we clutch each other for the last time. I was determined not to implicate her, when to my amazement, we were surrounded by

Union infantry. Unable to contain our joy, laughter was combined with tears. Within an hour, I delivered my belated dispatch to an inquisitive General Sherman, who listened with rapt attention.

After a tearful farewell, my nurse extraordinaire was escorted through the lines and provided transportation back to her native Philadelphia. Ironically, after the war, I wound up as a diplomatic courier for the US government, which to the benefit of my welfare, proved a lot less exciting.

BOY SCOUT HEAVEN

I was inducted into the Boy Scouts of America at the tender age of ten. You see, we lied about my age. Under that famous dictum "It'll do him some good," I found myself marching in nameless ranks in the school yard every Tuesday evening, and after a while, I actually got to like it. The best part was when four or five of us would gravitate over to Herby's house and drink Kool-Aid until all hours of the night.

Our troop was sponsored by the St. Francis of Assisi parish, predominantly Italian American, and adjacent to us was the St. Agnes parish, predominantly Polish American, who sponsored their own scout troop. It was to this troop that Norbert Wozniak belonged. Norbert was my best friend and lived four doors down from us on the same street. Both his parents spoke English with a heavy Polish accent but were well received and very much a part of the neighborhood. Norbert was always referred to as a good-natured kid, but the most distinguishing thing about Norbert was that he was lame. His foot and ankle were congenitally deformed. His parents had neither the money nor the inclination for an operation, and as a result, he could not join in most games.

Whenever my mother thought about Norbert, she always felt so sad. The fact that Norbert would not be able to spend seven days at Camp Ti-Wah-Yee along with his troop made her even sadder. His parents were very protective and did not have money enough for such things, and so it was that my mother offered to pay half his fee and extolled the virtues of the experience. His parents reluctantly accepted, and Norbert had to be peeled off the ceiling.

Our troop was the first to complete a week at Camp Ti-Wah-Yee. On the day of our departure as we were loading onto our buses, Norbert's troop arrived. He emerged dragging a duffel bag, his eyes wide as saucers. He reminded me of a wounded World War I German soldier emerging from a troop train. We met and embraced and wished each other well. Looking after him as he marched off, I could see that he was leading the pack, his right foot being dragged along beneath the duffel bag. A lion had emerged.

On the second night in camp, Norbert, along with four other boys, sneaked off after midnight for a swim. The site was a small concrete dam that served as a pedestrian bridge. Off to one side, the water was deep enough for diving. Norbert swam well in the water, his foot not hindering him in the least, but something went terribly wrong that night when he caught his foot in a grating. That same foot that had so hindered him in life, now took it from him.

The mailman, who had just come from the Wozniak house, broke the news to us. I never saw my mother so distraught. For two days and nights she would not eat and slept very poorly, if at all. She said she could never face Mrs. Wozniak again. It fell to my father to beseech Norbert's mother. Mercifully Mrs. Wozniak came to our house and in the spirit of God's will, absolved my mother.

Years later, as a newly minted US Marine, I would again see Norbert's wide-eyed look of anticipation in newly arriving recruits.

THE LANGUAGE TEACHER

I was the first to arrive, followed close behind by our Russian-language teacher, Ludmila, assigned to us by the Soviet Foreign Ministry for the purpose of language instruction. In all probability she was as much in the employ of the Soviet KGB as she was the Foreign Ministry, and that was why I came to be a member of this class. Acknowledging her presence, I clicked my teeth and gave her a menacing look to keep up appearances. I was a marine sergeant stationed at the American embassy in Moscow, USSR. She smiled coyly, but we were not unlike two leopards infringing of each other's territory. In this musty conference room, in the nonrestricted area of the consular basement, she conducted a Russian-language class for American military noncommissioned officers. We were both a little early, and so to amuse herself, she reclined in a chair and began to thumb through a Sears and Roebuck catalog, crossed her legs, pumping one leg up and down in a slow steady cadence, not without a hypnotic effect. We were still smarting from the Cuban Missile Crisis, and I found it difficult to resist being mischievous. I referred to the catalog. "It's amazing what the marketplace can do when they're not constrained," I intoned. Her eyebrows shot to the top of her forehead. She uttered a sound, but it was unintelligible. I persisted. "Ludmila, this Berlin Wall you have constructed across Berlin, twenty-eight-miles long with adjoining mine fields—a bricklayer's nightmare. Why is it everybody is trying to escape Communism? They all go one way; nobody goes the other way. Why is that?" I replied, feigning ignorance. She sighed heavily, her bodice seeming to swell to the bursting point. With one leg now pumping to double time, she answered, "Some people don't know what's best for them; it is the responsibility of the Communist Party to show guidance." "Guidance— you mean they have tour guides on the wall?" She was unable to constrain her smile, and the tempo of her leg shifted down to second gear. An assortment of US military noncommissioned officers began filing in, and soon twelve seats were occupied around the square conference table. They were all technical experts in various fields and represented the crème de la crème in military intelligence. A tour here when entered in their service records was analogous to a close encounter with the enemy.

I watched as Ludmila seemed to take care to position herself alongside Warrant Officer Thorner, a denizen of the army attaché's office. He was a good-natured Jewish American and his warmth soon pervaded the group. He removed his class materials from the black plastic flip-top case with combination clipboard and left it empty on the table between himself and Ludmila. The class soon became lively, and we began to trade our customary subtle insults. There was no presentation that was not rewarded with a barrage of snickering. Halfway through her presentation, she removed a plastic case from her bag and laid it on the table beside her, covering it immediately with a few pages of notes. I was struck by the likeness of her case to that of Warrant Officer Thorner. I was now riveted to it, watching it indirectly. At a point where a distraction engulfed the group, a switch was made. She now had his case, and he now had her case. Her complexion was now flushed and her demeanor now that of a shoplifter after having completed a successful lift. I spoke not a word but enjoyed the sensation of sugar plums dancing in my head. Being careful not to alert her that she had been detected, I afterward conferred with my commanding officer and began a delicate counterintelligence operation. In hushed silence, Officer Thorner was met by three marines and the head army attaché. A banter of aimless conversation was maintained as the case was silently examined. A seam that ran around the case was delicately probed with a sharp knife. It revealed a false bottom into which had been tucked a specially designed ultralight-weight microphone, transmitter, and battery pack. We maintained, during office hours, a convincing conversational chatter for the benefit of our Russian listeners. This counterintelligence bonanza was now turned over to a certain agency that specialized in disseminating disinformation. As a result, for a period of time thereafter, a number of Soviet operations began to go awry, but eventually, they surmised what had happened.

Late in life, even now, whenever I saw a black plastic case, I oftentimes would think of Ludmila with her hypnotic leg, forever beckoning.

JASMINE AND THE GLOBE AND ANCHOR

I was a US Marine, a sergeant, considered a noncommissioned officer. This distinction I earned through years of interfacing with my fellow marines. By military occupational specialty, I was an artilleryman, a forward observer to be exact, one who combined the stealth of a python with the endurance and intelligence of a wolf. Operating behind enemy lines, my only tools were a high-powered radio, binoculars, a compass, a grid map, a carbine, and a handgun. By observation and communication I would rain down artillery fire on enemy targets behind the lines. Fortunately I was never subjected to being hunted down by enemy patrols. You see, the fun-seeking side of my personality requested a transfer to Subic Bay Naval Base in the Philippine Islands. The marine barracks there had a guard detachment responsible for manning the gates and conducting jungle patrols of the naval reservation.

It was 1961, and I was twenty years of age, standing on the bow of the USNS *Barrett*. We were now gliding into the port of Manila. This was the era before the frenzy that was Vietnam, and we were some of the last marines to be transported by ship. Thereafter, air transport would assume ascendancy.

I was enchanted by the tropical breezes lightly scented with jasmine. The smell of oriental cooking wafting up from the hundreds of restaurants and outdoor stands. The bustle of hundreds of people swarming over jeepneys—the standard taxi/bus made from converted jeeps—and everywhere these alluring exotic females with what seemed to be an amalgam of body parts designed by no less than the devil.

Within minutes I was racing down the gangplank with a duffel bag slung over my shoulder to a waiting US Navy bus. Everywhere was the crush of women. I brushed against more thighs than in my entire lifetime. Could it be that these women saw me as a piece of grilled salmon? I fervently hoped so. It was possible that I might not miss the United States.

After arriving at the base and receiving a military indoctrination that consumed the entire day, I was taken under wing by Sergeant Cramer, my immediate superior. Now, Cramer had been here so long that he knew everything that had ever happened, might happen, or was going to happen. At twenty-nine years of age he was still as agile and as nimble as the youngest of marines.

On the way out the gate, I was introduced to some of the sentries who would soon be under my command. Beyond the gate, over the bridge that spanned the Dung River, lay the town of Olongapo. Now, the town of Olongapo was not quaint, and it was not sleepy being the equivalent of Sodom and Gomorrah and Coney Island during the height of the tourist season. Through swarms of American sailors we were assailed by mango girls carrying trays of the ripe fruit. Beneath nearly bare and exposed bosoms we were invited to fondle the fruit. At two dollars a mango it was a great way to ward off scurvy. Next come scantily clad teenage boys selling barbecued meat on a stick. I was advised to pass it up, the meat being anything from roadkill, monkey, lizard, cat, or dog. In fact, since the trade began, no one had ever turned up a filet mignon on one of these sticks.

Next we descended on half a dozen bars. Cramer knew everyone. The interiors were dimly lit and churning with prostitutes. Everywhere I looked I was enticed with exposed body parts. "Watch your step," Cramer said. "It's slippery in here." I was nudged to make way for a boy with a floor squeegee. He quickly squeegeed semen from beneath the tables and moved on with his load. We stopped at the bar and made conversation with a siren who was picking little bones and feathers from between her teeth. She was eating a balook, a partially incubated chicken egg, a popular delicacy with prostitutes. She offered me some, but I declined, pleading that I had already eaten. She spread her legs wide apart on the stool. I looked down between her legs and manage to say "Later." I offered her a breath mint. She declined, saying it gave her indigestion. I dropped my comb on the floor and bent over to pick it up. She proffered a bare, beautifully pedicured foot against my face. This was a free promotion, and I found myself kissing the foot and with more kisses I began the ascent. Three quarters of the way up her leg, I came to my senses and lamely asked, "Is there anywhere in this town where I can get a library card?" It was apparent that she was taken aback by this, her leg being quickly withdrawn. She stood up, spit a few feathers into the air, stuffed her business card down my shorts, and sauntered off.

It was now nearing 2:00 a.m. and all military personnel must be back on base. We flagged down a jeepney, this one loaded with a few chickens and a guy with a goat on his lap. This was considered first class, coach being a straw-ladened cart drawn by a water buffalo. We smugly passed US sailors being loaded into cattle cars destined for the marine brig at the base—these the result of raids on bordellos whose only violation may have been noncompliance with board of health regulations.

The approaches to the main gate were chaotic. Hundreds of drunken sailors were converging there at the same time. Many instead of using the bridge would swim the Dung River as a rite of passage. The river being little better than an open sewer festering with hepatitis and other contagion, marines would direct these sailors to naval medical personnel awaiting them with fire hoses. Many would have shards of broken glass in their pockets. The remains of pints of rum shattered there in place by the blow from a marine corps night stuck. So overwhelming was the throng that Sergeant Cramer and I had no choice but to pitch in and help. When at one point all seemed lost, I remembered blurting out "Hit the Road Jack." From that I got an inspiration. The Ray Charles hit "Hit the Road Jack" was currently the rage in all the bars. I ran to the loudspeaker and turned up the volume to the extreme setting, took the microphone out on the platform in full view of the throng, and at the top of my lungs began to wail out the strains of "Hit the Road Jack." The immediate effect whether upon drunken sailors or marines was temporary cessation of whatever it was that they were doing. Slowly but surely, drunken and sober alike began to pick up the strains. Soon, all were singing in unison, more desirous of maintaining the chorus than the mischief. The powerful chorus then took on a life of its own, like the liturgical chant of warriors ending a night of revelry. Long processions of sailors filed onto their cattle cars like the druids of olden days marching off to Stonehenge.

I spent a year and a half there, and from that little place, I learned a great deal about human sexuality and the entire world and would on no account have given up the experience.

THE POWDER MONKEY

Ah, "Trick or Treat," how well I remembered it. They were the Halloweens of my youth. I was twelve years old, and my younger brother Jerry was ten. It was an era of children packing the sidewalks with a shopping bag in one hand for the collection of treats and a hunk of paraffin in the other used to mark up glass surfaces. Whether the adults gave out treats or not didn't matter, their windows were marked up regardless, and yet all was taken in stride.

A lot of thought always went into my costume, and this year was no exception. We built a large paper-mache Civil War–era cannon—a Dahlgren gun, to be exact, in the classic soda-bottle shape. This mounted on an axle with large plywood wheels and the entire assembly painted black. My brother Jerry held the ramrod, a broom handle with an oatmeal box affixed to the end, also painted black. Each of us wore a kepi, the classic Civil War military cap. Draped over my shoulder was a woolen sack containing charcoal representing the standard ten-pound bag of black powder. Around my neck hung a sign "Powder Monkey."

In reality, I was the typical age of a powder monkey serving aboard a Civil War naval vessel—a twelve-year-old boy. His small frame gave him speed and agility. His task was to carry ten-pound woolen bags of black powder from the magazine below to the guns above, a task made all the more slippery traversing the blood and gore that often covered the decks in battle. Many a powder monkey lay mangled and writhing in pain after an engagement.

A nine-inch Dahlgren gun weighed five tons and required twelve sailors using a block and tackle to pull it back from the gun port for loading and then to run it forward. When withdrawn from the port, the powder monkey threw his woolen bag of black powder into the muzzle followed by a wad of dry cotton, then a soaking wet wad, then a nine-inch-diameter red-hot iron ball, and then another wad of wet cotton. The entire contents were then rammed home with the rod.

The gun was then run forward, the touch hole filled with black powder and lit. The blast would cause the gun to hurtle backward, and woe to the powder monkey who had slipped and had yet to move from its path.

Our first stop was always the American Legion, where children after receiving their candy at the door were paraded across the floor. The reception our cannon received was phenomenal. It created a sensation, and we were mobbed by legionaries with beer can in one hand and the stuffing of dollar bills down our shirts with the other. There was not an eye that wasn't waterlogged. There were so many tears that I was concerned that the paper-mache might begin to run.

A block away, we evoked similar emotions in about a dozen Quaker families but for what seemed to me, opposite reasons. To them, the employment of children in warfare was a demonstration to society of man's inhumanity to man. There wasn't an eye that was not attended by a hanky, and we were provided with an abundance of freshly made doughnuts and homemade apple cider.

It seemed that wherever we went we were greeted with an enthusiastic reception. As the evening waned, we headed home. Parking the cannon in the garage, it was discovered that Jerry had left the ramrod behind. It was at that point that I left on my own to retrace our steps, hoping to find the rod.

I soon found it, but as I reached down to retrieve it, I was seized by the neck, a hand was clamped over my mouth, and I was lifted bodily. I kicked in a frenzy and attempted to scream with little success. Carried swiftly into a house, I managed to break free as my assailant locked the door. He glared at me with a crazed look, his breath was heavy with whiskey. In a split second of inattention, I managed to grab a toaster and bring it crashing down on his head. He was stunned and staggered backward. I bolted for the door, escaping a loop of chain he had thrown over my neck and shot out into the darkness like the cannon ball from a Dahlgren gun.

I ran home as fast as I could. With a torn shirt and having lost three buttons, I avoided my mother. Traumatized, I was terrified at having to face my assailant under any circumstance. Desperately I pushed the nightmare from my mind. An hour after I crawled into bed, my mother entered, shook me, and asked if I had seen little Mikey Hunter. His mother was on the phone. He never returned from trick or treat; he was missing, and the police were now searching for him.

I said I did see him first with a group of other youngsters and then again later alone. When my mother left, I could not sleep. The thought that Mikey may be trapped in the very same house from which I had escaped kept recurring. When finally I could stand it no longer, I broke down in tears and confessed to my mother, showing her the torn shirt and missing buttons.

She called the police, and officers who were already searching for Mikey descended on our house. When the police captain had heard enough, he took me in an unmarked car to the location, and I pointed out the residence. A search warrant was obtained, and a SWAT team was poised to barge through the front door. At the sound of a shrill whistle, the team battered open the front door to find an adult male in the living room, clad only in panties and clutching a whiskey bottle in one hand.

The officers raced through the house from room to room. Descending into the cellar, they found a newly constructed room with a large padlock on the door. They pried open the door to discover a room totally soundproofed from within. A child's screams and moans filled the room that was in total darkness. In a flurry of flashlight beams, a light switch was found, and the room was lit to reveal a steel dog kennel with little Mikey naked and pathetic confined within. Mikey's hysteria did not subside, and he was taken to Children's Hospital where he was reunited with his parents.

The miscreant was shackled hand and foot and literally thrown into the back of a police car. His conviction with a life sentence was now assured. The toaster, still lying on the kitchen floor, was scooped up by the police, its outline matched nicely with the lacerations on the side of the culprit's forehead.

The police captain told me that I was a hero and had most certainly saved that little boy's life. But hero or not, it was the year I lost my innocence forever, and I couldn't help thinking there were far worse fates in this world than having been a powder monkey.

LAND OF OPPORTUNITY

I was five years old and lived in the town of Calvello, in the province of Basilicata, a mountainous and impoverished region in southern Italy. My parents, barely able to eke out a living, have resigned themselves to the common practice of selling their children to impresarios in the belief that they will be trained in America as child musicians. Many do so from pecuniary motives alone, but there were many like my parents, who fervently believed that it was the ultimate sacrifice a parent could make to enable the child to escape a life of abject poverty. So I slept with a small violin and bow and was given rudimentary lessons from the village music teacher whose sole vocation in life was the teaching of child musicians. It was a brisk trade in this 1881 milieu. Our parting was a tearful one, and had I known that I would never see my parents again, it would have been more tearful. A year later, they were struck down in a cholera epidemic. This fact mercifully remained unbeknownst to me, as the thought of someday reuniting with them always remained a shining hope,

I was in the company of five other boys, and we were transported by carriage to the port of Naples by two strangers who seldom spoke except to bark orders. We were packed deep in the hold away from all other passengers, and when a light chain was fastened with a padlock around one ankle and then to a steam pipe, we began to cry. Slaps to the side of the head stifled our anguish. Once under way, the chain was removed, and we were allowed up on deck in their company. The food, though humble, was sustaining.

Upon arrival in New York, we were sold after much bickering to the highest bidder. I fetched a high price because I came complete with my own miniature violin; my parents had used my purchase price to see that I was so equipped. I was appealing to my music master, Vittorio Vincenti, because by this time I had a forlorn look, and he knew that a waif-like demeanor would bring in more money as I played and begged on the streets. I was made to perform in all kinds of weather. In winter, being skimpily clad and shivering evoked pity in passers-by and resulted in more-generous donations and I was thus duly clothed. As I grew older, I was allowed to perform solo and farther from the boys' dormitory. But at the end of the day, I had to hand over at least eighty cents; this was later raised to a dollar a day, and woe to me if I failed to earn this amount. Vincenti would become livid, and after my being stripped of all clothing, he would lay into me with a merciless ferocity using a thick razor strop that left me criss-crossed with deep purple welts. Following this, I would be made to sit still naked on a stool, facing the corner, practicing my violin while the others were permitted to eat their dinner. I say to you in all sincerity that never were there more forlorn notes given vibration on a violin than my lament. On these occasions I was sent to my bunk without eating. On similar days, throwing myself beneath a streetcar became a temptation.

On one winter's day, near frozen and shivering and in the midst of a blizzard, I was drawn irresistibly to the warmth and splendor of an upper-class wedding reception being held in an upscale section of New York bordering Five Points. The smell of food and the sound of a five-piece band were overwhelming. Unnoticed by the celebrants, I gravitated to the tables ladened with food. While gorging myself, with my mouth full, I suddenly realized that the band had stopped playing, and all eyes seemed to be now riveted on me. I was mortified that in my eating I had forgotten my obligation to play my violin. So I put the bow to my instrument and began to play. This brought no return to normalcy, but instead intensified the silence. Save for my violin, you could hear a pin drop. When I had exhausted my repertoire and half expected a beating and being thrown from the room, a sudden thundering ovation rocked the hall. I was swept off my feet by the mother of the bride and taken from table to table. My tattered clothing was stuffed with countless dollar bills. When the mother, a well-known socialite in the New York glitterati, had a thorough understanding of my circumstance, she had me legally removed from Vincenti's custody along with the other boys. We were placed with the Five Points House of Industry, an orphanage where we received food, clothing, shelter, and an education.

But the mother was not done with me and perceived that I truly did have extraordinary ability with the violin. She saw to it that I received advanced violin lessons and that I was adopted by a childless couple of means so that in the end my parents' fervent and selfless desire to have their child escape a life of poverty came to be.

GOOD EATING

Ah, those gourmet treats of yesteryear—how well I remembered them. It was 1954 and I was twelve years old. Being a newspaper boy in this German, Italian, and Polish working-class neighborhood required the delivery of the *Evening News* to Mello's Bar and Grill located at the intersection of Bailey Avenue and Clinton Street, an intersection not without its share of traffic accidents. Two of the most noteworthy were caused by our neighborhood ragman who still plied his trade using a horse and wagon. You could hear his hoofbeats a half block away. On two separate occasions, two different horses had balked and run amok. The bar and grill had quickly emptied as patrons came out to watch.

The bar was owned by a good-natured German American by the name of Otto Obermeyer. Now, Mello's Bar and Grill was an eating institution in that every Friday and Saturday night people stood in a line that oftentimes extended around the corner. The attraction was a mammoth roast beef sandwich inundated with lavish amounts of gravy. The beef was roasted and so thinly sliced that you could almost see through it. The slices were then piled three inches high on a freshly baked hard roll studded with rock salt the size of raisins. All this, together with a large stein of beer, came at a very reasonable price. In the rear of the establishment, along with large roasting ovens, was the largest vat of gravy we kids had ever seen. Having seen its simmering contents, one of our young wags presumed that this was where the mob dumped their bodies. But being wiser than most and because it never tasted funny to me, I dismissed the idea out of hand.

As their newspaper boy, once a week as a tip, they'd sit me down at a vacant table and serve me one of their Goliath sandwiches. It was always an extra special treat in that the waitress, a well-endowed, full-bosomed German lady, would always lean over with the gravy ladle, begin to pour, and tell me to say when. Too distracted by what was only two inches away from my face, I never did learn to say when on time. It did help to get the juices flowing, always an aid to digestion.

One early evening, shortly after dark, as I walked through the rear lot of Mello's Bar and Grill, I saw in a poorly lit area a furniture van in the process of being unloaded. Peering into the cargo compartment, I saw meat carcasses hanging from hooks toward the rear and bins loaded with what appeared to be large roasts wrapped in blood-soaked butcher paper, some of which no doubt were intended for the bar and grill. Fascinated, I climbed into the cargo area, past drums filled with blocks of ice. Looking up, I remembered thinking to myself that these had once been live animals vibrant with life. As I left, I looked down at a hand truck. On a metal tag welded to the handle, clearly legible, were the engraved words *Mulligan's Horse Ranch*. Dumbstruck, I stepped off the truck to hear a stranger bellow, "Boy, git, you got no business here." The next day, deeply disturbed, I went to the library to see my friend Jennifer who worked there. Using her phone to inquire the state agricultural bureau about Mulligan's Horse Farm, we determined that Mulligan raised no cattle.

We mulled over the huge servings of beef proffered to customers, and then it hit me like a ball-peen hammer. The ragman's traffic mishaps—two of his horses on two separate occasions had balked and bolted at that location. I had heard that Indian ponies will balk at the smell of horse blood. There were days when Mello's garbage cans were loaded with bloody butcher paper. I thought of the patrons who had left the bar and grill to watch the spectacle. The horses were trying to tell them something, but they were not cognizant enough to understand.

Upon informing the county health department, an unannounced inspection was conducted. The samples proved conclusively horse meat. They were immediately closed down and their license suspended. Needless to say, they canceled their newspaper subscription. But it wasn't long before the demand for the large roast beef sandwiches, smothered in gravy outstripped the original repulsion, and the lines for admittance to the newly opened establishment again wrapped around the corner. Periodically, over the years, they were shut down for the same offense and always managed to reopen, which proved the old adage "It's all in your head."

FAREWELL MY LOVE

There was no time to lose. I was a marine corps sergeant serving at the American Embassy in Moscow, USSR, and must respond to a security crisis. A shoulder holster with a .45 caliber semiautomatic handgun was strapped on, and in one continuous motion I dragged a suit jacket off the back of a chair. There were three of us: two marines and one Foreign Service officer. We shunned the elevator, bolted down the stairs, and arrived in the compound to a waiting black embassy limousine. I excused the Soviet driver, and a marine, who could have had a promising career driving a getaway car, got behind the wheel.

We weaved at high speed in and out of traffic, with two KGB vehicles in hot pursuit. They were the tail on our kite. We screeched to a halt in the parking lot of the American House Club whose main purpose was housing for single American non-commissioned officers working in the military attaché offices at the embassy, these in the upper floors while the ground floor served as a social club where American military personnel could bring their dates as guests. Because fraternization with Soviet nationals was forbidden, the women who frequented the club were usually very alluring secretaries from the NATO nations, and we did our best to keep up the alliance.

I flew through the door past tables adorned with secretaries ensconced behind shrimp cocktails. I unleashed the customary cacophony of hoots and whistles and bolted up the stairs. They responded in kind with a flutter of eyelashes. Opening the door to the second-floor office, I found the security officer, two marines, and the source of our crisis—a US Army staff sergeant named Larry Bonner. Sergeant Bonner's sole purpose for being in Moscow was to administer the club and the enlisted living quarters. To this end, he had in his employ two maids and one waitress, all of whom were female Soviet nationals. His illegal attentions toward the Soviet waitress, which began as carnal desire—his status as a vegetarian not withstanding—soon blossomed into a full-blown emotional attachment. The KGB on learning this soon coerced our unfortunate Tamara Gudenko into plying Sergeant Bonner for confidential information. The KGB resorted to their usual methods: threatening to send her elderly parents and three-year-old daughter to a gulag if she did not cooperate.

At this stage, Sergeant Bonner was an emotional wreck. There was no doubt that he was truly in love with her. Unwilling to betray his own country, in a stressful breakdown, he confessed all to the security officer. He pled for one last meeting with her. She was here in the building, working on the ground floor. The security officer sent for her. She entered the room, rushed to Bonner's arms, and they both broke down and sobbed. He made a tearful apology for bringing such misery upon her and her family. The security officer apologized in turn and told her relief would come and soon. Sergeant Bonner was told to pack one bag, and she was dismissed with generous severance pay. He was to be taken immediately to the airport under escort, which was why I was here. I looked out the window to see a full array of KGB vehicles and personnel and watched as Tamara was bundled into one of the vehicles. It was apparent that our trip to the airport would be contested. Four of us filed into the limousine, Sergeant Bonner, the security officer, myself, and our marine driver who took off like a rocket with our KGB entourage in hot pursuit.

A mile farther on, a police roadblock loomed ahead. The marine instinctively took a hard left into an alleyway suitable for a golf cart. Two more hard rights and we were back on our route beyond the blockage. I looked to see that we had acquired a clothesline complete with undergarments. I stifled a chuckle and tried not to intimate that anything was amiss. We arrived in time to meet a Scandinavian Airways flight to West Berlin but not without racing out onto the tarmac with our diplomatic flag flying in synchrony with the clothesline. Simultaneously, three KGB cars came to a shuddering halt surrounding our car. It was apparent that their day in the sun had arrived.

We exited and headed toward the airplane staircase. The doors of the KGB cars flew open and Tamara was jerked out by the arm and began to plead with Sergeant Bonner to stay. A KGB agent on a bullhorn elaborated on incentives they would give Bonner if he defected. His defection would be a propaganda victory and a destabilizing blow to the morale of the Western intelligence community. Sergeant Bonner was in agony with eyes red, tears flowing, and his gait bordering on a stagger. For him, it was a long climb up that stairway and a great relief for me when he disappeared within.

As for the marines, it was the usual catcalls to the KGB as we got back into our vehicle. It felt good settling back into the routine. Eventually back in the West, Bonner received a summary court martial, which was the lightest. Found guilty, he received a letter of censure to be entered into his service record and was reassigned to a different military occupational specialty. The comely, voluptuous Tamara blended back into Soviet society and no longer of use to the KGB, was ignored by them. However, not by her future husband who lavished so much attention on her that she bore him five children. As for me, I continued to do all I could to foster good relations within NATO by continuing a close liaison with a lovely secretary from the Swedish embassy. Ah, the things I did for my country.

THE BOXCAR

It was 1933, what we would come to know as the height of the Depression, and I was an unemployed farm equipment mechanic on the outskirts of a small town in Kansas. Fate had dictated that it was not enough that I lost my wife and child in a bus accident a year and a half ago. I now stood amid the ruins of what had once been our home. The tornado was gone now, gone as quickly as it had come. A small shed on the property was the only thing left standing, and it served as my shelter. It was the remnant of what had once been a full and complete life. It was dusk, and the light was fading and it seemed with it, my life.

A distant train whistle shattered my reverie. A resolve to cast my fate to the wind took hold. It was the call of unknown fortune. I would relinquish all further attempts to design my life. Where now went the wind, I too would go. If it led to my final demise, then so be it and the sooner I would join my wife and child. I filled a knapsack with a dozen cans of sardines, a few bottles of water, a bag of oatmeal, a sack of cornmeal, and a large bag of shelled walnuts. I arrived at the freight yard in time to board a slow-moving outbound train. I boosted myself into an empty boxcar, and with the aid of a small flashlight, I determined I was its only occupant. There were empty wooden pallets scattered in disarray. I arranged a nook in a darkened corner and drifted off to sleep to the cadence of clicking iron wheels and the rocking motion of the car. With no lavatory facilities or dining car, I was reduced to a bare-bones human existence.

It was about 3:00 a.m., and as the train slowed up, I heard a commotion at the open doors. It was a young woman carrying an infant in a bundle. She let out a scream as she almost lost her grasp. She was propelled upward by a great hulk of a man who seemed to have no regard for her safety and that of the precious bundle she held tight to her bosom. It was obvious that the woman was terrified, and instinctively, I intuited that he was most likely not her husband nor was he the father of the baby. By his demeanor, it was apparent to me that my life was now in danger and that at best, I would be flung unceremoniously from the moving train. If I was at all to prevail, I must resort to stealth. The interior of the car was partially lit by the moonlight streaming through the open doors. However, my desire to remain concealed became strained as he began to force himself on her. The infant was tossed to the side and rolled along the splintered plywood floor, narrowly missing the open doorway. I decided I could wait no longer.

I searched desperately for a club and found a four-foot length of two-by-four. The train was moving at a high rate of speed, and my balance was precarious as I lunged forward. I delivered a glancing blow to the top of his head. He turned to me, and I saw a face severely scarred surrounding a mouthful of rotted teeth. He lunged forward, and I delivered a devastating kick to the groin. The thought that for him sexual intercourse may never be the same crossed my mind. He attempted to gouge my eye, but I broke his thumb, and he howled in pain. He delivered a blow to the side of my neck, and I lost all sensation, crumpling to the floor. He lifted a heavy wooden pallet over his head, intending to crush my face, when I heard a merciful thud and saw his head deflected forward. He lost his balance and together with the pallet toppled forward through the open doors. We were passing over a trestle, and he plunged three hundred feet to the rocks below. I slowly focused my eyes to see the woman standing over me as she dropped a two-by-four to the floor.

She returned with the infant, and for an instant, I was reminded of the Madonna with the Christ child. She was beautiful and enchanting. I shared with her the contents of my knapsack. It was the first meal she had had in two days. She and her husband had fallen on hard times and they, like me, had boarded a boxcar in hopes of going to California. Unbeknownst to them, the ogre was lurking in the shadows. Her husband was strangled and thrown from the car.

That night, the three of us huddled together cloaked only in the moonlight that showed through the open doors, and I fell in love with her and she with me. Awakening before they did, I gazed in wonder at the beauty that had befallen me and resolved that it was time to take root. As the train stopped at what was apparently a sizable metropolis, we left the train and I surrendered my little troop to a Baptist church. I spoke earnestly to the minister seeking only sustenance for the infant. Taking pity on us, we were all given a hot meal, allowed to bathe, and were given fresh clothing. We were allowed to stay in two rooms in a small cottage used for storage.

When I told the minister that I was a farm machinery mechanic, his eyes lit up and he exclaimed, "If this isn't the way the Lord works!" Now convinced that this was divine providence, he went on to tell me that one of his flock owned a farm machinery dealership and was hard pressed to find a well-qualified mechanic to replace the one who was about to retire. An interview soon followed, together with a trial period of employment. Passing with flying colors, I found permanent employment, and eventually through hard work and perseverance, I would own the dealership.

My beautiful Genny of boxcar fame and I married, and the infant—now our daughter Lisa—grew to be a beautiful young lady. Genny, in celebration of our union, bore me a daughter and two sons. In parting, let me say that in all the times ever after when we traveled by train, there was never in our minds any great distinction between coach and first class.

YOU NEVER KNOW WHAT

It was 1870. A gang of six highwaymen were in the midst of hijacking a wag-onload of gold bullion. The wagon was attacked in the Punta Gorda area of Florida while traveling the Tamiami Trail. The thieves were both brutal and efficient, leaving none of the guards alive. Quickly, they left the great trail, disappearing down winding side roads and arrived at a predetermined hiding place. The wagon with its precious cargo was maneuvered under an overhang along a creek bed. A well-placed stick of dynamite caused the overhang of rock and soil to collapse, completely engulfing the wagon, masking it entirely from view. A nearby majestic oak was scarred as a permanent landmark. They now rode long and hard to a cabin hideaway. But in three days' time, the cabin was surrounded by US Marshals at the head of a large posse. In a firefight lasting several hours, the last of the six desperadoes succumbed to his wounds, and in perishing, as if in retribution, they took the secret of the wagon's location with them into eternity. An exhausting check of the cabin and the surrounding area produced no clue. It was now a mystery that would not be solved in their life-time, and as the decades passed, it became almost forgotten and passed into the realm of legend—an area of half truth and half romance.

It was 144 years later, and the year was 2014. I was a volunteer church member clearing trees and underbrush along a ravine on church property. I encountered two rusted iron bands protruding from the bank. They were wheel bands from an old farm wagon. With my curiosity now aroused, I dug further, exposing smaller iron hub bands and then what was probably a rotted wooden hub. Further along, another iron wheel band with more smaller hub bands announced their presence. The dimensions of the wagon were now defined. More excavating revealed two heavily rusted seat springs along with smaller pieces of rusted iron hardware. There were still-remaining badly rotted timbers that once formed the wagon's bed, most likely oak or hickory. A large area at the center of the timbers had caved in downward, no doubt from a heavy object. So heavy was that object that it had settled into the earth three feet or more below the lay of the rotted timbers. Moving closer, I stubbed my toe on a rusted shovel and discovered a rusted canteen. What had been a wooden box now revealed itself. In it were two heavily corroded revolvers. I recognized them as Colt model 1851 navy revolvers. Before the production of this model, there were no gunfighters as we know them today. It was the first six-shooter light enough to carry on a belt and in fact light enough to carry two. With a seven-and-a-half-inch octagonal barrel and a .36 caliber, it carried a potent wallop.

I now hovered over the cavity and began to excavate. At a depth of three feet, the tip of my shovel struck a very solid metallic mass. I reached down and used my fingers to clear away the last remaining crumbs. I was astounded at what seemed to be lustrous yellow bars. I ruled out New York State cheddar and was left with the word *gold*. A wave of elation and indecision swept over me. There appeared to be dozens of bars, but I pried loose one with a screwdriver. I needed time to think and so covered the site with cut branches. At home, I put the bar under the kitchen faucet, revealing a bar of bright-yellow metal. It measured seven inches long, three and five-eighths inches wide, and one and three quarter inches high. Lain on my bathroom scale, it weighed 27.5 pounds. I rubbed a piece of unglazed china against it, and it left a yellow streak, a required characteristic of gold. On the underside, a date was stamped—1868—together with the letter *P*, indicating it was cast at the Philadelphia mint. All data indicated a bar of pure twenty-four-carat gold. At today's value of $1,300 per ounce, each bar was worth $ 572,000. I was now weak in the knees and poured myself a glass of bourbon. Was it really possible that this bar I held in my hands was worth half a million dollars and more, and how many more of these bars lay quietly there?

The vision was overwhelming, and so I must unburden myself. It so happened that the church elders were holding a meeting on the upcoming church bake sale. Without introduction, I announced, "Ladies, put away your cake pans. I have an answer to your financial woes." I laid the bar on the table and touted it as the ultimate paper weight. The revelation that it was worth $ 572,000 and that there were at least a dozen more produced a stampede in whose aftermath the sheriff's department, an FBI agent, and two officials from the Florida Bureau of Antiquities descended on the site, not to mention that several cupcake molds were trampled in the pandemonium. A metal detector revealed thirty bars for a total value of $ 17,160,000, surpassing all Sunday collections.

How much the church will actually benefit from the discovery was unknown as it was still in litigation brought about by the descendants of the original owners of the gold. Even though the jury was still out, I thought it was summed up nicely by our choir director who exclaimed, "You never know what!"

THE ELEPHANT'S TRUMPET

It was 55 BCE. Pompey and Crassus presided as elected consuls. It was the age of panem et circenses—literally bread and circuses as a means of maintaining political power over the Roman masses, using a variety of gratuities, not the least of which were violent and bloody exhibitions for the public's amusement. The Roman working class held gladiators in high esteem. Gladiators were typically ex-soldiers both from Rome and its allied provinces, slaves so talented, and a smattering of Rome's citizens. Indeed, there were even a few women gladiators who fought other women but more often male dwarfs, and woe to the dwarf who lay maimed and helpless for it was always her prerogative to castrate the dwarf and then prance about with her prize held high in hand.

It was common practice among male gladiators, who were star attractions, to endure forced infibulation—a metal bolt implanted through the foreskin—one week prior to the event to ensure an abundance of pent-up hormones, thought to ensure maximum aggression. This technique was performed by the locksmiths of their day – a service no longer performed by modern day smiths.

A popular form of execution and highly amenable to exhibition was the practice of exposing convicted criminals to the ravenous predations of dogs, lions, and bears. The crowd would roar with approval as limbs were torn from torsos, large swaths of flesh disappeared with one swipe of a massive claw, and intestines were unwound from abdominal cavities to the shrieks and screams of the still-live victims. So engrossed was the crowd that many spectators held off going to the restrooms until it was too late. The bloodier and the greater the suffering, the more the gratification.

There was a class of gladiators known as the bestiani and the venatores who specialized in combat with wild beasts, a combat in which many gladiators were horribly maimed. And as always, the more violent and bloody, the more ecstatic the crowd. The classic encounter between two star gladiators was held in great regard. More often than not, it was a gladiator with the traditional armament of the Roman soldier—armor and short double-edged sword called the gladius and the rectangular shield called the scutum—confronted by the villain whose ensemble included a broad brimmed helmet, a trident, and a net, and woe to his assailant who became entangled. If a gladiator lay injured and subdued at ground, it was the custom of the victor to beseech the emperor for a thumbs-up—he shall live—or a thumbs-down—death sentence. The emperor in turn usually took his cue from the sentiment of the crowd. If the crowd found him to have been fearless and aggressive, he would be spared.

Against this milieu of blood and gore, long before the advent of the Humane Society and the Civil Liberties Union, Pompey's new theater, the first perma-nent theater in Rome, built to accommodate forty thousand people, was to be dedicated. It was to be celebrated with a stupendous pageant and an exhibition of combat between men and beasts. Five hundred lions and twenty elephants were to be dispatched by groups of spearmen. The five hundred lions were first to meet their fate but not without the loss of numerous spearmen. The crowd loved it so that when the twenty massive elephants were led out, their appetite for blood had only been whetted. Among these twenty elephants were many who had had human masters and had been broken and trained as beasts of burden. Unbeknownst to them, they were now to be put to another use. Now herded at spear point into a confined area, the elephants panicked as their numbers on the outside of the herd began to be dispatched with lethal wounds. The trumpeting and the wailing of the elephants were like nothing the crowd had ever heard. These elephants, accustomed to human reason and now finding their escape cut off, began with uplifted trunks to beseech the crowd for mercy. Accustomed to human masters attendant to their needs, they were now reduced to a state of ill-understood hopelessness. It was the combination of the trumpet-ing wail with beseeching uplifted trunks that struck an unknown chord in the human psyche, and inexplicably, the crowd rose to their feet, the majority in tears, and brought down curses on the emperor's head.

In this most blood thirsty of crowds, the political pundits of that time were at great loss to explain it. But happen it did. It nurtured a belief, among budding psychologists, that there exist entreaties that the human psyche may well find almost impossible to resist.

MY BEAUTIFUL JONAH

I was the owner-operator of a shrimp boat harbored in Bokeelia, on Pine Island, Florida. A live-in girlfriend, Meg, a very attractive blue-eyed blonde, whom I was head over heels in love with, served as my assistant when at sea. I was proceeding to familiarize her with the rigging, machinery, and day-to-day operations. Although intelligent in her own way and well meaning, she was plagued by ill-fortune whose constancy suggested the root cause was genetic. But love being what it was, I persisted in encouraging her and minimizing her errors as best I could—no small task as she was acutely aware of her predisposition and was quick to fall into despondency.

It started out with little things at first like the time she mistook the gallon of pancake syrup for floor wax and wanting to surprise me, coated all the wood decks. In remembrance it was known to me as the "sticky time." I blamed the manufacturers for poor labeling. Then there was the time she hung her laundered panties and bras on an outrigger to dry. Still in the harbor when the rig was extended, the harbor master had a few anxious moments attempting to make sense of what he thought were improvised signal flags.

In the galley, it was apparent she was not a cook even though she managed to produce a few innovations, one of which were fried eggs so rubbery that they would have been the envy of the B. F. Goodrich Tire and Rubber Company. At one point, I contemplated using them as temporary gaskets for lug nuts. But so in love was I that I never let on and always managed to beam at this gastronomical delight.

There was the time she draped a loose rope end over the helm- wheel to keep it out from under foot, so that when the winch was turned on, it snagged the wheel and yanked it from the steering column. One look at her forlorn face and I found myself chiding the manufacturer for shoddy materials. The next day, she opened a drain cock thinking it went to the hot-water heater. The bilge slowly began to fill with seawater, and the boat took on a noticeable list. I caught it just before capsizing, and with her in my arms, I reminded her that life was not always on an even keel.

That night in bed, with her tightly in my arms, I succeeded in convincing her that she was not a Jonah and that I would always trust her with my life. A tender lovemaking session followed, and she awoke the next morning exuberant and with renewed confidence in her abilities. Riding high on this crest of confidence, I determined this would be a good time to allow her, by operating the winch, to lower the outriggers, the long steel beams, one on either side of the boat. At the end of each outrigger were two bag nets, each funnel shaped with closed end to contain the trapped shrimp. As the lines were let out, the bag nets descended to the very bottom and as the boat moved, they trawled the surface of the sand for bottom-feeding shrimp.

Not long after the bag nets began to scour the bottom, the sound of groaning metal from an outrigger indicated it had snagged something very heavy. As I cut the engines to impede forward movement of the boat, she engaged the winch, and the heavily ladened net bag moved up from the depths. I was faced with the choice of cutting the line and losing both net bags, or retrieval and cutting the object loose, saving the nets. I opted to retrieve the nets. As the bag net broke the water, it was not clearly discernable what this long slender object was. Using the winch, we arced the outriggers up and the offending net swung onto the center of the boat. It was at this point that the sound of groaning metal split the air as the outrigger buckled and allowed a World War II German U-boat torpedo to burst free from the net. It hit with a resounding thud on the hardwood deck. The point of impact was on the warhead and with 617 pounds of hexanite explosive that could still be potent, I involuntarily shut my eyes and grated my teeth. It was now heavily corroded and weighed a fraction of its original 3,400 pounds.

I had to work swiftly and proceeded to cut away the net. I jury rigged a combination of block and tackles and winched it over the side. The splash as it hit the water produced an overwhelming catharsis. I turned over the engine, and we headed back to port.

I could see the gloom on her face, but her despondency was no match for my obsession for her. In a clinch, holding her tightly, I whispered in her ear, "Meg, that kind of thing happens all the time in the Gulf. Oh, Meg, how I hate when that happens." She belly laughed, and I pledged never to leave her. "I like the challenge you bring into my life."

MOMMA DON'T LEAVE

It was 1803, and the United States of America had completed the purchase of the Louisiana Territory, a colossal 885,000 square miles. The whole obtained for $15 million. It was fortuitous for me because I had had an illegal homestead in what would come to be known as the state of Arkansas, for some seven years now. I was twenty-eight years of age, the son of a colonist who had fought in the Revolutionary War against the British. Because the territory was now American, it boded well for my claim to ownership of the homestead. I was elated and saddened as I recalled that my wife, who had died two years ago of yellow fever, was no longer with me to savor the moment.

When the team of horses pulling my supply wagon lurched forward, I was jolted from my reverie. The road was an accumulation of well-worn wagon ruts, and a fair number of homesteaders plied this route into the wilderness. Not far up ahead, I watched as a woman and what was probably her small daughter emerge onto the road. The woman, of blond hair and blue eyes, though seriously ill, was not without attraction. The daughter, a lovely little girl with long golden curls, appeared to be about five years of age.

I halted the team and stood transfixed. The woman, who was very ill, was in a state of delirium but seemed to have a set purpose in mind. Two weeks ago, she had buried her husband—a victim of typhoid fever- in a shallow grave. Now that she in turn was infected, she knew that she must get the child to the road, lest the child die a lonely death of hunger and thirst with only her mother's rotting corpse as solace. She knew in her heart that a passing wagon would in all probability pick the little girl up, but not if she was huddled next to her mother. In those days, typhoid symptoms were all too apparent, and people tended to shun victims lying along the road. I watched from a distance as the mother seated the little girl on a log beside the road. Sobbing, she explained tearfully to the little girl that they must now part and that she must ask for a ride on a passing wagon. The child, not comprehending why the mother would abandon her, burst into tears. Terrified, the child grasped on to her mother's leg in a viselike grip. Mother and child now melded, and the mother, now extremely weak, could not free herself from the child's grasp.

It was at this point that I was able to put my large hands on each of their shoulders. They looked up at me in confusion and listened intently as I told them, "Now, now, it's not all that bad." I carried the mother to the wagon and laid her gently on a blanket, and the child I mounted on the seat with me. My homestead was less than five miles away, and we headed there at a gentle pace. I had survived typhoid and knew well the look on the mother's face. Though gravely ill, her beauty, still manifest, reminded me of my late wife.

Even though the reader, from another age, now knows that typhoid fever is caused by the bacterium *Salmonella* Typhi and is shed in the feces and urine of its victims, whereupon flies transmit it to food, in those days, we could only wildly speculate. As fortune would have it, I did everything right, keeping the child at a distance and the mother's soil and urine quickly disposed of. I nurtured her on a hearty broth made from game, which I shot daily. In three weeks' time, she was well on her way to recovery, and the child had remained unscathed. The daughter's name was Cheryl and the mother's Sharon, and I found myself saying "Sharon" over and over again. In time, we each developed a high degree of affection for the other and temptation being what it was, our bond was consummated long before we took the oath. We eventually married and raised a large family. In all those years, I could never shake the reality that all this love and good fortune was brought about by a bacterium in the guise of a matchmaker.

THE RED FURNACE

It was 1963, shortly after the Cuban Missile Crisis, and I was a State Department code clerk assigned to the American embassy in Moscow, USSR. Ostensibly, I handled code traffic, outgoing and incoming messages. In actuality, I was a CIA case officer, a foreign spy handler, the spy's umbilical to an espionage agency. I was assigned Colonel Vladimir Sarkovsky, a Soviet army GRU officer who had secretly defected. GRU was Red Army intelligence, a parallel organ to the KGB and frequently in competition with it. Sarkovsky was in his early forties, married to the daughter of a Soviet general, his father and uncle were retired generals, and he belonged to the privileged class, the nomenklatura, who had access to expensive cars and imported Western luxury items.

His assignment in the Soviet military was to frequent Western trade shows spotting Western businessmen, engineers, and scientists ripe for espionage recruitment. The reason he had given for his defection was a deep-seated hatred of Nikita Khrushchev. For the time being, we would take him at his word. Our Colonel Sarkovsky, as a young Red Army officer, was mentored by Marshal Barentov, chief of artillery. Barentov was now the head of the Russian ICBM Program, and our Colonel Sarkovsky had access to these most secret of files. The ICBM Program was the most secret facet of the Soviet military and one that we least understood. He was a treasure trove on two legs, and we could hardly believe our good fortune.

On his next trip to the West he was provided with two specially designed Minox cameras and a dozen film cassettes. Each cassette held forty-four frames. By holding the camera exactly fourteen centimeters above the document, he would achieve perfect focus. He also received a pad of fifty sheets; each sheet was the same containing numbers opposite which a particular instruction was inscribed. Radio Free Europe, broadcasting from Munich, Germany, would send out his code name, "Ludmila," followed by several numbers indicating the message. Also in his possession was an "off-the-shelf" Soviet-made shortwave radio receiver on which he would receive these messages.

When he had a half dozen exposed cassettes, he would deposit them at a drop point called the drop, where I would saunter along on a mission of retrieval. It was of the utmost importance not to have been followed. Our US Marines were often employed to create minor diversions enabling the case officer to slip away undetected. This operation had now been ongoing for eighteen months and producing invaluable information. The following was what occurred the night of the very last pickup, a description not for the squeamish.

It is eight o'clock at night, and Sergeant Martelli, a US Marine guard, after taking a cologne shower with a bottle of Johnny Walker, staggered out through the main entrance feigning drunkenness, throwing packs of cigarettes and dollar bills to passersby. An unruly crowd gathered, and when Sergeant Martelli socked a Soviet policeman in the jaw, I slipped away undetected into the shadows. After making certain that I was not being followed, I took the Metro, Moscow's subway, and then exited through another subway station. The drop point was the darkened vestibule of an apartment building. The film cassettes were bound up in a newspaper and tucked behind a radiator. What was not known to me at the time was that Colonel Sarkovsky has been arrested. A long series of minor slip-ups on his part had accumulated, resulting in his exposure. On entering the darkened vestibule with a small penlight in hand, I reached behind the radiator. At this point, five KGB agents emerged into the hallway. I was grabbed with the utmost ferocity. In quick succession I received massive blows to the abdomen, losing all capacity for breath. Multiple blows to the eyes caused closure, and my eyes now looked like two slits in a jelly doughnut. I was bundled into the back of a large black Volga. I was vomiting. A large hand was clasped over my mouth and nose, and I found it extremely difficult, if not impossible, to breathe. Suffocation was a favorite tactic with the KGB and made for a very unpleasant ride. I was taken to the basement of Lubyanka Prison, and accommodations did not improve. The questions were incessant. They wanted to know everything about my role in the operation. I persisted in denying knowledge of everything. I endured powerful blows to both sides of the face. A towel wrapped around my head and face was pulled back taut and water was poured from a pitcher onto the towel. I coughed and choked, and with each gasp I drew more water into my lungs. Both lungs were now enflamed. I was drowning in a waterlogged towel. This was waterboarding without the board. The Soviets called it the wet submarine.

I was held for two days and two nights and then released into the custody of two US Marines and two Foreign Service officers. As for our beloved Colonel Sarkovsky, he was tried in a military court, found guilty, and sentenced to be shot by a firing squad. However, he did not experience so merciful a death. In the highest traditions of the Red Army, he was strapped to a wooden board, given three minutes to contemplate his espionage, and then tossed feet first into a roaring furnace. We learned that he used his three minutes to hyperventilate himself, sucking air rapidly in and out, causing an eventual loss of bodily feeling culminating in fainting. How much pain he suffered we would never know. His cries never escaped the furnace. He served the United States for approximately eighteen months and photographed some four thousand pages of top-secret ICBM data—an invaluable service.

As for myself, four of my cohorts and I were declared persona non grata and made to leave the country. My only legacy from this period was a slight apprehension upon entering dimly lit hallways.

THE BATTLE OF THE LIGHTS

It was early November 1961, and I was a marine corps sergeant stationed at the US naval base in Subic Bay, Philippine Islands. Having just been told I would carry the American flag in the marine color guard at the marine corps ball, my head had swollen to one hat size larger. It was the most prestigious position in the most solemn of military ceremonies, and so we practiced night and day in full dress blue uniforms. There were four marines. The American flag was right center, the marine corps flag left center. These two were flanked each by a sentry with rifle with chrome bayonet affixed. The two flagstaffs were each topped with golden bronze eagles. It was an unspoken mandate that these eagles must never be taken by the enemy in battle and are to be defended at all hazards.

It was the evening of November 10, and a standing crowd in suits, dress uniforms, and evening gowns filled a huge open area, its eight-foot ceiling with exposed fluorescent light bulbs posed a challenge to the flag bearers. The marine band then struck up the sacred hymn, and there was no spine, male or female, that did not shiver. With the band blaring, the color guard stepped off smartly in its procession to the stage where our commanding officer awaited us with speech in hand. With a military precision that would have made Napoleon's Grande Armée jealous, notwithstanding, I decided to indulge myself by glancing over at a particularly inviting décolletage to my right. The distraction was crucial in that my bronze eagle, now fully erect, caught two fluorescent tubes causing both to explode. It was a "marines have landed moment"; the crowd went wild, and a myriad number of flashbulbs went off as people sought to capture the scene. The blinding flashes lit up the phosphorescent particles in the air, and with the house lights already dim, we lost our bearings. The thronging crowd soon masked the original corridor so that when we stepped off, it was anybody's guess where we were headed. We were striding briskly when a Filipina, who weighed no less than three hundred pounds, loomed up to our front. She raised her arm stiffly and pointed in a direction. "Thank God," I thought to myself, and we step off in that direction. After a half minute of marching, to my horror, we arrived at the ladies' room. I wheeled about in a U-turn, and the crowd parted like the Red Sea. The crowd was ecstatic and now convinced that we were a renegade color guard, raised their glasses on high and began to chant, "You got balls. You got balls." Marines dispatched to our aid could not catch up with us, and soon they themselves became disoriented. With the press of the crowd, the flagstaffs began to look like two saplings in a hurricane.

After what seemed like a fifty-mile march, the stage suddenly loomed into view, and we stiffened our gait. We took our positions to either side of our commanding officer, and our colonel, never lost for words, exclaimed, "Proving once again that the marine corps will overcome all adversity." The rest of the night, we were treated as celebrities, and to make it all so worthwhile, my Miss Décolletage showed up as one of my admirers. It was the first and last time I ever served on a color guard, but it was enough to last me a lifetime.

THE COMPANION

A twelve-year-old boy, together with his dog, had resolved to run away into the night after both had endured a beating by his alcoholic father. The boy's mother had died of tuberculosis when he was nine years of age. The dog, an inseparable companion, was very protective of the twelve year old and in some ways, in judgment, seemed his equal. Now alone on the streets, the dog always seemed to find a nook providing shelter from the wind and rain, and provided security while the boy slept. On that first chilly night, as on all subsequent nights, they curled up together in a small darkened alcove, the fur of his golden retriever providing warmth and its heartbeat reassurance. In time, they came to enjoy their newfound freedom, and in their camaraderie, an even closer bond developed, so that each day they awakened to a new adventure. Theirs was a symbiotic relationship providing all the needed sustenance in the days to come.

Gradually, the boy acquired a small tarpaulin, a blanket, a raincoat, and a warm jacket. A small mess kit from a secondhand store served for eating implements so that here and there, he was able to establish temporary homesteads. The boy, with the dog as an accomplice, now took the art of shoplifting to new heights. In the urban outdoor markets, the boy would deftly pick out a small food item and stuff it under a cloth band that encircled the dog's upper waist. Thus impregnated, the dog would leave and await the boy outside the market. Neighborhood hose bibs provided water for the metal bowl he carried in a backpack. In time, their presence became known to the locals and halfhearted attempts were made to bring them to bay, but they seemed always to be one step ahead of their pursuers and would make good their escape.

Then one night, perhaps three or four o'clock in the morning, with the boy and dog ensconced in a hollowed-out thicket, he awoke to the sounds of an altercation. Behind the tavern, he could see a man on the ground being mercilessly beaten by two other men. He could hear the man pleading for his life. At first, the boy was gripped with fear and moved to calm the dog, opting to stay hidden. But no sooner had he come to this resolve than he recognized the man's anguished pleas as that of his father. Choking back tears and gripped by a powerful emotion he little understood nor could resist, he stood up and exposed himself, yelling at the top of his lungs, with the dog now joining in chorus. As one of the assailants stood over his father with a large rock, about to crush his head, the boy let fly a stone the size of his fist. It grazed the attacker's head, knocking him to the ground. With the dog now attacking in full fury, both men fled. Although an object of hate, the boy was irresistibly drawn to the crumpled-up form that he knew to be his father. He now seemed to him so pitiful, so helpless. He felt his protective instincts welling up within him. The dog seemed to concur by profusely licking the father's face in a sign of recognition and forgiveness.

When the father recognized his rescuer as his own twelve-year-old son, he sobbed uncontrollably. He hugged his son as he had never hugged him before. "I am so sorry, son, so sorry," he exclaimed over and over, and upon hearing this, the son resolved to forgive his father's sins. With the help of his son, he made it to his feet. Slowly, arm in arm, they walked the four blocks home, and always the dog led. It seemed he had never forgotten the way. The boy and the dog entered the house as though they had never left it. The dog leaped onto the boy's bed and dozed contentedly while the boy filled the dog's dish with kibble. After three bowls of clam chowder, a glass of milk, some chocolate chip cookies, and a hot bath, it all seemed like a dream. The father after his brush with death could not take his eyes from the boy. An epiphany had taken place causing the father to join the local chapter of Alcoholics Anonymous. The boy was reenrolled in school, and the father began to provide the love and support he had so long withheld and the dog, good sport that he was, went along with everything.

PEG STUNFORD COMMEMORATION DINNER

Unless my long-term memory has failed me, Peg Stunford was the most remarkable woman that I have ever been affected by. After a great deal of ponderous thought, I came to the inescapable conclusion that she was truly the most selfless and good-natured person within my sphere, past and present.

She was a lady of remarkable stamina and endurance and of a wholesome intelligence, not to mention being well endowed with the physical feminine attributes, an excellent cook—and I have a waistline that provides irrefutable proof. But Peg was much more than what met the eye.

I remember the time we went hiking on the trail at Spanish Point in the middle of August. I was hot, exhausted, and drenched with perspiration and whined every minute. I looked over, and there she was, standing tall as a trooper, hands on hips with a baseball cap perched squarely on her head. I half expected her to say, "Is there a problem?" As an ex-marine with plenty of jungle patrol experience in the Philippine Islands, I thought silently to myself, "If this isn't role reversal."

Endurance wasn't her only attribute. Peg was also very handy. I remember the time she rewired the bathroom ceiling exhaust fan. The noise was excessive, but what I liked the most was how it would snatch toilet paper from your hand and draw it up to the ceiling.

At the Bayshore Exercise Center, the attendants still marvel at the time, during calisthenics, that Peg caught her ankle in the ceiling fan. It was the opinion of the electrician that the fan got the worst of it, although he could never be reached for further comment.

The time she stubbed her toe on the concrete parking lot car stopper, it took the contractor a month to repair it, while Peg was in and out of the emergency room in less than an hour. The evidence of her indestructibility is all around us.

Although hardworking and frugal, when Peg first came to Florida, she had absolutely nothing, and today, she still has most of it left. Then, I don't think there was a handful of people who knew her, but today, her name is in every phone book in Charlotte County.

With regard to ambition—and I quote Peg—"I started at the bottom, and I liked it there." And who among us can forget the time some heartless individual stole the penny out of one of her loafers? It's not easy!

Who can forget her contributions to technology? Her jalapeño dip is now used by NASA engineers to caulk the stained-glass windows on the shuttle! Her chicken soup is reputed to have grown back a limb!

And to those who would say, "We're not getting any younger," she would reply, "You better hope we're not, 'cause you need the experience more than anybody."

Peg always admired my facial features and would often tell me she wished she had a nose like mine full of nickels.

Peg was always very helpful in those times when I needed transportation and would often tell me that if the turnip truck ever came back through for me to get back on it. On those winter days when it was so cold that the flashers in the park were describing themselves, she would gather them up and take them over to the local bakery where they were content to watch the buns rise in warmth and comfort. Yes, her compassion knew no bounds and lastly Peg was instrumental in getting me my first job as a bookend at Barnes & Noble. Peg, I am the richer for having known you!

THE WOUNDED BIRD

They say love is where you find it, so it came as no surprise even to those marines stationed behind the iron curtain. Though restricted from fraternizing with Soviet citizens or citizens from any iron curtain country, it did not preclude chasing after secretaries from the Western embassies, and the marines at the American embassy in Moscow, USSR, took full advantage of that option. Tall, blond, blue-eyed vixens from the Scandinavian countries were highly sought after. Although none of us were married, we were all physically well practiced for that eventuality. Though most of us could maintain a precarious balance, like a moth caught up in the flame, there were a few who would fall head over heels in love and be unable to escape its gravitational pull.

A case in point was a newly arrived corporal, George Hernes, a very competent and engaging marine but with an appalling lack of life experience when it came to those of us garnished in skirts. He was vulnerable in that he idealized women to a fault and seemed incapable of assigning any ulterior motives to the fairer sex. This, coupled with the sex drive of a brontosaurus, did not bode well for George's emotional health. Because there were only eight of us, it was only natural that we all looked after each other on the social scene, being careful not to tread on each other's turf. But it was soon apparent that we could not stand by while our beloved George got sucked down the maelstrom. He had fallen hopelessly in love with Ingrid, a Swedish secretary who frequented our American House Club. Ingrid had a body that was conjured up by the devil using only a drafting board, a 115 pounds of protoplasm and a French curve. It was said that her gaze could levitate the olive in a martini, her high-heeled feet paralyzed a foot fetishist, and her near proximity could cause spandex to lose its elasticity. She also had a static electric effect in that whenever she came near me, the short hairs at the nape of my neck would stand on end. She was also known to produce a stutter in what had otherwise been an eloquent male, but I got over it.

So with visions of the girl next door dancing in his head, our corporal George mortified our noncommissioned officer in charge by declaring his desire to marry Ingrid. Because yes was the most-used English word in Ingrid's vocabulary, it came as no surprise to us that she had answered his marriage proposal in the affirmative. The rest of us held an informal meeting in a heartfelt attempt to resolve the crisis. Knowing Ingrid's sex habits, there was no doubt in our minds that she would chew him up and spit him out in short order. It was decided that the only way to open his eyes was to let him discover her engaged in her favorite pursuit with a fellow marine. There was no shortage of marine volunteers, and because she seldom passed up an opportunity for coitus, success was almost assured.

Upon his arrival at the American House Club, Corporal Hernes was told his beloved Ingrid was awaiting him on the second floor in bedroom C. When George opened the unlocked door, there was Ingrid in all her glory entwined with our volunteer. A mixture of shock, disbelief, and betrayal contorted George's face. More marines appeared to make sure there was no bloodshed. What we had not anticipated was Ingrid's perverse pleasure, once she was caught, in inflicting emotional pain on George. Those marines who were there would never forget her sardonic smile.

The corporal bolted from the club and took a car back to the embassy. Responding to an overwhelming desire to talk to somebody, he took the embassy elevator to the restricted area. I was on duty at the desk and unbolted the door allowing him access, the equivalent of lowering the drawbridge. Having been informed by telephone, using a code word, I was prepared to administer a verbal unguent. He was despondent and tears followed one another in tandem down his cheeks. I told him, "Had it not been for your brother marines, you would have married that sack of shit. They did what they did for your welfare. Think about it," I implored. I could sense that he knew I was right, but I also knew that his pain was immense.

An hour passed, and I told him to watch the door while I took a leak. When I came back into the room, he had his back to me. He abruptly turned and faced me. He had the short-barreled shotgun, what we called a street cleaner, gleaned from a bottom drawer, jammed into the roof of his mouth. As I raised my arm in a staying gesture, he pulled the trigger. A shock wave assaulted my eardrums; simultaneously a circular pattern of various shades of gray, pink, and red impinged on the ceiling above. Globules of splintered bone and brain now hung from the ceiling. The top of his head was gone, and for an instant, the body stood upright as though in disbelief before surrendering to gravity. Blood spurted in distinct pulses from the wound cavity, and the air was rife with the acrid smell of sulfur. I reached for the emergency phone to the marine apartment. "Get up here," I exclaimed. "George just blew his head off. This is no joke." In less than a minute, five marines in various stages of dress appeared. A pall of shock and disbelief hung over the scene. Gallows humor prompted a wag to exclaim, "Wait till the cleaning lady sees this."

In the aftermath, Ingrid was told in no uncertain terms never to show her face there again—or was it her rear end? Corporal Flanagan, our volunteer, was never the same man, and as for the rest of us, it was like so many decisions that we made in life, fraught with irreversible consequences. We all had the best of intentions and inadvertently helped to pave the road to hell.

THE MAY DAY FLOAT

It was the year 1953 at the parish of St. Francis of Assisi Catholic Church, and I was a deeply religious eleven-year-old boy enthralled and devoted to the Blessed Virgin Mary, who, as everybody knows, is the mother of Christ. I prayed to her often with mundane and magnificent requests, and one way or the other, they were resolved. The Virgin Mary was as real to me as Grace Kelly was to you, so that when the first Sunday in May rolled around, I always found myself passionately assisting my father, the artist, who every year was assigned the prestigious honor of decorating her May Day float, a flatbed trailer parked in the lot next to our house with an eight-foot statue of the Blessed Mary mounted at the front end.

Early morning on the day of the parade found us hard at work on a trailer lit up with spotlights. A few dedicated volunteers assisted our efforts, but as wind gusts reached twenty-five to thirty miles per hour, they began to drift away in total discouragement. My father, now visibly thwarted as the crepe streamers were blown asunder, succumbed to this trial of wills and eventually dropped everything and went into the house. I soon followed in bewilderment, and I found him prostrate, sobbing on the living room couch. I pleaded with him that we must keep trying because only a few hours remained before noon. My father, seemingly oblivious to my presence, moaned aloud, "One day out of the year in her honor and she couldn't be damn considerate enough to hold down the wind." Frantic that the float be completed by noon, I summed up our predicament with the only thought that came into my little noggin, a theme that my father was only too familiar with: "Dad, you know how women can be. Look at Mom." When I saw a smile bleeding through his anguished face, I knew I had struck a chord.

Seeming to make no difference in my father's condition, I staggered through the wind and mounted the float with crepe paper in hand. Alone now, it was evident that the mother of Christ now had only one small boy working on her float. Suddenly, the roll of tape was wrenched from my hand by the wind, leaving only the rolls of crepe. Now without tape, I began to tie the crepe ends. This proved to be our salvation, the wind being unwilling to break the bond. I was making small headway when I felt my father's powerful hands relieve me of some of the rolls. Through the gusts, we steadily wove our crepe, and the design began to take on a life of its own. As we neared completion, my father seemed awed and astonished at the overall effect. By his silence, he seemed humbled by the spectacle of his own creation. As the wind began to subside, our volunteers began to reappear, and it became apparent that they, too, were struck by the float's inordinate beauty and radiance.

By noon, the winds had died, and the sun reappeared. The tractor was methodically hitched to the float, and crowds began to throng Lovejoy Avenue. Now with the full brilliance of the sun, the crepe streamers took on an unearthly glow. My father would always say that during the seven years that he designed the float, nothing would compare with that year of trial and tribulation for its magnificent beauty and emotional impact. Sadly, my devotion to the Blessed Virgin lasted six more years, and then with the onset of atheism, an irreconcilable breakup occurred which has lasted to this day.

THE DOG WALK

It was 2014, and I was walking my dog in the town of Port Charlotte, Florida. The walk almost always began a little after midnight when there were few encounters with pedestrians. My dog, a German shepherd, had long decided he did not like people or dogs as much as he once did and must now be restrained at any chance meeting. The route we took was down a scenic lane that meandered through a condominium complex studded with massive oak trees.

One night, I encountered an attractive woman coming toward me. She was walking an Afghan hound and was the epitome of high fashion, though a fashion somewhat out of date. She was stunning with a slightly ethereal aura. I suddenly realized that my dog had made no reaction to her or her dog. Encouraged, I moved closer to engage in conversation. Her dog moved in to sniff my dog, and I braced for an eruption. There was none. We exchanged glances, and a light conversational banter ensued. She told me her name was Sonia and that she often walked her dog late at night, the hour seeming to have great significance for her. As time passed, I began to look forward to our nightly encounters. We always seemed to meet at the same place about the same time.

Soon the attraction blossomed into a full-blown infatuation, and I offered to take her to dinner and a movie. Her eyes saddened, and her voice became subdued as she declined the offer, saying that she was not available for such things.

Now realizing how she managed to stay unattached for so long, I changed the subject.

One night, I was late for the rendezvous and despaired of meeting her. When I saw her standing with her dog in the usual location, I began to wonder whether she had been waiting there all that time. As I approached, we waved to each other, and even after I'd dropped my hand, I could see that she was still waving. It was at this point that my concentration was shattered by the thunder of an aircraft engine. I looked up in horror to see a twin-engine aircraft clipping the treetops. Its trajectory ended in an earth-shaking fireball that consumed the area where she stood. I was thrown to the ground and found myself prostrate in the grass. Still clutching the leash, I looked over to see my dog standing upright looking at me in wonderment. I raised myself from the grass and was amazed to see no wreckage, no crater at point of impact, or evidence of a fire. She and her dog had vanished into thin air. I staggered home but on arriving could not resist the compulsion to go back to the spot. But she was not to be found, and the area still appeared unscathed.

The next day, I was having homemade doughnuts and coffee with Mrs. Lanahan across the street, who had been in the area so long that she was reputed to have dated Ponce de León's grandson. Halfway through the coffee, I unburdened myself, telling her about the vivid hallucination I had while walking the dog on Forest Nelson Boulevard. To my surprise, she seemed fascinated, telling me that indeed there had been a plane crash on the boulevard some thirty years ago. The pilot had been killed and so was a woman on the ground walking her dog. She knew the year to be 1984, it having occurred the same month and year her brother died. Astonished and intrigued to the point of obsession, I visited the public library, and using a computer terminal called up newspaper editions from that year and month. The article came up, and it hit me like a wooden mallet. The picture was of her. An Afghan hound was included in one of the photos. A picture showing the smoldering wreckage, the remains of a twin-engine plane, was framed by the stone buttresses defining the entryway to the condominium. It was the same location where we would meet. My mouth was now so dry it felt like cotton, and the librarian was moved to ask me if everything was all right. I nodded weakly and stared off into space.

For years afterward, I walked the same route at the same time of night, but never again did she appear. I was left with the haunting memory of her last moments. Her lingering wave, long after I had dropped my hand, right up to the moment of impact. The experience left me with the unshakable conclusion that there is more to the universe than we are capable of conceiving. I miss you, Sonia, wherever you are.

THE ILL WIND

A breeze blew from seaward onto the shoreline of a small Malaysian fishing village located on the island of Penang in the Malacca Strait. It was 1980, and a mysterious affliction had this close-knit community in a state of terror. Its onset was sudden. The victim became weak and nauseous, losing control of all bodily functions, including the ability to breathe, with death from asphyxiation soon following. Malaysian health officials beseeched the World Health Organization, who then enlisted the laboratories for the Centers for Disease Control in Atlanta, Georgia. Their findings were startling. The cause was a sarin nerve gas of a distinctive type, a chemical warfare agent five hundred times more powerful than cyanide produced only by Nazi Germany in the early 1940s. But where could the source be? In 1943, the Japanese navy had set up a submarine base on Penang Island some fifteen miles from the village. Allied naval intelligence had known that the base was also the destination of long-range U-boats bringing vital commodities such as tool steel, mercury, and optical glass to a needful Japan. Could a cache of nerve gas have been delivered and eventually buried somewhere near the village? The area was evacuated, and chemical warfare personnel scoured the vicinity with toxin detectors but to no avail, though the air was still laced with traces of sarin. A light northwesterly breeze blew in from seaward, and all eyes now turned toward the watery depths.

Investigators foraging over U-boat archives in Germany uncovered an intriguing cargo manifest for the U-490, a long-range U-boat with a reach of some twenty-three thousand miles, whose last voyage entailed the delivery of war material to Penang Island. It never arrived and was listed as presumed lost with all hands in the eastern Indian Ocean. Along with its cargo of optical glass was a staggering sixty gallons of liquid sarin, the concentrate. Small boats now set out from the shore looking for telltale bubbles from the deep. The boats spotted nothing, but on the return, about three hundred yards out, an intermittent trickle of bubbles revealed itself. A marker buoy was set in place, and a Portuguese patrol vessel from the World Health Organization arrived to take a sonar signature. The operator in front of the sonar screen became agitated. At a depth of 225 feet, the image of a massive cigar-shaped Leviathan, on a scale of a World War II submarine, suddenly dominated the screen. The exclamation "Mother of God!" escaped his lips. Four divers in protective clothing and toxin-proof respirators assembled on the deck and in a flurry of "sign of the crosses" rotated over the side and into the murky depths. At two hundred feet, they saw the outline of a U-boat. It lay situated in an upright position, the visage, a secret kept for thirty-six years. Bubbles could be seen emanating from the intake vents. A close inspection revealed a small engraved brass plate affixed to the conning tower betraying the designation U-490. A chill ran through the diver as he contemplated the sixty gallons of sarin within. The divers traversed the U-boat from bow to stern but could find no battle damage. All hatches were buttoned up securely in a state of watertight integrity, and the entire crew was presumed to be entombed within. But what caused this submarine to settle here in its final resting place? Official speculation on its fate settled on one theory, that as it made its underwater approach, a catastrophic leak of sarin gas overcame the entire crew. Only an internal explosion could have resulted in lethally incapacitating the entire crew within seconds. What could have caused such an event? Each crew member of a U-boat had in his possession an emergency respirator with an attached oxygen bottle. If accidentally impacted on the threaded nipple, the sudden release of gas would have caused considerable explosive damage. With a crew of sixty-two souls, it carried on board seventy-five such units.

After the German relatives of the crew were notified concerning the final fate of their loved ones, a not-too-inexpensive removal of the sub to deep ocean depths began. All intake vents were filled with marine concrete injected under pressure. Tunneling allowed four ten-foot-wide support straps to girdle the sub.

These, in turn, were fastened to massive inflatable flotation collars. When res-urrected to the surface, it was towed through the Malacca Strait and in turn across the Andaman Sea to the Indian Ocean where it was sunk to a depth of sixteen thousand feet, far from any population centers. In retrospect, it could be said to have been the last chemical warfare gasp of the Third Reich.

THE SHOESHINE BOY

Yes, I was once a shoeshine boy, an endeavor that now seems very unlikely in retrospect. I sallied forth into the business world as a sole owner-operator. My mobile shop consisted of a green ammunition box with a cast-iron footrest bolted to the top, with a large leather strap that allowed me to carry it along on my shoulder, with its contents of brushes, shine rags, and polishes locked inside beneath the hinged top. It was my very first job as a breadwinner. I say breadwinner because my earnings augmented the family income. You see, I at twelve years of age was the oldest male in the family with three younger sisters—Ann, Mary, and Carol, aged nine, seven, and five, respectively. Our father had been killed abruptly in an automobile accident two years prior to my twelfth birthday. Our family was now being carried along by my maternal grandparents. Though themselves not wealthy, whatever they had, they shared with us. My mother was now not well and had been bedridden for the past two months.

It was a cold winter morning when my grandparents took us aside and ever so lovingly told us that Mother would not survive her cancer. The doctor predicted she would not survive through the night and that we must be strong for her sake. Grandfather pleaded with us not to wail in front of her as this would only add to her anguish. There would be time enough afterward. To me, it meant she would not be here to receive the bottle of lilac perfume that I had so long intended to buy her. I became obsessed with the thought that if she could only smell the lilacs, somehow everything would change for the better.

Grabbing the shoeshine box, I ran out the door and arrived at the beginning of my route. It consisted of one drinking establishment after another, henceforth referred to as bars. In these bars, I had a smattering of regular customers. In those days, it was a macho-male status symbol to have your shoes shined while imbibing at a standup bar. A shoeshine was thirty-five cents, and together with the tip, you might wind up with one or two dollars per shine. Usually, the higher the level of inebriation, the better the prospect of a large tip. Because these bars were frequented by prostitutes, a shoeshine boy working as he did at ground level usually got more than an eyeful, and the prostitutes were more than willing to indulge in prurient mischief. But I survived it and if nothing else, it enhanced my sense of anatomical correctness.

In a few hours, I had earned enough to buy the perfume. Racing down Lovejoy Avenue I entered the pharmacy where my treasure was displayed in the window. Breathlessly, I explained to the saleslady that it was for my sick mother and that she would know if it was not fresh. She let me smell it, and because it seemed fresh enough to me, I bought it. As I ran down an alleyway, a shortcut to home, I was knocked to the ground from behind. Terrified, I peered up to see two older shoeshine boys, competitors, who administered a swift kick to my head, stomped on my legs and arms, and before leaving, smashed my shoeshine box. After a short agonizing interval, I rose and gathered together the contents of my box as best I could. A sudden panic was abated when I was able to focus my eyes on the little bag lying in the snow. The perfume had escaped their destruction. In this manner was I able to stagger home.

I arrived home as the sun was setting. It seemed to forebode that there was very little time left. My grandfather, who met me at the door, was shocked at my appearance. I feebly explained how I had fallen in the snow and that I would be only a minute cleaning up in the bathroom. "Hurry," he said. "There is precious little time." I washed the caked-on blood from my hands and face and pulled the baseball cap low on my forehead, hoping to conceal my black-and-blue eyes. In the hand with the two broken fingers, I clutched Momma's perfume. The hairline crack in my skull gave me a throbbing headache. Two partially fracture ribs and an arm added to my woes. But it was imperative to me that Momma should be spared this visage, and so I steeled myself as I entered her dimly lit bedroom. My sisters and grandparents, who were clustered around her, parted as I entered. My mother was conscious, and it seemed to me that she smiled at my approach. She could hear and think clearly, but her vision was very poor. "Momma," I said, "I brought you something; it's your favorite," and with that, I extended my broken hand, opened the bottle, and thrust it under her nose. Instantly, a beaming smile swept across her face. It was apparent to me that the perfume was working its magic; soon, she would be restored. But seeming to ignore this change in her fortune, she began to tell me to brush my teeth twice a day and to make sure that I ate plenty of green vegetables. She emphasized that although soon she could not be with us that she and my father would always be with us in spirit. "You must be strong to take care of your sisters," and with that final thought, she died before my eyes. Instinctively, I thrust the perfume under her nose but to no avail. I remember resisting my grandmother as she took the bottle from my hand and led us out of the room.

Years later, my grandmother gave me back that bottle of perfume with its contents still locked inside. To this day, whenever I want to commune with my mother, I open it, inhale its precious fragrance, and suddenly it's as though she is there in front of me. I miss you, Momma.

THE LITTLEST CAMERA

My name is not important, suffice it to say that I was a marine corps ser-geant stationed at the American embassy in Moscow, USSR. Our guard detachment consisted of eight marines, all handpicked for various capabilities. It was 1963, I was twenty years of age, and was second in command, and although I could not legally drink in Florida, I tried not to let it bother me.

There, living in an upper-floor apartment of the embassy as a dependent of an American army attaché was a five-year-old boy named Jerry, whose termi-nal, debilitating neurological disorder left him with both legs encased in steel braces. Jerry had one interest left in life and that was the marines, to which the detachment responded with salutes and so many donated medals that his mother, when pinning them to his chest, had to make sure they were evenly distributed lest he topple over. His ultimate thrill came when he grasped the handle of a .45 caliber handgun and with both my hands clasped around his, cranked off a round hitting a tin can. But his most prideful possession was the large white circular ceremonial cap complete with the golden marine emblem affixed to the center. I had cut down the inner band so it accommodated his head snugly, and there were few people who could look directly at him without tearing up.

A heavy ambience hung over the embassy following the recent Cuban Missile Crisis, and when military intelligence learned that Soviet military hard-ware to be displayed in the October Revolution Parade, would of necessity because of unforeseen road construction, be required to pass directly across the front of our embassy, it unleashed a paroxysm of photographic determination. This Soviet equipment usually paraded only in Red Square could now be photographed like never before. From the storage areas came a plethora of heavy highly sophisticated tripod cameras. All marines were given crash instruction on their operation and cameras were sighted from advantageous windows for the proper angle. It was not unlike the sighting of artillery pieces, my occupational specialty.

The day of the parade dawned to find all of our military personnel ensconced behind their cameras. So dire was our need for support that the wives and older children of military attachés were employed to carry wicker baskets full of film cassettes up and down the stairs, keeping us continuously supplied. The shooting soon attained a frenzied pace, and at one point, I turned to see little Jerry standing behind me holding a wicker basket containing one film cassette, his mother having carried him up the stairs. His marine cap perched squarely on his head in stark contrast to his leg braces. I turned to him. "You came to fight the Cold War. Wow! What a brave marine!" I made it very apparent to him that I was awed and at the last second was betrayed by two tears wending their way down my cheeks. He looked at me curiously, and I reached over and squeezed his cheek and looked up to see two matching tears on his mother's face. In an instant, the mother and son were both gone.

I returned to the camera and nursed it much as I would a machine gun. The Soviets made it as difficult as possible, passing by at speeds averaging fifty miles per hour, but our ultrahigh-speed film seized their images in place. This exposed film would be sent to West Berlin via the diplomatic pouch for imagery analysis. The science of photogrammetry using electronic, mechanical, and optical photo enhancers and stereoscopes provided a wealth of detail not apparent to the naked eye.

Jerry and I parted when his father, an army major, was sent to a posting at the Pentagon, presumably where little Jerry could receive the best available medical care. About a year and a half later, his mother wrote to me at the London embassy, where I was posted. Jerry, she wrote, had passed away two weeks ago to the day. It was as though I had lost a son; the tears flowed in an endless stream and could not be stanched. I always thought of him as he was that day with his marine cap, with leg braces and all, holding that wicker basket with a lone film cassette. Of all those who were on the firing line that day, he was the purest of heart.

Forever after in my thoughts, he was known to me as the littlest camera.

THE ERRANT LOAF

It was the fifties, 1951 to be exact, and I was nine years old. This was the era before the proliferation of supermarkets. A simpler time when the corner family-owned grocery store was our main source of victuals. Then, you simply stated to the proprietor what you wanted, usually sight unseen, and he would dutifully march out from behind the counter, pole gripper in hand, and with military precision light at the exact product location. For some unknown reason, the product, as though not wanting to leave the store, would be perched at the highest level. This seemed not to daunt the proprietor, and it was evident that he took particular pride in this exhibition of mercantile prowess. The straining to reach the product was always accompanied by a loud grunt or the passing of gas. The flatulence seemed to quicken his gait and on the whole seemed to increase the rapidity of the service.

This particular corner store was owned by Joseph Farina, an Italian American from our parish, a very diminutive man, and his Swedish-born bride, a very tall, buxom blond lady. She I found very distracting in that in her presence, I often forgot what I wanted. Yes, I did develop a crush on her but no matter.

It was a hot summer day when my father gave me eighteen cents to get a loaf of Italian bread on the double. Being nine years old, I had long since forgotten how to walk and therefore ran everywhere. I ran into the store, put the money on the counter, grabbed a loaf, and was back home in a flash. My father met me at the door where I handed him the loaf. The bag contained a Vienna bread, not Italian. Seeing this, he slapped me across the side of my face with an open hand. The force caused my head to bounce off the door jamb. Unbeknownst to him or me, it had opened up a cut on the side of my head. I fumbled for the loaf off the kitchen floor and ran back to the store, dropping it on the counter, and blurted out the mistake. As the loaf hit the counter, it caused a spattering of blood. Mrs. Farina, horror stricken and speechless, grabbed a loaf of Italian bread and gave it to me. When I arrived home, it, too, was covered in blood. Now realizing that I was injured, he became grief stricken and remorseful. A quick trip to the emergency room followed. After being stitched up, the nurse filling out the report in my father's presence asked me how it happened. A short silence ensued, and then I looked over at my father and said, "My father can tell you." The nurse and my father then conferred in private. To my satisfaction, when he emerged, I could see that he had cried.

Long afterward, as I looked back on this incident, I always felt sorry for my father. You see, my father very rarely hit me, and even then, it was never very forceful, and yet this man who had exhibited a remarkable degree of restraint was subjected to a humiliating exhibition of child abuse. Most unfair, I thought. Needless to say, I harbor to this day no resentment, and if nothing else, I am now a highly discriminating bread shopper with a fetish for tall blondes.

THE PAPER BOY

As a budding writer, I feel I would be remiss if I did not reveal to you one of the most powerful experiences in my early sexual development. The names need have no significance, and the times have long changed, but the images and frissons evoked remain as poignant as the day they occurred.

At the time, I was eighteen years of age, though I looked much younger and prospering as a newspaper delivery boy with my own paper route. I purchased the papers wholesale from the *Buffalo Evening News* and delivered them to my customers each afternoon. The retail cost I personally collected from them at the end of each week. Equipped only with large pockets and a coin changer fastened to my belt, I would often find myself standing in their kitchen or living room with the lady of the house in her various modes of dress. In some cases, the mode was more than skimpy and in those days represented a complete disregard for catching pneumonia.

Being of Italian extraction, my emotions are very transparent, and women seem to be able to read them much as they would the signs on an expressway. So when I stood before her barely clad figure, she was more than in control, and she knew it. She was in her twenties, married although her husband was away on business, and this was her last week. They were moving to another city. Her figure, well endowed and statuesque, was further enhanced by a face that was both beautiful and exotic. Green hypnotic commanding eyes that seemed capable of transfixing a light beam peered from beneath a tussle of strawberry-blond hair.

Ruby-red lips matched her impeccably manicured finger- and toenails. High heels with ankle straps added to her already-impressive height. A loose blouse exposing most of her bosom complemented a loose translucent skirt revealing an absence of underwear. She said not a word, locked the door behind me, and gazed at me intensely. By this time, I had lost the capacity for speech and was being rapidly overtaken by paralysis.

She proffered a ten-dollar bill, puckered up her lips, winked, and dropped the bill on her feet. After an eternity, I bent down to retrieve the bill. With lightning speed, she raised her skirt and dropped it over me much the way a hunter drops a net to snare an animal. It seemed as though I had been transported to another world, the Elysian Fields. I remember the captivating scent of what I now know to be Chanel N° 5. The translucent skirt provided just enough illumination to reveal two beautiful alabaster legs that seemed to go on forever, like two marble columns in a Greek temple. My wonderment was short lived as I felt her hands on the back of my head. With one forceful motion, she pushed my face between her legs. It was then that I finally knew the true meaning of the phrase "First Communion." Periodically, I was allowed to come up for air, and the oxygen deprivation seemed to have had no lasting effect.

It was here that I first learned a skill that has served me well throughout my life. I call it the "graceful exit." At a point where it was apparent that we were both satiated, I decided that this was the time to make change for the ten-dollar bill, and so it was that from beneath the skirt was heard the ringing of the coin changer. I could see by the jiggling of her thighs that she was laughing. When I emerged from under her skirt, I was ready with change in hand. I thanked her profusely for her business and wished her well in her relocation. Yes, I did look like a glazed doughnut when I left the house, and to this day, the glazed doughnut occupies a special place in my psyche.

THE PRICE OF PORK

It was 1989. I was forty-seven years of age and made my living in Florida as a landscape contractor. Even though my business was prospering, there was something missing. It was the element of adventure whose active ingredient was raw unmitigated danger. Having become aware of a two-week hunting season for wild boar in the Big Cypress Swamp adjacent to the Everglades, I resolved to confront the most vicious of feral hogs, the razorback, descended from domestic hogs brought over by the Spanish during the 1500s and then escaped into the wilds. The razorback is powerful, aggressive, and agile and will viciously attack the hunter if left wounded. I was advised to seek safety in the nearest tree because another shot may not be enough to arrest his charge. A few hunters who have chosen to attempt a second shot have been disemboweled by his sharp tusks.

"This is perfect," I thought to myself, thinking that in the confrontation the boar may have as much chance as I do. What could be more sporting? Regarding the danger of being disemboweled, I consoled myself by reasoning that because I didn't have a potbelly, I would present a smaller target.

Because penetrating the watery wilds of the Everglades alone is considered near suicidal, I prevailed upon my younger brother Gary to accompany me as backup. His first reaction was to suggest that it would be easier to pick up a tray of pork chops over at our Publix supermarket.

Convincing Gary that the all-important exciting interval between beginning the journey and consuming the pork would be lost and after he pondered that thought, he agreed. And with this accord, we began the purchasing of firearms, body armor, and all the related accoutrements considered judicious for the expedition.

My high-powered rifle was a Remington .270 Model 700; my sidearm, a revolver, was a Smith & Wesson .44 magnum. Seamless, knee-high rubber boots overlaid with hard plastic snake guards for footwear, a lensatic compass, a large bowie knife, two canteens of water, food rations, a floppy full-brimmed hat with attached mosquito netting, long-sleeve shirt, mosquito repellent, and a set of binoculars made up my kit. Gary was similarly attired.

After obtaining the necessary hunting permits, we arrived at what we hoped would be the scene of the carnage. I parked the truck on a marl road that ran through the swamp east to west and we descended on foot into a watery world, the water level being just below the knee. Using the lensatic compass, I sighted on a distant landmark and navigated around obstructions to that point. Arriving at that point, I sighted on another distant object all the while maintaining a constant bearing, which was exactly due north. We would walk for four hours out, and then doing the reverse azimuth, it would take four hours to get back to civilization. This skill was not new to me having been a marine jungle patrol leader in the Philippine Islands.

As we trudged through this eerie world studded with massive bald cypress trees, laced with Spanish moss and protruding cypress knees, we were ever vigilant for poisonous snakes—the water moccasin on watery surfaces and the large diamond back and pygmy rattler on higher ground.

Within the close confines of three cypress trees, I suddenly heard a loud hiss. Directly in our path, five feet away, was a wide-bodied cotton mouth water moccasin coiled around a cypress knee. I drew my revolver, cocked the hammer, took careful aim at the head, and squeezed lightly on the trigger. Simultaneously with the explosion, the head disappeared, manifesting itself as dozens of little red specks on adjacent tree trunks. The body released its coils and collapsed into the water. The .44 magnum had proved its efficacy as a snake gun.

We moved on and began to encounter islands of elevated land studded with hardwoods, these being known as hammocks, and as we approached the bank, we were subjected to our first nightmare. With sudden realization, not fifteen feet away lay a massive ten-foot alligator whose girth was more impressive than its length. Frustrated in my attempts to make the sign of the cross by low over-hanging branches, Gary and I could only remain frozen, not by choice, but by sheer instinctive fear. Alligators, when aroused to attack, can attain speeds of forty miles per hour, chomping down on an arm or leg and then torqueing their powerful bodies resulting in the removal of an entire limb as easily as removing the leg from a grasshopper. How long we remained frozen I cannot say. Our dilemma was brought to a conclusion when Gary involuntarily broke wind with a loud pop, causing the alligator to explode in a paroxysm of motion and disap-pearing into the water. This incident was known to me ever after as "saved by a can of beans."

As we crouched down in the grass, the binoculars revealed three to four black boars on the edge of the next hammock. Upon our stealthy approach, they withdrew into its interior. Having waited over an hour for them to emerge and with a limited amount of time to get back before darkness fell, we decided it would be necessary to go in and flush them from their cover.

Gary insisted on taking the lead. I walked fifteen paces behind and seven feet to the right. As we closed with the hammock, the tension became almost unbearable, and in half disbelief I heard Gary's audible voice, as clear as a bell, begin to sing the strains of a Nat King Cole recording: "At the end of a rainbow, you'll find a pot of gold. At the end of a story, you'll find it's all been told. But my love will go on till the end of time." It was at this point that four razorbacks burst forth from the hammock. Amid the snarling of tusks and a cacophony of multiple gunshots, three hogs now lay dead and the fourth lay dying. There, too, lay my brother mortally wounded, a massive neck wound severing his jugu-lar vein. We established eye contact before he died in my arms.

So you see, I got my pork, but it was my brother who paid the price.

I AM NOT ALONE

There was something medieval about the building. Many of the interior walls were four-inches thick and filled with rubble, presumably to withstand bomb blasts. It was the American embassy in Moscow, USSR, and it was not the Middle Ages. It was 1962. The dust had just settled from the Cuban Missile Crisis, and I was a newly minted US Marine sergeant, a security guard. Even though I wore a suit and tie, diplomacy was only my second nature. Beneath my jacket, cradled in a shoulder holster, was a .45 caliber semiautomatic pistol, and I was as adept with it as you are with a fork. However, I could not draw blood unless my life was threatened, a limitation we liked to think the Soviets did not know.

This building served as our embassy during World War II and during receptions had seen the likes of Stalin, Malenkov, Molotov, Beria (the head of the Soviet secret police and intelligence services), Mikoyan, and untold others. It had seen numerous American ambassadors including Averell Harriman, Llewellyn Thompson, Charles Bolen, David Bruce, and Foy Kohler. Although gloomy and massive, these walls had witnessed agreements that affected the welfare of millions of people for good or for worse.

Though a ten-story building, only the bottom two floors conducted routine consular and visa activities; floors three through seven contained apartments for the dependents of military attachés, American women and children; and the top three floors were composed of some of the most highly restricted office space in the world. It was the wee hours of the morning, and I was making my rounds in the restricted zone. I flicked on the fluorescent lights, and a whole pantheon of desks, typewriters, map tables, black electronic boxes, and waste baskets boldly marked "Top Secret" greeted my eyes. Here before me was the entire US intelligence and counterintelligence effort in the Soviet Union. Here, before the computer age, lay row upon row of filing cabinets whose drawers were hindered by steel bars secured with combination locks. During the day, this area was a beehive of activity, the cigarette and cigar smoke seeming to aid in masking these most secret of endeavors. Here, master sergeants, chief petty officers, warrant officers, and attachés of the army, navy, and air force toiled in a relentless struggle for survival. Here, too, under another veil of secrecy was the Central Intelligence Agency whose station chief's identity in all probability was known to no more than three people in the entire embassy. At that moment in time, the entire complex depended for its security on one marine sergeant, and I felt the full weight of the responsibility.

As I walked through the complex, there was a presence that I felt but could not explain. I would describe it more as an intuition than a rational thought, a feeling that I was not alone. My hearing at that time was very acute, and there were times late at night when I thought I heard murmurings. It did not sound English but more suggestive of Russian. Was this my imagination playing tricks on me late at night or was it the long-lost cries of Russians tortured to death during the Stalinist purges of the thirties urging us on in our efforts? I was over-come with a sinister feeling of foreboding and instinctively reached up to caress my handgun. Reassured that it was still there, I walked to the exit, turned off the lights, and opened and then slammed the door shut. Having feigned leaving, I pasted myself against an interior wall, with gun drawn, and strained my hearing in the darkness. Thirty-five minutes passed, and I began to hear the murmurings. Not thirty feet away I was astonished to see a steel-framed alcove, holding a fire extinguisher and canvas hose, begin to slowly swing out-ward into the room. It was adorned with two dancing flashlight beams. A little voice inside me asked, "Don't you wish you'd left when you had the chance?" I quashed it, and my fingers mounted the light switch. There were two of them, and I waited until only one of them had fully exited. I flicked the switch, bath-ing the room in brilliant light, and shouted in classic Russian, whose equivalent translation was, "What the hell do you think you're doing?" He bolted for the trap door, and I brought my handgun crashing down along the side of his head, lacerating his ear. It was at this point that he must have urinated and grazed his scalp on the steel frame, leaving behind skin and hair. Unable to get a grip on the welded steel ladder, he tumbled head-first down the shaft, taking his accomplice with him. I could still hear the shrieking. Both died upon impacting the floor nine stories below, having fallen the entire length of the shaft. I shone a flashlight beam down the shaft to see hands removing the bodies. I sounded the alarm, and all personnel reported to their posts in various stages of dress. A long drawn-out investigation of damage assessment began. I was now in dire danger of reprisal by personal colleagues of the two deceased Soviet agents. Quickly, in less than an hour, I assumed the identity of one of two diplomatic couriers about to leave the country with the diplomatic pouch and was covertly whisked away aboard a Lufthansa airliner.

Ironically, as the decades passed, I lost most of my hearing and now leave it to younger generations to listen for those murmurings.

THE PASSOVER

It was 1872 in the New York slum of Five Points, and a small eleven-year-old girl, clasping her mother's hand, tramped through the snow and slush. She was poorly clothed and malnourished. Her Irish immigrant mother, a laundress, had resigned to give her up to the orphanage now that her husband had died of cholera and she could no longer afford to support her. The child had lived in dreadful conditions and had often endured beatings from her alcoholic father that left her with one eye crossed, a legacy that caused her childhood to be even more tormented. The orphanage was a Methodist undertaking and was directed by the Reverend Isaiah Crane, who periodically took thirty children on train trips to the Midwest, telegraphing ahead his intentions. At each stop, hopefully, one or two children would find adoptive parents.

The girl was trim and pleasing to the eye and responded quickly to the love she received at the orphanage. She proved to be bright and inquisitive, exhibiting a delightful personality. As such, it was with high hopes that she was selected for the excursion. At each station, one or two children would be taken from the train and welcomed into loving homes with new adoptive parents. But at each stop, she would be passed over, and with each crushing rejection, the hurt began to weigh more heavily on her soul. At one stop, three teenage boys began to mock her and persisted until they brought tears to her eyes. It was typical of the cruelty that children visit upon themselves, but being only eleven years of age, this mitigating perspective and its accompanying wisdom was not available to her. She had overheard in several instances the issue of her crossed eye deciding her rejection, and because she was only a child and they were adults, who attached such great weight to this characteristic, she convinced herself that she was indeed inferior, and soon she found it difficult to look up, let alone make eye contact. This resignation accentuated her forlornness, so that by the end of the trip, the only child returning with the reverend, she sat comatose in her seat.

The reverend was a man of great compassion and deep intellect. His heart ached to see her so depressed, and so he told her how beautiful she was, how delightful her personality, and how someday she would make a very lucky man his wife, and in so doing she would herself become a mother and in turn have beautiful children. He explained how the people who turned away from her, because of her eye, were shallow minded and not worth her concern.

Back at the orphanage, over time, she rose above her depression and began to excel in her schooling. Unbeknownst to her, Reverend Crane had written a long impassioned letter to a good friend and classmate from Harvard who was now a renowned eye surgeon teaching at Princeton University, inquiring whether anything could be done to correct her eye. The surgeon, who held his friend the reverend in high esteem, was touched by his entreaty on behalf of the innocent and the helpless. In a return letter, he stated that "It is ironic that I have perfected an experimental surgery for this very thing," further adding that it was not without risks. "However were this my own daughter, I would not hesitate to avail her of this life-changing procedure." He offered to put the child up at his own home, explaining that his wife would be delighted at the prospect. They had remained childless for years and an emptiness had begun to pervade her life. And so it was that the young girl and a volunteer governess made the train trip to Princeton.

When the surgeon's wife saw the girl for the first time, her eyes lit up like a Christmas tree, and the surgeon perceiving this, knew then and there that in reality he would be operating on his own adopted daughter. In due time, all three fell fast in love with one another, and the girl, with a pair of eyes that now moved in unison, began to experience the parental love that she had never known. She was duly adopted and made to understand that in any case, crossed eye or not, they would have made her their own. And so it was that a forlorn and tormented little girl became a very poised and confident beautiful young woman.

I THOUGHT YOU LEFT

It was 1964, and this was the American embassy's marine apartment in the West End of London. I was a marine sergeant having recently served as an embassy guard in Moscow, USSR. The Beatles was all the rage here. The London detachment consisted of twelve marines. For all of us, it was the second year of embassy duty, the first having been served behind the iron curtain. London was our recompense for adrenaline expended, wounds incurred, and hardships endured. By comparison, it was elysium. There was no shortage of beautiful women, and the marine apartment, hosting many a bacchanalian party, had a regular following.

It is the day of our semiannual inspection by the European regional commanding officer, Major Thomas Dunavy, who was flying here from his headquarters in Bern, Switzerland. He was due here at 10:30 a.m. with the inspection to commence at 11:00 a.m. He would leave us immediately afterward. A lot of things were tolerated here, but flunking a regional inspection was not one of them. With this in mind, the detachment rose at 4:30 a.m. to the sound of the "House of the Rising Sun" blaring over a loudspeaker. A chorus of groans and cursing now competed with the sound system, and it was not unlike the disturbing of a beehive. Amid the chaos, Corporal McCloskey emerged with his lover, Angela, from his bedroom. She had slept over illicitly. She was partially inebriated, well endowed, skimpily clad, barefoot, and carried her purse and high heels in her hand. He gave her a deep kiss, and at a point where I thought they were both going to choke, they parted without a cough, and he saw her to the door.

We had our own cook and part-time maid, both British matrons. One by one, marines filed into the dining room, lined up at the pass-through to the kitchen, and gave their order to the cook: eggs cooked to order, sausage, bacon, pancakes, chipped beef on toast, fruit, milk, and coffee. Everyone and everything must be in readiness by 10:30 a.m., and to that end, a flurry of scrubbing, dusting, and vacuuming ensued. Bathroom fixtures were polished to a gleam, culminating after a shower, in the donning of dress blue uniforms.

The major arrived, and the inspection was conducted with the utmost pomp and formality. Being second in command, I stood on the major's left side and escorted him from one bedroom to another. Each marine stood beside his bunk and in crisp military precision saluted the major in his turn. On each bed, in three neat rows, were the marine's military uniforms and accoutrements laid out in a specific order. The major picked up an item here and there and examined it for serviceability and appearance. If found deficient, a demerit was recorded. Any derogatory comments he may have made were recorded in the log. Each individual inspection was then terminated with a crisp salute.

Last, he arrived at our vacant guest bedroom, and as I opened the door, I imagined I heard a flurry of footsteps, but to my relief, I found the room empty. I explained the room's extraneous use to the major. He entered and opened the closet door. Standing there was Angela, still well endowed and skimpily clad, now wearing her high heels. She blew the hair away from her eyes and stepped out into the room. As I thought to myself all was lost, she raised her arm to reveal a feather duster and began to titillate the furniture with it. As she sauntered across the room to the door, I heard myself telling the major, "It's the cleaning lady, sir. I thought she had the day off." She was almost to the door when the feather duster dropped from her hand. She bent over to pick it up, revealing the absence of undergarments. I remembered thinking to myself, "Now we all hang." I called out to her, "That's enough for today, Angela. Corporal McCloskey will show you to the door. Thank you." McCloskey appeared out of nowhere. I looked over to see the major looking straight up at the ceiling. A half minute passed, and he walked over to the bed, looked under it, and with his swagger stick lifted out Angela's panties and said, "See that the cleaning lady gets these, will you, sergeant?" "I certainly will, sir," I replied.

After a few minutes, the inspection was completed in good order, and no mention of the incident was made in his report. Ever afterward, the feather duster, draped with a pair of pink lace panties, and mounted on a plaque was hung above the marine bar with the inscription "Beware the Cleaning Lady."

THE BARREN LAND

There was something ethereal about a Montana wheat field, especially this one that stretched off to the horizon. The wind caused undulating waves in the grain, a locomotion that suggested a larger and more-vibrant life form. I was thirty-two years of age and married to Peg, the love of my life. We had two little girls, aged four and seven. My employer, known as old Wade Jenkins, had given me title to a farmhouse at the edge of the barren land, but oddly enough not the land on which it was built. I never questioned this strange gift.

Old Wade, the patriarch of the family, had four sons who each worked a portion of this immense and prosperous wheat farm. I was employed as a foreman supervising twelve day laborers. Though the farm's prosperity was due to its high fertility, not all of the land was prime agricultural. There was a portion, about one-fifth, that was barren clay with almost the consistency of loosely aggregated rock, laced with quartz deposits. We were planning to convert this land to agriculture by plowing in large quantities of manure from neighboring livestock farms, but we were hampered by the quartz granules which abrade the plow tines in short order.

In time, my relationship with old Wade evolved into one of father and son, and it became apparent that the four sons resented my influence. Relations with his sons were strained and often rife with enmity. By contrast, ours became closer as I gave him the respect and admiration he could not get from his sons. I knew Wade to be fond of practical jokes and knew that he loved sardonic humor as well, so that when he'd tell me continually that in his will he would make me wealthy and wise, I'd laugh it away. His favorite saying was "Sometimes the forest can't be seen because the trees are in the way."

Years later, when old Wade died of a sudden heart attack, it didn't take long for the four sons to squabble among themselves. A wave of satisfaction spread over them as the executor of the will announced that I had been awarded the section of barren land. I was saddened as I recalled old Wade's sardonic smile. His prophecy that he was going to make me wealthy and wise now stung. I was immersed in deep thought when the executor handed me a sealed envelope from Wade. He was instructed to deliver it to me upon his death.

It read:

The contents of this letter will make you wise, and its wisdom will make you wealthy. Dan, my good and faithful son who gave to me what my biological sons never gave, I bequeath to you my most valuable possession, whose existence I have known about for more than thirty years, a secret that I have kept, knowing full well that if revealed, it would change my whole way of life forever. My love of farming precluded its revelation. The yellow clay in your barren land has a name in the mineral world. It is called kimberlite. It represents the surface expression of an explosive volcanic vent whose contents found this outlet some twenty million years ago. The volcanic cone at its surface has long since flattened by erosion. Your barren portion encompasses the entire top of the vent, and in time you will come to know this geological formation as a kimberlite pipe. You will find this effusion is choked with diamonds, which formed at great temperature and pressure at depths of as much as 280 miles below the surface. It was not quartz that caused great havoc with the plows but diamonds. Remember now how I'd slap my forehead whenever you suggested plowing manure into the clay? After all, we shouldn't make mining any more unpleasant than it is. Contact a sizable law firm. Let them set up a large mining corporation and make yourself chairman of the board or some such thing remembering that you and only you have the mineral rights. Though they do not deserve it, be lenient with my sons.

I took his advice, and all these things came to pass. In regard to leniency toward his sons, I felt a compulsive need to be magnanimous and took pains to make sure they were allotted a reasonable portion of the wealth. So as time passed, as Wade would have it, the trees merged with the forest.

WET INNOCENCE

It was a lazy, hot Saturday afternoon, and I was meandering along the banks of Ellicot Creek with tackle box and fishing pole in hand. I was an eighteen-year-old high school student and was well endowed with male appendage. It was tucked away securely in my shorts and was not in conflict with my fishing pole so that I glided through the reeds with a minimum of effort. At this age, there was a vague pulsation in my loins that occurred with a regular rhythm and if left unchecked, bred a plethora of erotic thoughts. But I endured it and took consolation knowing that it was a device begot by the Supreme Being. Who was I to question divine wisdom?

I heard splashing sounds up ahead and gravitated there. At a bend in the creek, where the water flowed swift and clear, I saw my classmate Janene Comely bathing in the nude, her clothing piled neatly on a blanket with a large white towel. She did not see me, and I sank weakly to my knees, transfixed by her image. I knew her to be my age, very bright and beautiful, and realized that her house was not far down the road. She had been raised by her grandparents from an early age, had long auburn hair that hung down to her shoulders, deep languid blue eyes, and a smile that showed off a near-perfect set of teeth. Her figure was well proportioned with round, pert, impetuous breasts and thighs, buttocks, and hips of a proportion offering great promise. She was well tanned, and I was hard pressed to find anything about her amiss.

As she began to soap up, I sensed my appendage beginning to stir in my shorts like a wide-bodied snake. She took an inordinate amount of time scouring every little nook and cranny and from time to time seemed to look in my direction. Could she have seen me coming and knew that I was here? I wondered and hoped at the same time. At a point where I felt her steady gaze approximated eye contact, I announced my presence by rising into full view. She was not alarmed but seemed pleased. Her facial muscles blossomed into a beckoning smile. Attempting to get on her good side and hoping to allay any fears, I confessed an admiration for her impeccable personal hygiene. Her smile broadened, and I assure myself that I had struck the right chord. Sensing that there was no shortage of soap, I began to divest my clothing and entered the water in the full spirit of the Roman baths of old. With a resemblance not unlike that of a small rhinoceros in full anticipation, I glided to her as if drawn by some unseen magnetic lines of force. We clasped, and our lips fused. Her hair began to drape over my shoulders, and I imagined myself an insect caught in a Venus flytrap. After a frenzy of soaping and scrubbing, we were so clean that we squeaked as we left the water. I stood her up in the middle of her blanket and began to pat her dry. She had become my goddess and I her priest. She beckoned me to kiss her feet, and not wanting to commit sacrilege, I complied. As her devotee, my lips slowly began the journey that was her leg. I traversed her calf and thigh, drinking in deep draughts of passion. Out of the corner of my eye, I saw a round shimmering buttock, and I was challenged much the way a climber was drawn to Mount Everest. I began the scaling and was humbled by its magnificent grandeur. In almost a state of delirium, I began the descent, over and across her taut abdomen, pausing to admire that magnificent dimple that was her navel. Ever onward, I scaled toward those twin rounded peaks that cast a shadow across my foraging tongue. Arriving in turn at each nipple, I had a vague feeling that early in life I was well practiced at this for reasons more akin to survival. At last my lips arrived back at their starting point. Our tongues now duel like two swordsmen, and at a point where I felt I had achieved dominance, I laid her down on her back, and the rhinoceros horn disappeared into a warm, dark, velvety cocoon, this known in the vernacular as "hiding the sausage." After interminable frissons of passion, we were both spent and gazed into each other's eyes with a new awareness, that of carnal knowledge. Because our little escapade fitted nicely into her biological rhythm, we did not pay the ultimate price. Although we never pursued a permanent relationship, the memories of our liaisons—and there were many—would endure a lifetime of trials and tribulations erasable only by the twin thieves of death and dementia.

THE MUSICAL REPRIEVE

It was the place of my roots, the foothills of the Alps in northern Italy, and my grandfather, Antonio, together with his four brothers, my great uncles, were preparing to bolster the Italian army. World War I was raging, and the invasion by a well-equipped Austrian army was imminent.

Even though none of the brothers had any military training, it was agreed among them that without their help, their large but humble farm that supported all five families would be overrun. In addition to the killing, rape, and pillaging, horror stories were circulating of Austrians indiscriminately bombing pasta factories, of whole loaves of Italian bread being ground up for stuffing Austrian turkeys, of children being garroted with rosaries. The list of atrocities went on and on.

As the five brothers—Antonio, Vincenzo, Tommaso, Domenico and Pasquale—together with their families gathered for one last communal dinner, it was difficult to find a dry eye. Men, women, and those children old enough to comprehend knew full well that these brave husbands and fathers, their sole providers, may never return. When the last slice of bread and morsel of cheese had been washed down with the last glass of wine, the families knelt down and prayed to the Blessed Virgin for their safe return.

My father, Luigi, Antonio's eldest son, was a small boy at the time and remembered them trudging off down the hillside in a slurry of tears from well-wishers. Soon, they faded off into the valley below to board the carts provided by the Italian army. As they approached the staging area toward nightfall, they could hear the booming of the artillery and the merciless clatter of the Austrian machine guns. Everywhere they looked, they saw the wounded and heard their mournful groans.

Italian nurses moved among the carnage providing water and sustenance and distributing rosaries. Although not part of the Italian army, being considered militia men, they each were issued a Locarno bolt-action rifle equipped with an eighteen-inch bayonet and four rounds of ammunition. Antonio, in disbelief, held the four rounds in the palm of his hand, but because everyone received only four rounds and he did not want to appear greedy, he did not complain.

Within minutes, they had taken up their position in the trenches that faced the Austrians only some two hundred yards distant. It was possible to see the faces of their enemy. Amid the sporadic artillery barrages and the incessant clatter of the machine guns, an occasional whiff of sauerkraut would waft in from the Austrian side. At the first sign of Vincenzo crinkling up his nose, Antonio would remove a flute from his pack, knowing it was dinnertime in the Austrian line. Antonio was a gifted flute player, and it was often said that he had been a snake charmer in another life. As he played, the intensity of the sporadic firing began to drop off.

But inevitably, the command came down the line to fix bayonets, and they now were poised to go up and over. In truth, all men experienced fear and terror in this moment. Antonio felt compelled to call out to his brothers, "What will be, will be!" The charge was sounded, and a swarm of humanity surged forward. The composite sound of their yells was deafening but was soon drowned out by the staccato clattering of the machine guns. The carnage was horrendous. Capping this was a creeping barrage of Austrian artillery. The dust was so heavy that visibility was reduced to three feet. Antonio, Tommaso, Domenico and Pasquale somehow made it back to the trenches. Even though all were spattered in blood, their wounds were not mortal. The four brothers strained their eyes to try to find Vincenzo's location. He was finally spotted. He was alive but immobilized midway between the Austrian and Italian lines. Trying numerous times to crawl out to him, they found the firing to be withering. The Austrians were in no mood to tolerate an act of mercy. A feeling of helplessness and anguish gripped the four brothers. Antonio called out to Vincenzo at the top of his lungs, "Wait, Vincenzo. We are coming!" Antonio told Domenico and Pasquale to fashion a litter to carry Vincenzo and for Tommaso to put a white undershirt on the end of a stick. They would not leave this place without Vincenzo. "This I swear!" As the four brothers crouched in preparation, Antonio put flute to mouth. All along the Italian line as the strains of the Italian equivalent of "Edelweiss" filled the air, the firing from the Italian line subsided until there was nothing. From one end of the line to the other, soldiers looked on in disbelief and strained to hear the improbable. At first when Tommaso raised the white flag, it was shot off, but gradually as more Austrians strained their ears to listen, their firing diminished entirely. Slowly, the little party rose and began their journey to Vincenzo. Antonio with his ethereal flute was in the lead, next with Tommaso bearing the white flag, followed close behind by Domenico and Pasquale bearing the litter. As they loaded Vincenzo onto the litter, Antonio played on. The strains of "Edelweiss" seemed to get louder, clearer, and more mesmerizing as he played. Now the little party began to trudge back, the wounded carrying the wounded. As they did so, Antonio walked backward and remained facing the Austrians much the way a snake charmer never takes his eye off the serpent. Incredibly, an entire battle had been extinguished with an enchanting melody. As they walked back through the Italian rear areas, an officer approached. He seemed to have tears in his eyes. He told the five brothers they were free to go home. "You have done your share here. Wounded as you are, if you stay, you will only be a burden to me. Go home and raise wheat for the army." And so it was that the brothers set off on foot, on a compass bearing that would take them directly to their farm in the foothills. They journeyed that day and through the night. At dawn the next day, the dogs on their farm began to stir. With the dogs visibly agitated, the five families rose and stared off into the distance. Having caught the scent, the six sheep dogs bolted down the hill. Now the wives, sons, and daughters caught sight of the little troop, and they, too, bolted down the hillside bearing loaves of fresh-baked bread and goatskins of homemade wine. Even though all were wounded, the brothers managed to sweep a few wives off their feet before collapsing onto the grass. Again, the hillside was awash in tears, but this time, they were tears of utter joy.

To the soldiers on both sides who heard "Edelweiss" the day of the battle, those brothers became a legend, and their story was told countless times at dinner tables both in Austria and Italy. More Austrian soldiers claimed to have been one of the combatants who held their fire than could possibly ever have been in that unit. The distinction became a badge of humanity. Years afterward, school buses would arrive at the farm to hear the flute that had pacified the Austrian army.

A HIGH FLY

I was shaken awake by a highly agitated Corporal Travis. Having been asleep
for only one hour, after working the wee-hours shift, I was not in the best of
moods. As a marine corps sergeant serving at the American embassy, USSR, I
had the added responsibility of being the assistant noncommissioned officer in
charge of the security guard. We were on the ninth floor in the marine apartment, and from Corporal Travis's room, using a pair of naval submarine binoculars borrowed from the offices of the naval attaché, I was shocked at what I
saw. There, thronging Tchaikovsky Street, a twelve-lane-wide circular loop, six
lanes one way and six the other, was a mass of humanity not unlike a lava flow.
The Soviets had let out entire factories and in well-organized cadres, complete
with banners, were moving en masse to engulf the embassy. Our detachment
consisted of eight marines. It was apparent that they had all distinguished themselves by some act of bravado, and in some instances, it was not always prudent.
But if there was one trait they all shared in common, it was tenacity.

It was a month after the denouement of the Cuban Missile Crisis, and the
Soviets were protesting our threatening attitude toward Cuba. Gallows humor
took hold and Custer's last stand was mentioned more than once. A festive mood
soon took hold, reminiscent of the last hours at the Alamo. A collective groan
rose when we were told not to carry firearms. A wag asked if we were allowed
to rattle off biblical verse. The heavy see-through wrought-iron gates of the two
entrances were swung shut and chained with heavy padlocks, and I shook hands

with the Soviet militiamen on the outside who guarded the gates, each a superb product of anabolic steroids. Heavy desks were moved to stairwell landings as barricades to protect our most-precious commodity: the wives and children of military attachés who occupied apartments on floors three through seven. They were visible, gawking from windows from above.

We were all wearing civilian garb complete with a floppy Russian work-ers' cap. Our identity was known on sight to all embassy staffers, but to the demonstrators we were incognito. This tactic was known among our wags as "If you can't fight 'em, join 'em." All military personnel from the attaché offices reported to their posts to prepare, if need be, for the rapid destruction of all encoding machines and all classified material. The demonstrators soon swamped the four lonely militiamen and began to batter the gates. Through the bars, I offered a breath mint to one of our tormentors, but it was ignored. If the gates were breached, all would be lost. To prevent this, marines with nightsticks warded off attempts to cut the chain with bolt cutters, and many a knuckle was brutally crushed in the attempt. I moved back into the compound to get a better overall view and converse with our noncommissioned officer in charge, Gunnery Sergeant Weber, using a walkie-talkie.

It was at this point that I saw it arching into my area—a high-flying canis-ter hurled by a Goliath of a Soviet workman. I yelled at the top of my lungs for bystanders to disperse and began to run clear of the area. As I looked back, to my chagrin, several embassy staffers, which included two young ladies, stood in place frozen with fear. There was nothing left for me to do but perform the most dangerous and foolhardy of all procedures, and I found myself running straight to the device. Even though highly dangerous, it was faster than trying to convince bystanders to leave. Though it took but a few seconds to scoop up and heave into an open area, moving it seemed to take forever. Heavy enough to confirm my worst fears, I cocked my arm back before heaving. Here time seemed to stand still, and everything seemed to pass my mind in slow motion. After an eternity, release came and it sailed out of harm's way. This little act of panic did not go unnoticed as the gawkers in the top-floor windows began to applaud, and it was not unlike a baseball outfielder being cheered after a suc-cessful retrieval. Soon, the demonstrators wore themselves out and with energy spent began to slowly disperse. The worst was over and the storm weathered.

Using rifle fire to riddle the canister, a form of low-budget bomb disposal, it was found to contain only a rock and some letters of protest. For my efforts, this act having been duly noted, I received a letter of commendation from the Department of State for "due diligence in an emergency" and this to be entered in my service record.

Afterward, with a cigar in one hand and a beer can in the other, Gunnery Sergeant Weber lectured me that if that canister had contained explosives, he could have gotten me a Bronze Star, and if I had been killed in the attempt, a Silver Star. The marine corps was always pointing out missed opportunities. To this I replied that I much preferred the letter as the other alternatives were too harrowing to even think about. As the years passed and youthful exuberance waned, the consequences of what might have happened grew more and more unsettling.

CAN I MOW YOU?

I was a lawn maintenance contractor en route to Punta Gorda Isles with a truck and trailer fully ladened with lawn equipment. Daily, in doing so, I passed an area of sparse run-down homes. Even though the area was unsuitable for business prospects, I found myself continually drawn to a young woman, who when occupied on her front lawn, far surpassed any garden ornament. Later, I would find out that she owned that run-down home, was a waitress, unattached, was fiercely independent, and had a three-year-old little girl, and I knew from sight that she was physically attractive.

The lawn was usually overgrown, and many a time I have passed by to see her struggling with a small hand mower. I never saw a male or another car in the driveway. Attracted and drawn by this apparition, it became the highlight of my workday and her absence a disappointment. It was a communion with something desired from a distance. One day, as I passed the house with truck and trailer, I saw her halfway through the mowing. The mower was stalled, and she was yanking hopelessly on the cord. As I passed, her arm shot up in a beckoning wave. I knew that wave well. It was the wave of a damsel in distress, and even though it was not likely that she had two nickels to rub together and even less likely she could sign an annual maintenance contract, I pulled over. Though I managed to get the mower started, the blue smoke indicated badly worn rings and with it a significant loss of compression, so that against an overgrown lawn, it could make little headway. I offered to mow the lawn and weed-whip the edges for $15, a bargain considering the grass length. She told me she did not have $15. I said, "Perhaps your husband or your boyfriend could help you out?" "I have neither, and until today, I was doing just fine," she barked. I confessed that even $15 was not worth my while, but there was something. "Can you cook ?" I asked. "As a matter of fact, I am an excellent cook," she snapped. "I'll tell you what, then. If you're not doing anything tomorrow night, let's say six o'clock, I will bring from the supermarket two T-bone steaks, two lobster tails, two baking potatoes, butter, sour cream, a magnum of champagne, and a kiddie dinner for your little girl. The cooking will be payment in full with no obligation. It's been a while since I've had a home-cooked meal. You can trust me. I was an Eagle Scout at the age of ten."

She blossomed behind a smile and said, "And I suppose I'm going to be the dessert." I feigned innocence and pleaded that if she was going to be the dessert, I would have included whipped cream. She took it all in, smiled, and said, "Well, in that case, bring the whipped cream in case one of us gets a sweet tooth." I was thoroughly titillated but managed to maintain an even calm. I made short work of the lawn manicure and reminded her I would return tomorrow evening for payment.

I arrived ladened with groceries and pondered how many times this scene had been repeated since the beginning of time. She was ravishing and suitably attired to allow easy transition from the kitchen, to the living room, and to the bedroom. I held her three-year-old daughter in my arms and then delighted in feeding her a kiddie dinner. Just before the steaks and tails were ready, we tucked her into bed. We got comfortable on the couch and fed each other alternating chunks of lobster and steak and washed it down with champagne served in coconut-shell goblets. The lighting was soft and subdued, and in the music in the background, a woman was singing, "Summertime and the living is easy." With another deep draft of champagne, her top slipped away, revealing two beautifully bronzed orbs. I was not disappointed and began to scan them with the surface of my lips, the lips sensing what vision alone could not. I drifted into a mild delirium. Her eyes were large and hypnotic and continually locked on mine. At a point where the T-bones had been denuded and the tails fully stripped, I heard the unmistakable sound of a motorcycle roaring up the driveway. Could it be her long-lost cousin Beauregard come home at last? I could not believe my ill fortune and lamented quietly to myself until the door burst open, revealing a stunning young female decked out in clinging leather attire. It was her special friend Mary Lou, and I do mean special. She looked at me and exclaimed, "Oh, he'll do just fine." I heard myself feebly saying, "See here!" But they paid me no heed. The next half minute was a blur of assorted clothing flying through the air, and in no time at all, in the low lighting, it was difficult to discern what body part belonged to whom. But when all was said, and a great deal done, a good time was had by all. For the next few years, we would repeat our escapade, and during those years, I would often contemplate how truly wondrous was the lawn business.

EMBRACEABLE YOU

A fourteen-year-old girl stroked her pet Burmese python. The two were very much attached to each other. She had a great affection for the python, and people swore that it was requited by the snake. When watching television, the snake would curl up with her oblivious to the parents. Even though it was nine feet long and very powerful, they almost always slept together. She lived with her father and mother on a remote ranch. He was a biologist engaged in research on the gray wolf. The mother was a homemaker and very devoted to the family.

It was about four in the afternoon when a drifter approached her kitchen window. He startled the mother. He appeared to be homeless. Instinctively, she knew enough to tell him to wait there while she got her husband, who had fortuitously arrived home early. The husband took pity on the man's plight and allowed him to stay for dinner and even offered to allow him to stay overnight in the warm, dry barn. His appetite was ravenous, and the husband indulged him with second and third helpings. Although the conversation was sparse, the drifter made it clear that he had a great hatred of snakes. To the girl's gratification, her father pointed out that the snake helped to keep down the rodent population. The drifter grudgingly acknowledged and washed down the last of the scalloped potatoes with a large glass of apple cider.

Shortly afterward, the father took the drifter out onto the front porch, where he lit up a pipe. An amicable conversation followed, but as the father bent over to tap out his pipe, the drifter sprang at him from behind, snaring him by the neck with a loop of baling wire. The father pulled backward, was unable to utter a sound. The drifter, an ex-marine, now used his military skills in the pursuit of abject evil. With a small pocketknife in his right hand, he slit his victim's throat from ear to ear. He released the wire, and what had once been a father and a husband now slumped to the floor in a slowly accumulating pool of blood. Only soft gurgling sounds broke the eerie silence as blood bubbled and spurted from the gash in the neck, all unbeknownst to his wife and daughter who were dutifully washing the dishes in the kitchen. With the ghastly fate of the father now sealed, the drifter burst into the kitchen. His leer was that of unquenchable evil. Through the screen door, she could see her husband's body surrounded by a pool of blood. Compulsively, she screamed. The snake, nestled around the girl's neck and shoulders, now slid to the floor between the girl and the drifter, instinctively hissing at her aggressor. In an instant, the drifter turned on the mother, picked up a cast-iron frying pan, and bashed in the side of her head. She died instantly. The girl, now trapped in a corner, watched helplessly as he picked up a heavy hat rack and began to administer what would have been lethal blows to the snake had the snake not retreated and slithered out through an open window.

He now turned and grabbed the daughter in a fit of demonic rage. His powerful arms tore off her clothing with no more concern than if he had been husking a cob of corn. In the next hour, he raped her multiple times. At a point where his lust had been sated, he grabbed her by the ankles, swung her in a circular motion over his head, and allowed her skull to bash against the wall. She died at the instant of impact and lay crumpled like a rag doll.

Incredibly, he rifled through the refrigerator and fried a skillet full of bacon and eggs, the same cast-iron skillet he had used to bludgeon the mother. He seemed gratified as he took the keys to the pickup truck and tucked their cell phone into his pocket. He was still gloating as he slid behind the wheel of the truck and turned the key. The engine turned over as though nothing had changed in the world. But just as he was backing out, he felt a searing pain in his leg. He looked down, to his horror, to see the head of the snake grasping his upper thigh. Dozens of razor-sharp backward-pointing teeth held him fast. Simultaneously, a nine-foot length of snake slithered out from under the dashboard. As it did so, the powerful, muscular coils enveloped the drifter in a death grip. In his panic, he managed, nonsensically, to punch the 911 on the cell phone, but it was already too late. As the operator came on the line, his ribs were already splintering, and his blood pressure had skyrocketed so that blood vessels were hemorrhaging throughout his body. The emergency operator heard only distinct hissing. She would describe it as a mournful hissing. The open line enabled the operator to get an identification and a geographic location for the phone.

When a sheriff's deputy, who knew the family well, arrived on the scene, he found the snake coiled up on the girl's body. As he approached the body, it began to hiss loudly. It was evident to him that the snake was not responsible for the girl's demise. When the investigation was completed, and it was apparent that the snake had killed only the assailant, the snake was venerated in much the same way as a German shepherd who had dragged a child from a burning building. A good home was found, and to this day, his high excitement is confined to catching an occasional raccoon on a large farm.

A LITTLE PATCH OF GREEN

It was 1982. I had been divorced for two years and was still doing process engineering when I decided to start a landscape maintenance contracting service for a predominately upscale residential clientele. This flowering of a passion for gardening I had held all my life, a passion that released prodigious amounts of energy for a workload that would have daunted those of lesser inspiration. I was sole owner-operator with three high school seniors providing my labor force on a part-time basis, and in time, I became of necessity proficient in manipulating teenage hormones. Being able to think on an upscale level, I soon developed a rapport and a reputation for expertise and high quality, and in very short time, the accounts multiplied by word of mouth alone. Contracts were signed on a yearly basis and divided into twelve monthly payments. Being divorced with two dependent daughters, I often looked longingly at the idyllic family life of many of my clients, many in the prime of life with young children. It was the stability and continuity that I envied the most.

A case in point was Mr. Montrose and family. A beautiful young wife was always ready to greet me with checkbook in hand on the appointed day with two beautiful young daughters, probably six and eight, whose spontaneity always seemed to add a festivity to our appearance. Mr. Montrose, in his forties, was an executive with the Spencer Kellogg Corporation and an inveterate gardener, as fastidious in detail as he was energetic. We were contracted to do the general pruning, shearing, and mowing with one odd stipulation: that little patch of green lawn, twenty by twenty-five feet at the rear of the house, a very fine-leafed Kentucky blue, was reserved for his mowing alone. To this end, he maintained a small three-and-one-half-horsepower push mower, which he kept polished to a high luster as you would a small sports car. After gazing at the house, I would often think, "What more could a man want?"

A sunny, balmy spring day in April found us mowing a home three doors down and across the street from the Montrose residence, when a sudden explosion, whose shock waves assaulted our eardrums, caused me a momentary flashback. It was not unlike the blast from a marine corps .105 mm howitzer. Breaking my reverie and seeing a black puff of smoke rising like a mushroom cloud from the rear of the Montrose residence, I grabbed a fire extinguisher from the back of the truck, and the four of us raced to the scene like a small herd of antelope. We were greeted by the sickening smell of burning human hair and flesh. The wife, screaming, had emerged from the house and was attempting to untangle a garden hose. The upper half of the husband's body was engulfed by the conflagration fed by a five-gallon gas can, which now on its side, had spewed forth its contents. The boys pulled him out by the ankles only to find that he was so badly burned as to be unrecognizable. These monster flames now succumbed to the CO_2 extinguisher. The EMS trucks soon materialized, and she was entrusted to the counsels of a minister. The speculation was that he attempted to gas a hot mower and with fate and conditions being in confluence, he paid the supreme penalty. It was hoped that he died instantly in the initial blast and was spared the agony of burning flesh. The irony was that if I had been allowed to fulfill my contract, by mowing the rear, his life in all probability would have gone on and on. In all the years that passed afterward, very rarely did I gas a mower without a passing thought to that incident.

THE PARISH

It was a weekend to remember, and in fact, the only one I remember concerning my Catholic boyhood. The year was 1954, and I was twelve years old. There at St. Francis of Assisi Parish in Buffalo, New York, an Italian American enclave, were two very powerful personalities in my formative years. One was Sister Mary James, our school principal, always shrouded in the black nun's habit and encircled around the waist with rosary beads the size of walnuts. She is most remembered ringing a large handbell while uttering that Shakespearean quotation "No podado chips in the schoolyard." The other was our pastor, Father Balenti, a hard-driving, charismatic cleric, who with slapstick antics always got a rousing welcome upon entering our classroom. It was rumored he had roomed with St. John the Baptist at the seminary.

In those days, confessions were always held on a Saturday afternoon to allow the shortest time interval between confession and holy communion the next day, allowing confessors less opportunity to resin. It so happened that the day before, the adjoining floor areas to the confessional were waxed and buffed by a cleaning contractor. A teenage scamp working for the contractor, knowing full well the inner workings of a confessional, took the wired microphone for the outdoor loudspeaker system and hid it under the confessor's bench with the switch in the on position. As confessions began the next day, an assortment of people engaged in outdoor activities began to pause one after the other to listen to astonishing revelations, and while most agreed these repentances were admirable, they were perplexed as to why they had decided to go public with it. Belatedly, the plug was pulled on the sound system. As it was, only one confessor demanded the parish reimburse him for having to move to another city.

A close childhood friend of mine was a boy named John Bartini. Now, John Bartini, who was twelve years of age, was about as dedicated an altar boy as they come. He had an unusually large head, the condition having been caused by an alcoholic mother imbibing during pregnancy. But John's real problem was that he could not keep away from snorting the altar wine at any opportunity, and apparently on this Sunday morning, he had been caught. When he emerged, attending the priest, there was little doubt that his ears had been boxed, and large tears streamed down his cheeks accompanied by a low-but-very-audible whimper.

Having arrived early for nine o'clock mass that Sunday morning, I was greeted by the familiar scattering of little old ladies dressed in black, most of whom were widowed, and arrayed in black kerchiefs. The aroma of olive oil and garlic was always the perfume of the day. They always seemed to inhabit the first two rows at the front and always reminded me of the raisins studding a fruit cake. For some reason unbeknownst to me or posterity, Father Balenti descended from the altar in a mild rage, grasping several little old ladies and ushering them to the rear of the church, exclaiming, "Sit in the back, all of you. Let the young come forward." Because I was the only "young," I was beckoned to come forward. It made me feel special as well as very sad for the way the women were treated, and as if all this wasn't enough, as Father Balenti began to say mass, with his back to the congregation and holding up the chalice for consecration, our neighborhood bag lady, Sophie, decked out in a long trench coat and holding a large shopping bag, strode up the aisle, mounted the altar, and not twelve inches from the priest's back, announced in a loud raucous voice, "Boost Buffalo." She then stepped down and strode out the front doors. The priest, having convulsed, had two altar boys come to his aid to dab the wine and oil that now speckled his face. The incident is still remembered today as "the day Buffalo got boosted."

Now in my old age, in the grips of fame and fortune, basking in the warm waters of financial security, looking backward, and enveloped in the warm glow of nostalgia, there isn't anything I would change.

DELIVER US FROM EVIL

My fascination with canine emotional intelligence was heightened into a state of great awareness as a result of a romantic liaison with a very alluring lady named Kate Thresher. Not that Kate possessed this kind of intelligence, but it was her little dog Amy, being half toy poodle and half Pekingese, a pekapoo, who never allowed us to forget her heritage. With Amy being temperamental and ready to lash out at the slightest affront, I found myself more in deference to the dog than to Kate. Soon, Amy and I formed a strong emotional bond. How strong was demonstrated to me in no uncertain terms by an incident. After a heavy lovemaking session with Kate in the bedroom, witnessed in its entirety by the dog, I slipped on my briefs, went out into the living room, and plopped down into my usual padded chair. To my astonishment, I had nestled into a puddle of dog urine, Amy's urine. Kate, bless her, being the psychologist that she was, quickly explained that it was Amy's way of showing that she, too, was available for extracurricular activities. Ever the diplomat and in the spirit of the occasion, I pleaded exhaustion at the moment but that this little expression of affection had been duly noted. I was impressed. Needless to say, Amy quickly acquired a place in my heart.

One afternoon, after Kate put her out on a length of chain in a shaded patch of lawn, she disappeared without a trace. Kate was frantic when she phoned. She called animal control and gave them all the necessary information and related circumstances. Jumping into my truck, I conducted a thorough search down every street in that area to no avail. Kate bought a "lost and found" pet ad, which would appear in the very next edition of the local paper.

Disheartened and disappointed, I paid a visit to the county animal control officer and expressed my frustration and remorse. He listened patiently and then beckoned me into his office. Shutting the door, he lamented to me that within the past three months, thirty-seven pets, mostly dogs, some cats, had mysteriously disappeared from backyards. He feared an animal experimentation procurement ring was operating in the county.

He had no leads concerning who might be involved, but there was a remote area that he felt should be checked out. Tips had been received from a few residents who lived on the fringes of this area. Every Friday night between midnight and 3:00 a.m., they could hear a cacophony of dogs yelping—not ordinary yelping but clearly that of dogs in distress, described by one resident as chilling.

His attempts to get the sheriff to investigate had come to naught, the area being considered too remote and alligator infested to be of concern to his undermanned department. However, he would respond if the animal control officer uncovered a serious breach of the law. Looking me squarely in the eyes, he asked if I could help organize a group of volunteers. It would consist of himself and preferably five others. "They would have to be men who have hunted at night and are savvy to the wiles of the alligator." "I know such men," I replied. "But they will want to arm themselves with magnum handguns and bowie knives." "That's all right with me as a defense against alligators," the officer replied. "I understand," I said.

Finding four of my fellow landscapers willing and able and with the necessary background was not difficult. At ten o'clock on Friday night, the six of us assembled in the ample light of a three-quarter moon. Though now easier, it would make a stealthy approach more difficult. The area in question was a swamp through which an alligator-infested creek wend its way through the center. Access to the area could be attained by any one of four obscure marl roads coming from different directions, all converging on an area of the creek littered with fallen tree trunks.

Undetected, we emerged to find ten four-wheel-drive pickup trucks with oversize tires parked askance the conglomeration of fallen trees. Animal cages littered the beds of many of the trucks, but above all, it was the howling of terrified animals that assaulted the senses. Dogs were at various stages of being chained to the fallen trees while other men held the swarms of alligators at bay. Six-packs of beer adorned the hoods of many of these trucks. This was to them a form of entertainment harkening back to the coliseum of ancient Rome where in much the same manner the Christians were chained and at the mercy of wild beasts.

Although outnumbered almost three to one, our group attacked firing shots into the air to scatter the alligators, saving those dogs already chained to the logs. As the miscreants scattered after having their tires shot out, we began to gather up the remaining caged animals and free those chained to the logs.

It was at this point that I heard a familiar yelp that brought sheer joy to my ears. There was no mistaking it—it was my Amy embedded in one of the cages on a still-functional pickup truck. In the semidarkness, I arrived at the truck at the same instant that the owner did. We grappled instantly and parted only when I brought my revolver, a .357 magnum, crashing down on his head. He bolted for the driver's side, and I ran along the truck and shot out three of his tires. He got out and staggered off into the darkness. I jumped onto the bed of the truck, and there was my Amy tucked away in a cage. Using my bayonet, I wrenched off the lock, and Amy climbed up onto my shoulder quivering like a leaf and her heart beating like a ball-peen hammer. I assured her that she still looked good to me. Taking this to heart, she licked my neck all the way home. Six sheriff's patrol cars converged on the area after a cell phone call from the animal control officer. Most of the culprits were apprehended and their vehicles impounded.

When I got home with Amy, Kate was ecstatic. As for me, I was so exhausted that I told Kate she would read about it in the newspaper. Amy and I are still very close. I know because from time to time, she still pees in my chair. Ah, love takes many forms.

NO OTHER CHOICE

It was 1961, and I was a newly minted US Marine sergeant, recently arrived here at Subic Bay Naval Supply Depot in the South China Sea. It was my first day on guard duty. Marines man all the gates to the town of Olongapo and various restricted areas in addition to conducting jungle patrols of the naval reservation. I was assigned sergeant of the guard and was armed with a .45 caliber semiautomatic pistol. My khaki uniform was starched and was not unlike being clothed in a thin veneer of plywood. I was adorned with a pith helmet affixed with a gold globe, anchor, and eagle emblem. I loaded eight sentries into the back of a carryall. They eyed me intently looking for signs of weakness and irresolution, any hesitancy that for them could translate into needless casualties. I got behind the wheel and drove the now-familiar route to the various posts. Because urgency was a necessary ingredient in importance, we sped from one post to another. Arriving at a post, I jumped out with a relieving sentry, and standing abreast of the sentry to be relieved, I exchanged the ammunition from his rifle to the rifle of the sentry going on duty. In the middle of this ritualistic exchange, an armed forces police truck pulled up with flashing lights. A navy military policeman jumped out and interjected himself in the midst of this exchange, demanding my driver's license. The affront was highly unprecedented and was questionable. Incensed, in a lightning-like movement, I drew my handgun, cocked the hammer, and placed the barrel two inches from his nose. The trigger was now so sensitive that I feigned touching it with my finger.

My instructions to him came in a torrent. I said to him, "Don't ever, ever interrupt the changing of the marine guard. Get back in that friggin' truck and go back where you came from." True to his instincts, he turned an egg-shell white and departed as quickly as he came. I announced the start of World War III and proceeded to the remaining posts to relieve the sentries.

As we pulled up to the marine barracks, three armed forces police vehicles converged in the parking lot. I radioed into the barracks, "Send twelve marines out here with rifles, form one rank in the kneeling position, lock on five AFPs, no firing unless commanded." I was approached by a naval petty officer with a pair of handcuffs in hand. I told him, "Get back in the truck and leave." At this point, the marine officer of the day arrived followed by the naval AFP officer. I dismissed the riflemen, and the officers engaged in a heated exchange. They agreed it must be resolved by higher authority. The next day, I was ushered into a high-level meeting attended by all staff NCOs and officers and presided over by our commanding officer Colonel Jenkins. When all was said and done, I was vindicated. Afterward, he kept me over and said, "Son, I like what you did and how you did it," and then he looked up at the ceiling and laughed. Subsequently, in a meeting with the base commander, an admiral, he was able to convince him that because the incident was so unprecedented, it fell more into the realm of mischief than law enforcement, and henceforth marine vehicles were exempt from speeding regulations.

Now, human nature being what it is, my tribulation with the AFP in the town of Olongapo, where they could arrest me, was just beginning. To protect its own, the marine barracks had its own version of the witness protection program so that when I left the base to go on liberty, I was more often than not nestled among the bananas in a produce truck as it trundled its way out the main gate. Safely off the base, I made my way to see my lady friend Luling who was a hardworking prostitute in a bordello. Now, Luling was everything the marines were not, and I spent endless hours in her company sipping coffee in the back rooms. The backstage in a brothel was a continuous scene of activity, and many a time I found myself either holding the shaving mug or wielding the brush for some young lady bent on shaving her rear end. An endless succession of women emerging from the bath required pat drying. There were toenails to be painted, and I thought of my high school art teacher, Mrs. Hoolihan, for her endless encouragement and the way it had finally paid off. There were fannies to be spanked for good luck, a custom I introduced. I was on my last set of toenails when we heard the sirens. It was the AFP about to raid the brothel, having been alerted to my presence, no doubt, by all the giggling. In a fit of motherly love, Luling grabbed me by the hair, emptied a large hamper, deposited me in the bottom, and loaded the laundry back on top of my head. In ten minutes, the AFP had come and gone, taking all US military personnel with them. I alone had found a refuge in the laundry.

At Luling's cue, I burst forth like Lazarus risen from the dead. The aroma of perfume was intoxicating, and almost involuntarily I vocalized the strains, "Some enchanted evening, you may see a stranger." I looked to see a frown on Luling's face and realized I had two panties nestled on my head. I grabbed Luling by the wrist and offered my services. The offer was accepted.

After a couple of months, the AFP lost interest in my demise, and things returned to normal, if ever there was such a thing. The last I heard, the brothel was issuing green stamps, and the sailors were greedily accumulating kitchen appliances.

THE HOUSEGUEST

It was 2008. I was working as a heavy-equipment operator at a limestone quarry not far from my home in the state of Florida. The boundary of the Big Cypress Swamp was only two miles distant. I was twenty-eight years of age and married to a lovely lady four years younger than I. We had three children and the youngest, a five-year-old daughter, was the constant focus of my mind's eye. We lived on a small parcel of land in a bungalow raised above ground level by an eighteen-inch crawlspace. The crawlspace was enclosed, but there were several breaks in the latticework.

The bungalow's remote location at the end of a marl road allowed us to raise a small flock of chickens providing both occasional meat and fresh eggs every morning. Through the years, a good many hens had vanished, and I attributed the predation to thieves. In the past six years, we had lost two family dogs under mysterious circumstances, the only trace being one dog tag embedded in a trail of animal excrement. I conjured up the image of a predaceous black bear with a tooth for canines and left it at that. A 30-30 lever-action rifle, fully loaded, occupied an upper shelf in a closet, providing comfort for my wife who knew well how to use it.

Over the last several years, I had noticed a drastic reduction in the squirrel, raccoon, and possum population in my vicinity, although distant neighbors had noticed nothing. They were circumstances that I could only ponder until one night, in the wee hours, a longtime resident slithered from the crawlspace.

It was an eighteen-foot Burmese reticulated python weighing 220 pounds and was twelve inches in girth at its widest point. Motivated by hunger and curiosity, it darted a forked tongue repeatedly into the air rendering it a sense of smell. Sensing the warm bodies within, the head forced its way through a break in the window screen, the hole easily enlarged to accommodate its massive girth. The snake in an investigatory mood slithered over my wife and me as we slumbered in our double bed. At first sensation, I imagined it to be my wife's thigh, and I marveled at her ability to titillate, thinking the movement entirely in character. The sensation diminished to nothing, and I presumed she had withdrawn her offering.

The next in line in this human buffet was my youngest and smallest, my five-year-old daughter. The snake was enthralled with this bite-size morsel and struck at her shoulder. Dozens of razor-sharp backward-pointing teeth held her fast. I was awakened by an ear-splitting scream. Bolting upright, I hit the light switch to reveal the child enveloped in the powerful coils of a massive snake. I retrieved a .357 magnum handgun from between the mattresses but was frustrated in its use by close proximities. I unsheathed a twelve-inch bowie knife and began to pierce the forward quarter of the snake, taking care to hold the blade parallel to the snake's ribbing. After six piercings, the coils began to visibly slacken. At a point where the snake had succumbed to paralysis, I pried the jaws open with the tip of the blade. I snatched the child from the coils, and my wife doused the child's shoulder with hydrogen peroxide.

Using a pry bar, through a series of manipulations, I was able to leverage the carcass out of the house and down the front stoop. It was the opinion of the wild-life officer, who arrived that very day, that the serpent had probably been a resident of the crawlspace for several years, affirming the snake as one of the stealthiest of God's creation. As small compensation, I had the skin made into two pairs of cowboy boots and a lady's purse. But it wasn't until the crawlspace was sealed off with a fine-mesh chicken wire and all outside windows provided with removable wire frameworks that the family finally consented to sleeping with the lights out.

To date, it has been the only instance in a double bed where the sensations have been of the unpleasant variety.

HAASEN BAKERY

It was 1958, I had just turned sixteen and was working at an all-night bakery located in one of Buffalo, New York's working-class neighborhoods. Working the four-to-midnight shift, I saw things that you would normally not expect to see in such an environment. You see, Haasen Bakery was a hub of activity both above and below the counter. It was owned by Walter Haasen, a good-natured, big-hearted, hard-drinking Dutchman who was subjected to his share of humiliations, like the time the salesgirl brought a huge cardboard tray heaped with dozens of hard rolls. The boss, who had been crouching down, stood up abruptly, catching the underside of the tray and sending the rolls cascading outward in a ten-foot radius. Then there was the time he sat down on the commode and neglected to lock the restroom door, where upon a small boy opened the door, panicked, and ran off, leaving the door wide open and the boss with toilet paper in hand in full view of the patrons in the sales area. It was I who closed the door. Then there was our full-figured saleslady, who got turned on whenever the jelly doughnuts were being filled, who always found something extra in her pay envelope for sharing her charms. It was I who saw that they were not disturbed and picked up after them. In these ways did I ingratiate myself with the boss.

One night, I found our newly arrived German baker in the backroom with one leg pinned beneath an overturned flour barrel. Had I not arrived, he would have been there all night. Using a pry bar, I was able to free him instantly, and from that time on, he was always glad to see me and made sure the pry bar was always handy. There was the time a brawny homeless man gained access through the rear loading area. At a point where I thought I was going to have every bone in my face broken, he asked for a loaf of bread, and I realized that he was only hungry. I gave him a fresh loaf of Vienna bread, and as he turned to leave, I plopped down a pecan bun on the loaf and said, "Don't ever say God never gave you a break." He reached up as if to strike me but smiled and tipped his baseball hat instead. It was from this incident that I began giving a lot of thought to diverting day-old baked goods to homeless families. It was the homeless children who haunted my mind day and night, and this compulsion became a benevolent obsession.

To this end, I allowed the prostitutes to freshen up in the ladies' room in return for donations to purchase fresh-baked goods for the homeless. The police made donations in return for free coffee and doughnuts, and it was not uncommon to see prostitutes chatting with police officers in the back room over a cup of coffee and a doughnut. Our German baker began to set aside deformed loaves of bread, and the salesladies, day-old baked goods no longer destined for the tamper-proof Dumpster. I chose eleven o'clock at night to dispense this sustenance and soon had a dozen families participating. The children were each given a Danish pastry, and with two of the mothers in attendance, we'd take them into the cooler where the real-fruit fillings were kept, and on each Danish I'd ladle a thick covering of real-fruit raspberry filling. It's been years now, but I have never forgotten the look of wonderment and appreciation in their little eyes, some whose little faces hadn't been washed in days.

Decades later, I was gardening in the front yard when a black Mercedes parked at the curb. Two staffers wearing suits got out and asked if I was Daniel Cinelli. I hesitated but then acknowledged. I was beckoned to the car, from which Mayor Joseph Perdito, newly elected mayor of the city of Buffalo, emerged. As he approached, he seemed to recognize me, broke into a broad grin, and gave me a bear hug, telling me that he was one of those homeless children who partook regularly of the raspberry Danish, and then a strange thing happened. My eyes welled up with tears and so, too, did his. He confessed that as a small boy it was one of the few things he could look forward to. Rarely the recipient of such warmth, I was overwhelmed but managed to ask if he had time for some real-fruit filling.

BE ALL YOU CAN BE

He was born on a cold winter morning, one of a litter of six brothers and sisters. His mother, though he could not realize it, was a golden retriever, and his father, though he would never know him, was a German shepherd. Being a mixture of two pedigrees did not preclude his having to struggle for the ever-precious teat, whose sustenance alone seemed to slack his hunger. Sleep seemed to come so easily when nestled together with his siblings. The symphony of little heartbeats added to his feeling of warmth and security. After weaning, their owner, a widow, began distributing the puppies to whoever she thought could provide a good home, and so it was his fortune to be adopted by a young couple with a six-year-old boy.

The boy named the dog Tony, and they soon became fast friends. Whenever possible, wherever the boy went, Tony went, and it was often said that they were inseparable. If the boy became too rambunctious, Tony would pull the boy's shorts down around his knees and saunter off. The boy always found it sobering. But within a year or two, the boy lost interest in Tony and found other pursuits. Sad as it seemed, the mother decided to give Tony away to a young, married, childless couple.

By this time, Tony had matured so that his regal lineage was readily apparent. His large brown eyes were embedded in a large wolf-like head and complemented by a beautiful long-haired coat whose color I would describe as root beer. He was the quintessential wolf with none of its atavistic traits. It was apparent that the couple was enthralled with his beauty, and he was shown a great deal of affection. But in time, the couple began to have their difficulties and eventually split up. Neither being financially disposed to care for Tony, he was put up for adoption.

Within a week, he was adopted by a young man in his twenties who succumbed to drug addiction. The abuse began a week later. In many a drunken rage, with a thick leather belt in hand, he would chase Tony through the house, belting him mercilessly. With ears hunkered down and teeth bared in a perpetual snarl, Tony was able to find refuge only under the kitchen table. His food and water bowl remained empty for days at a time. He was not allowed out for long periods, inevitably resulting in defecating in the house which in turn resulted in more beltings. At a point when he could no longer bear it, he jumped through an open bathroom window never to return.

Now he found himself alone on the street. Having had enough of humans, he fled from anyone who tried to befriend him. He found that the nights were cold, the ground hard, and the food and water scarce. He scavenged from Dumpsters and drank water from puddles. That night, he was attacked by a pack of feral dogs, and even though he gave a good account of himself, he was now injured in four places. Though none were permanently disfiguring, he was now in abject misery. As he lay there, more dead than alive, he began to feel a foreboding that from here on out, this was as good as it was going to get. The thought of any improvement in his condition was beyond his comprehension. Mercifully, it was at this point that he felt the dogcatcher's snare tighten around his neck. Taken to the city dog pound, his fortune began to improve dramatically. The superintendent phoned Dr. Tomas, a veterinarian who operated an animal hospital nearby. "I have what you're looking for, a male, large stature, long fur, and about two years of age, but he needs rehabilitation." "Send him over," said Dr. Tomas. Dr. Tomas spoke not from the heart but from his pocketbook. This was a time when NASA was paying top dollar for dogs like Tony. Under expert medical care and a high-nutrition diet, Tony recovered quickly.

With the papers signed, he was transported to NASA at Cape Canaveral. Tony was about to be trained as an astronaut. Pretty heady stuff for a dog who not too long ago was eating and drinking out of Dumpsters and puddles. Almost immediately, he was befriended by the lady scientist responsible for his biotelemetry, the maze of biosensors and transmitters used to record Tony's vital signs. He was put into smaller and smaller cages to prepare him for his confinement in the nose cone. He was trained on a centrifuge to simulate the g-forces in rocket acceleration and then subjected to noise, simulating rocket propulsion. Always proudly he wore his flight harness.

Did he ponder about what his siblings would think if they could understand such things? Did he himself understand the importance of his role? It is doubtful. He only knew that there was something very earnest about the way his lady scientist spoke to him. At the end of each day, she stroked him and promised him that he would come back alive and that after this mission both he and her would retire together to her home on Cape Cod. The night before liftoff, she cuddled him in her arms, called him her "little soldier" and looking into his eyes told him to "be all you can be." The next day, Tony orbited the earth multiple times, sending back a wealth of biological information. He was safely recovered, and true to her word, he and the lady retired a short time later to Cape Cod, where Tony's favorite activity was entertaining the numerous Girl Scout troops that came to visit. But it was her endless love and devotion that told him he truly had become all that he could be.

THE POOL PARLOR

Of all the architectural wonders that made up my old neighborhood, it was the pool parlor, situated on Lovejoy Street in Buffalo, New York, during the early fifties, that still produces the most vivid image. It was 1954 to be exact, and I was twelve years old. The parlor was situated in the business district and occupied an entire second floor. Across the entire front of the building stood a massive concrete stairway that led to the second-floor entrance on high. It bespoke of the Roman love of concrete and an unspoken desire to replicate the Lincoln Memorial.

Upon these steps stood the cream of second-generation, working-class Italian American males, most in their twenties. They were our Italian stallions, clad in gold watches, chains and rings, peg pants, and expensive Italian leather shoes. They were the statuary in this Parthenon. It was an age when girl watching was an accepted practice and a fine art, and there was no shortage of nubile females passing in twos and threes and sometimes four abreast. They were almost always greeted by a symphony of whistles the likes of which I have never heard since, some shrill enough to knock the fuzz off a peach at thirty feet.

Because I had taken a shine to Phyllis, my schoolmate who was the daughter of the owner, I had in effect become the resident shoeshine boy, and for a twelve-year-old, I prospered. Phyllis could usually be found in and around the pool hall doing chores, and I frequently found myself there after hours where we did homework assignments together.

One Sunday afternoon, shortly after closing, a mafioso the size of a refrigerator entered the hall and demanded the monthly payment of protection money. It was evident Phyllis's father did not have it. The mafioso began to flail him with a pool cue as though he were beating a rug. Amid groans, her father began to lapse in and out of consciousness. Unbeknownst to the assailant, Phyllis and I were still on the premises cowering behind a counter. My first impulse was to restrain Phyllis who wanted to run out and assist her father. But at the first opportunity, I grabbed a pool cue and advanced on the assailant. I whacked him across the back with little effect, and he turned and delivered a blow that partially severed my ear and broke my collar bone. I lost consciousness but then managed to drag myself into the storage room. I saw a pot of water on a hot plate. It was for instant coffee and was boiling vigorously. I grabbed the kettle by the handle and slowly but steadily advanced on the assailant. He wheeled around to face me as I flung the water. His head sizzled in a cloud of steam. He was partially blinded and in agony. As he collapsed, I hit him over the head with the pot several times, and Phyllis advanced and hit him with a pool cue. When her father regained consciousness, he phoned the police, requesting an ambulance. The assailant was taken into custody, and we were all hospitalized. When the mob boss realized what an odious disaster he now had in his lap, he did what any sensible mob boss would do. In no time at all, the assailant, while in police custody, disappeared from the burn treatment center and was never heard from again. Because he never filed for social security benefits, we assumed he had an early and unexpected demise. Rumor has it he now serves as aggregate in a monolithic concrete casting on the Skyway Bridge.

As for Phyllis's father, he was never badgered again by the mob. The odious involvement of children was considered sloppy and very unprofessional, and the mob boss, as if in a ritual act of atonement, saw to it that her father had an immunity that was never broken. As for Phyllis and me, we continued to do our homework assignments after hours, though the older we got, the harder it was to concentrate on the subject matter.

THE REMAINS

Her name was Talia Yashem, the daughter of a once-prominent Hungarian-Jewish banker in Budapest. It was the winter of 1945, and a bleak peace began to take hold in this war-ravaged society. Her good looks and feminine allure had served her well at Dachau, the German concentration camp. A liaison with the camp commandant had ensured her preservation and ultimate deliverance. But now with a conscience tortured by a dark survivor's guilt, she longed for a life of redemption. With suitcase in hand and her only dress on her back, she walked steadily through the gate of this ruined compound and beheld the shell of what had once been the family mansion. Her father, Janos Yashem, had been the doyen of the Budapest banking community, one of many gassed and cremated at Buchenwald, along with her mother and brother. Now the only survivor, she was the legal heir to this home and compound. It was ransacked by the pro-Nazi Hungarian police and in turn by the populace, and eventually in March 1944, with the German occupation, had become a central sorting and cataloging center for looted valuables and myriad personal possessions from Jewish deportees. Upon German occupation all such valuables and property were to be surrendered. She remembers her father being mercilessly tortured in front of his family to reveal any hidden jewelry. She and her mother were subjected to the forceful probing of a midwife brought in to explore body cavities for contraband, her hand having all the delicacy of a grappling hook. Transfer of valuables to Christian friends was declared illegal. A few wealthy Jews succeeded in bribing SS officials for safe passage but not many.

With peace now at hand, Jewish orphaned children hidden and fed by a few merciful souls began to make their appearance. These she took in, clothed, and fed, supported by her own begging from the provisional government. Soon, the government began sending all Jewish orphans and in return gave her a meager food allotment, which was never enough. Food was to be had but at exorbitant black-market prices. With the help of a few volunteers, they baked their own bread, and by stretching the flour with the addition of sawdust, it was enough to fill their stomachs. The welfare of the Jewish community did not improve as the Communists attained ascendancy. It was apparent that any special consideration accorded to the Jews because of past suffering and injustice was resented by the Hungarian populace who were now themselves suffering. This was a bleak period before international Jewish relief organizations began to disseminate funds to alleviate Jewish suffering.

Now with 112 children in her care and more coming weekly, she began to despair. At one point, she broke down in a torrent of tears, and to avoid a further display in front of the children, she descended to the cellar. In a far corner, she lashed out at the world and its inhumanity. She remembered romping through this cellar as a child. As she dried her tears, her eyes began to focus on the opposite wall. Something was missing. She remembered the door to a storage room having been there. Memories of exploring it as a child began to play in her mind. "Why was it no longer there?" she asked herself. Drawing herself to the wall, she took a rag and began to remove a coating of dust where the door had been. The outline of what had once been an entryway began to manifest itself, defined by a coating of more-recent stucco. She found a small hand pick and in secrecy, began to chip away at what would eventually become a twenty-four-inch-diameter hole. Upon completion, she took a kerosene lantern and contorted herself through the opening. She was not prepared for what she saw and almost dropped the lantern. As she thought "Is this real?," her hand descended to one of the open crates. Lifting a bracelet, two necklaces, and a diadem, all heavily encrusted with the most exquisite of precious gems, she stood aghast. There were crates of magnificent pearl jewelry, all of which would prove to be genuine. Other crates contained more than a hundred thousand gold wedding rings; small gold ingots; jewel-encrusted cigarette cases; solid-silver menorahs; kiddush cups; torah crowns; breast and hallah plates; human dental gold in the form of crowns, bridges, and plates; charity boxes of precious metal; and last but not least, a gold-coin collection which would be assessed at $6 million.

She stumbled backward and threaded herself back through the hole. Deep in thought, she swept up the masonry shards and pulled an empty bookcase across the opening, concealing it. A resolve took hold, and surreptitiously, she began to use the gold coins to improve the lot of the children, and in the end, this treasure trove was secretly spirited out of Hungary from under the noses of the Communist regime, by Zionist agents, who then used the proceeds to fund holocaust humanitarian organizations. The gathering and concealment of the treasure by the German SS, in effect, kept it from despoliation by the Hungarian populace.

As time passed, a thought began to glow in her subconscious, a renewed sense of justice served. Perhaps there was a God after all, who in the end saw to righteousness. She imagined these wealthy, elderly Jews, who had relinquished their lives and fortunes, now beckoning her to take their wealth and use it to bring forth the young of a new generation, so that in the end, they will not have perished in vain.

THE SHORT STRAW

I was a US Marine sergeant stationed at the US embassy, Moscow, USSR, and I served in the capacity of a security guard. It was January 1963, the Cuban Missile Crisis still loomed in our consciousness, and our adrenaline levels had not yet fallen. Kennedy and Khrushchev were at loggerheads, and in the counter-intelligence community, it was an era of hardball, an era of brutal interrogations and contacts cultivated at great pains suddenly disappearing without a trace.

Marine guards, not being diplomats, did not rate diplomatic immunity. We carried only official passports. But like the foot soldiers in any army, we were the tip of the spear, and as such, it became apparent that our legal protection was not commensurate with many a chore. If caught facilitating an act of espionage and surviving a not-easily-forgotten interrogation, we could face a long stay in a Soviet gulag. Though referred to by the marines as an all-expense-paid vacation, the thought was always chilling.

With stakes as high as these and marines being great believers in fate, manifesting itself in the well-known adage "The bullet had his name on it," a ritual of drawing straws was accepted by all. So when a certain office in the US Navy esteemed for its intellectual capacities requested a runner to retrieve a package, it prompted our noncommissioned officer in charge to stand in the middle of a room clutching a bundle of straws. I went first and pulled up what was indeed the shortest straw. It was an impressive demonstration of fate, and I was resigned to it as though it were the will of a supreme being.

I reported to an area of the embassy known officially as Cultural Affairs and learned that it was a highly dangerous assignment in that they did not know whether the contact was legitimate or whether they were being set up for an arrest. I was given full latitude to break off if I felt compromised. He then offered to allow me to turn down the assignment, but the honor code being what it was, that choice was unthinkable. Our supplier of the packet of documents was a Russian national who was a secretary in the foreign ministry. She was well placed and may prove a valuable source.

The pickup would take place at 3:30 a.m. in the dark of a moonless night. I dressed in black, and with my face covered with a scarf, I crouched on the back floor of an embassy sedan. As we raced down back streets, the marine driver jerked to a halt at an alleyway, and in an instant, I rolled out the door. The sedan sped off as I ran down the alley and jumped several fences. At a point where I believed it was impossible for them to be following, and I discerned no surveillance aircraft, I began to make my way to the appointed drop point. Carefully, I eased into a place of concealment about an hour before the appointed time. The drop point was a little flower bed surrounding an ornamental tree adjacent to a marble bench. The area was deserted, but in no time at all, I began to notice the glow of several lit cigarettes coming from the surrounding trees, a violation of stakeout procedures the world over. A chill made its way up my spine, and I determined I must get out of here and quickly. I bolted from the scene; a dozen figures emerged from the shadows. The headlights in five vehicles flickered to life. Warning shots rang out, and a foot chase ensued. In a thick Russian accent, a loudspeaker admonished me to surrender. I heard the merciless growl of a Russian wolfhound at my heels and turned rearward. With a rigid arm bracing my bowie knife, the hound leaped and impaled itself on the point. It was lethal, and it fell to the ground. Another fifty yards and I leaped feet first into the Moskva River. I looked to see a barge with running lights being towed to my front. Swimming to the barge, I grabbed hold of an old tire affixed to the side and hung on for twenty minutes. Around a bend, I saw what looked like a derelict Russian Orthodox church in the midst of some abandoned outbuildings. I swam to shore and collapsed exhausted. As it happened, orthodox services were being conducted in the basement at that very moment. I was found by the wife of the caretaker who looked up to see police boats converging on the scene. She knew them to be the state security services, and she was consumed by a vile hatred. They were responsible for the tortures and executions of many of her relatives during the Stalin years. Instinctively, I was carried to the basement and moved to the center of the congregation. The incense was so thick that visibility was reduced to four feet. My head was topped off with a worker's cap, and I began to chant along with the rest.

Having escaped the dragnet, they now nursed me back to full vigor and pointedly ask me no questions. By a method that I will not deign to discuss here, I slipped back into the embassy, and a very appreciative US government saw to it that a significant sum of money in small-denomination rubles found its way into the congregation. You can believe me when I say it was but a small token of my appreciation.

WE LOVE YOU, DAD

Looking back on my childhood, it seems a lost civilization, its locus on the fabric of space time forever receding. Yet at this point in space and time, I am still capable of remembering, revising, and resolving, all with a few strokes of a pen.

Lest the universe totally forget, let me emphasize that I vividly remember riding in the backseat of our new Henry J. Kaiser automobile, my father's first car. There were four of us boys in the backseat, aged eleven, six, five, and four. I was the oldest. My mother sat in the front passenger seat and acted as a mediator between us and the forces of the universe. We began ascending a hill and as it steepened, the car being in third gear began to groan, buck, and ping. He could not shift back down to second gear, and we envisioned sliding backward down the hill out of control. Mercifully, a last shudder took us over the top. At last, we arrived at Hess and Bement dairy where we each got a triple-scoop blackberry ice-cream cone. At that age, it required two arms and a tongue like an anteater to manage. It was little wonder that Ronny, the youngest, wrestled it to the floor of the car. With a cacophony of curses, Dad picked it up and flung it out the window, and because he forgot to roll down the window, it bounced back onto his lap. My mother was now incapacitated with laughter, and we were treated to a new round of incantations. Dad was always expanding our vocabulary.

But I could never fault Dad. There was always some quality that beggared his redemption. To begin with, he loved a bargain and loved bragging about it even more. So when he gloated over what he called his "Japanny boots" and then put his foot through the bottom of one, it was an especially awkward moment.

As kids, we always gave special deference to our dad except that one time when he collapsed on the floor in front of the bathroom, incapacitated with a back spasm. Tommy, aged six in his bathrobe and slippers, stepped right over him, looked down, and said, "Hi, Dad," and continued on into the bathroom unconcerned. But Dad forgave him.

The only instance I can remember that Dad gave himself over to the devil was the time, a few years later, when an unbalanced barbell propelled itself off a weightlifting bench and cleaned out a double-hung window, frame and all. Telling him the window collapsed of its own accord fell on deaf ears. He took off his belt and proceeded to chase the four of us around the furniture. Relief came only when his pants settled down around his ankles.

But he also revealed a very tender side when he backed out of the driveway and ran over my pet kitten. At the sight of the kitten, whose head was distorted and still twitching, I perceived tears rolling down my father's cheeks. It was role reversal as I began to console him. That night, toward recompense, he took me to the movies, or should I say, I took him to the movies.

In those days, Dad worked second shift and Mom worked a day shift so that when Mom phoned midmorning to make sure everything was fine, he'd have to get out of bed, put on his flip-flops, run the length of the upstairs, down the stairs, and the length of the downstairs to get to a black phone bolted to the wall that only looked like it was armor plated. By the time he got there, she'd hung up, and he'd go back upstairs to bed. Fifteen minutes later, she'd call back. He'd get out of bed, exclaiming, "OK, we're gonna play games," and repeat the process.

Our house was in the city of Buffalo on a truck route and about a half block away from an active train track. In the summertime with the windows wide open, the house literally resonated with the vibration. As if this wasn't enough, Gary played the electric guitar, Ronny the drums, and Tommy ragtime piano. But this background noise notwithstanding, when Dad whistled for us to come home, so loud was it that it cut through everything.

Even though the house was prone to vibration, it had a lot of hiding places that came in handy for hiding my corn-cob pipe and pouch of tobacco. But to my surprise, my mother found it. Irate, Mom said, "Are you smoking?" "No, Ma." "Then how did this get up there?" "Pack rats, Ma!" "Well, believe you me, this pack rat has got some very bad habits." "I should say he does," I stammered. I always thought Mom would have made a great attorney general. She had a way of cutting to the quick of things.

To Mom, Betty Crocker was second only to the Blessed Virgin and was open to all innovations and considered herself a thoroughly modern woman so that when instant coffee came out, Mom relegated coffee grounds to the compost pile. This also led to Mom's experimentation with the pressure cooker, and many times I bolted from the kitchen forgetting to completely open the screen door as I fled.

Did all of this affect me for better or for worse? The jury is still out.

ALUMINUM FOIL CHEF

It is 1972 and I am a heating, plumbing and air-conditioning systems designer with Shaugan and Fitch consulting engineers. I was involved with the calculations and drawing of these systems on architectural floor plans. I was thirty years old, happily married with one daughter, and had developed a "been there, done that" attitude with regard to my drafting board.

I applied at an employment agency and expressed an interest in some sort of process engineering. She told me that they did have something in a Niagara Falls abrasives plant. "But I have to tell you," she said, "that in the last year, I have sent them five people, none of whom lasted for more than two months."

"I'll take it," I said, and off I went to Niagara Falls, a thirty-minute commute. As I stepped from my car in the parking lot, I was appalled at the sight of an industrial complex that conjured up an image of the birth of the industrial revolution—three-story buildings made entirely of concrete slabs, steel girders, and corrugated-iron sheathing with everything coated in a thin veneer of dust. If any surface had ever been painted, it was now barely visible.

In the office of the head chemical engineer, I confessed my complete lack of experience in the field but told him earnestly that I had a great capacity to absorb engineering material. So desperate was he to fill the position that he hired me, and I left with a stack of manuals a foot high under my arm to cram in a marathon session lasting the entire weekend.

Arriving at eight o'clock Monday morning, I was introduced to Big John, a black American who was the foreman of the foundry, a big man with a good-natured grin whose mouth lit up like the keyboard on a Steinway piano whenever he smiled. I got the impression that Big John would see to it that I didn't get killed for no good reason.

We walked out onto the floor, and I got my first glimpse of what Hades would be like. Five huge cauldrons ran the length of the foundry into each of which two huge carbon electrodes projected into a molten mass, the end product. This molten mass after hardening was essentially a giant ruby or sapphire but not of gem quality being opaque and riven with fissures. The hum of the exposed electric arcs was deafening. To this was added the loud clanging of overhead cranes and the incessant noise of crushing operations. The heat was near 110 degrees, and the dust permeated every cubic inch of air space. The overhead crane, using a wrecking ball, split the cool pigs asunder.

At this point, the breaking gang moved in. Five men, each toting a massive sledge hammer broke the remainders small enough to be conveyed away on a belt. These men were almost always blacks, the whites transferring out at the first opportunity. The image of these men was seared in my memory. Their glistening bodies reflected the eerie flickers of the electric arcs. Of the five, only four swung their sledges at any one time. The fifth belted out a refrain at the top of his lungs that served as an erotic cadence for the other four: "Here comes Sally with a red dress on. Whatcha gonna do? Whatcha gonna do? Here comes Sally with a yellow dress on. Whatcha gonna do? Whatcha gonna do? Here comes Sally with a green dress on. Whatcha gonna do? Whatcha gonna do?" Each then alternated.

Somewhere in between "Whatcha gonna do?" I would grab a couple of pieces for sampling back at the lab. No one ever alluded to what happened to Sally, but my guess was she had the time of her life. Back in the lab, Big John had a vested interest in staying close to my side to observe the test results so that corrections could be made if needed.

Now, Big John's claim to fame lay not in being a foreman but in being what we called an aluminum foil chef—the threat of Alzheimer's disease notwithstanding. John would take various pieces of raw meat, seasoned with his own special blend of spices, wrap it in aluminum foil, and perch it on top of an industrial space heater for a very slow cook. I can attest that my lab was soon filled with a most-appetizing aroma, and even such exotic delicacies as tongue and sow's ear were not beyond my desire to sample. The aroma would try the willpower of a vegan.

One early evening during an overtime stint and after a few forkfuls of rump roast, Big John's attention was called to a malfunctioning carbon electrode. Experience sent him to the transformer room as the source of the problem, and in all probability, he would have called for an electrician. Shortly after he closed the door behind him, the entire plant blacked out, and emergency battery lighting came on. I was one of six men who responded to a fire in the transformer room. Close examination with lanterns revealed John's smoldering, blackened body burned to a cinder, a victim of electrocution.

All of us who knew him were in a state of shock for a month or more. The whole thing was summed up philosophically by one of our sledgehammer guys, a sage by the name of Old Sam, who mused that "Big John dun liked da barbecue so much; he become the barbecue hisself."

I stuck it out a year more before heading for Florida's sunshine and fresh air. To this day whenever sow's ear comes up in conversation, I always think of Big John.

THE POUCH

It was August 1962, and I was a US Marine sergeant newly graduated from marine security guard school. I had been assigned to our embassy in Moscow, USSR, and had not the slightest premonition that the Cuban Missile Crisis was but two months away. I arrived at Dulles International Airport and wrestled two large duffel bags through baggage before boarding a Pan American 707 bound for Prestwick, Scotland. At Prestwick, I transferred to a BOAC Comet airliner. I was told the Comet was the world's first commercial airliner, and I made a mental note. In Copenhagen, Denmark, I boarded a Scandinavian Airways Caravelle. It was the first jet airliner with aft-mounted engines, and I marveled at its innovative design. In Riga, Latvia, I made another transfer to an Aeroflot TU-104 Soviet airliner. It was the world's first successful jet airliner, never having been pulled from service for design flaws.

But unlike the other aircraft, to my Western eyes, it was a mild culture shock. A maze of exposed tubing, terminating in an oxygen mask, dangled from the back of each seat. The rumpled clothing of passengers and crew suggested the steam iron had not yet arrived, and women with unshaved legs seemed to predominate. As it turned out, my TU-104 had had mechanical difficulties, and at the last minute, I was assigned another aircraft about to take off for Sheremetyevo Airport in Moscow. The KGB, who were conducting a clandestine operation aboard this flight, through an oversight were not informed that I was now on board. In the crush of passengers, a well-dressed individual, deducing that I was a Westerner, introduced himself. He was Tommy Newgate and was my counterpart in the British Security Service newly assigned to the British embassy in Moscow. He sat two seats ahead on the opposite side of the aisle. I jokingly told him that if I needed help, I'd give him a sharp whistle. We laughed.

While loading, I observed two well-dressed Westerners board, one of whom was handcuffed to a sturdy duffel bag affixed with an American flag decal. I immediately reasoned they were US State Department couriers. One sat ten seats behind me; the other, handcuffed to the bag, positioned himself in a rear area near the stewardesses' serving station. The pouch containing top-secret correspondence between Washington and its embassies must never be left unattended and was to be defended against all hazards.

I made eye contact with a comely stewardess, who despite having hairy legs and a rumpled uniform, did not lack for animal magnetism. We were not allowed to fraternize with Russian nationals, but I managed to stretch things and allowed the milk of human kindness to flow freely. Thus engaged, it was the sudden expression on her face that made me turn my head just in time to see something alarming. The US courier sitting ten seats away was harnessed to the seat with his head in a collapsed position resting on his chest. I bolted from my seat. As I passed the seated courier, I shook him. He was out cold. I looked toward the rear of the plane, focusing on the courier handcuffed to the pouch. He too appeared overcome and was now surrounded by three large males. It was clear they were not from the Bolshoi Ballet. Armed to the teeth with a fingernail clipper, I let out a shrill whistle, and Tommy Newgate sprang from his seat. It was now the American eagle and the British bulldog, NATO's dynamic duo, pitted against the three Russian bears. I hollered at the top of my lungs. Words failed me, and I dug deeply into the well of obscenities. The Soviets were confounded and embarrassed, and the question was begged: "Where did this son of a bitch come from?" It was clear we were unexpected.

Now caught red-handed in a dastardly breach of diplomatic etiquette, they melted away as if nothing had happened. Within twenty minutes, both couriers regained consciousness but with a mild headache. A medical investigation revealed they had both been jabbed with a small hypodermic needle, most probably mounted at the end of umbrellas wielded by two women. This incident was known ever after as the Mary Poppins attack, and I never looked at an umbrella the same way afterward, or women, for that matter. However, this precaution notwithstanding, I would marry one six years later. Each year, Tommy and I still exchange commemorative letters on Mary Poppins stationery.

THE VISITORS

It was early morning on a crisp autumn day in late November 1989, when a late-model Ford, its tires heavily encrusted with mud, pulled up in the parking lot of a convenience store. It was before the rush of customer traffic and neither of the two occupants was observed as they exited the vehicle. They were unshaved and weather beaten and their clothing was greatly the worse for wear. Tight to their sides, they each clutched a 30-30 lever-action rifle. Upon entering, they announced a holdup in crazed demonic tones. Cash drawers were emptied into a shopping bag, and the three women clerks were herded into a back room where two were raped, and then all three were shot point-blank in the back of the head.

They took bottled water, beer, and some canned goods, stuffed them into two knapsacks, and fled at high speed in their own vehicle. Ten miles down the road, they pulled into a parking lot, accosted another woman, and transferred to her vehicle. She was taken with them and further down the road, was shot in a grove of trees. They now headed south, intending to hide out in the Big Cypress Swamp for a week if need be.

It was 5:30 a.m. on that same day. My brother Gary and I parked our car on a siding of Loop Road/Route 94. It was an unimproved road that meandered south from Monroe Station on Route 41, taking us deep into the Big Cypress Swamp. We were here to hunt wild boar and deer, having obtained our hunting permits for the season. The area bounded by Loop Road and Route 41 was off limits to off-road vehicles. You had to enter on foot with significant risk. Having been a US Marine jungle patrol leader in the Philippine Islands with considerable skill navigating with a compass, it was for me a cake walk. However, this cavalier attitude was belied by my personal kit, which included a Remington .270 high-powered rifle, a Smith & Wesson .44 magnum revolver, a twelve-inch bowie knife with a hand-forged blade, and hard plastic snake guards that encased my lower legs like two stovepipes. A long-sleeve shirt and full-length pants, along with a floppy hat completed my ensemble. All exposed areas were slathered with mosquito repellant, and because this would have no effect in warding off coral snakes, water moccasins, pygmy, and diamond-back rattle snakes and alligators, a constant vigilance was maintained.

We penetrated deep into the swamp, maintaining the same compass azimuth so that the reverse would take us straight back to the car. We found a hardwood hammock elevated above a marl prairie, unloaded our gear, and made a campsite. This was our refuge come the night, the hours of darkness posing the greatest danger. We lay in an ample supply of firewood, a good campfire being the ultimate defense. When all was completed, we left camp to do an exploratory hunt, taking note of several promising boar trails. On the approach back to our camp, I saw two men, both carrying rifles, picking through our gear—not a good sign. They had violated common courtesy. I flashed Gary an ominous look and told him to keep his rifle in his hand, the safety off, and the muzzle pointing twenty degrees to the left of target. "You cover the left one; I got the right one." We strode in on them, and I was anything but meek and mild. I chided them for rummaging through our gear but suggested that we all sit down and have some coffee, offering to share our dinner. They showed no warmth, and the word *sociopath* came to mind. A long silence ensued. It terminated when I told them, "You boys best be on your way." They left and did not turn their backs to us until well into the bush. The psychological pressure had taken its toll, and we were both wringing-wet with perspiration. It called to mind engaging timber thieves in the Philippine Islands. The warrior in me told me they would be back, and we prepared a campfire surrounded by two dummy sleeping bags.

There would be no sleep that night as we cloistered in thick bush and await their return. I awaited my fate with bowie knife in one hand and a .44 magnum revolver in the other. Gary clutched a 30-30 lever-action rifle. At a little after 3:00 a.m., they rushed in on our campfire and riddled our sleeping bags with rifle fire. Almost immediately, we caught both of them in the open. I emptied all six rounds from the .44 magnum into both. Each round hit with the impact of a baseball bat, and they were buffeted this way and that. They collapsed, and their clothing began to take on a scarlet hue. Strange as it seemed, neither of us got up to examine our handy work, as if the act of not acknowledging would erase it from reality. We each fell asleep in place.

It was with foreboding that we heard the helicopters overhead. Would they believe our story? We had grave doubts. But on learning who they were, the convenience store videotape having conclusively identified them, a great relief swept over us, and it was generally acknowledged by law enforcement that this murderous lot had met their match.

We never hunted again; the memory bore too great a weight.

ASSUMPTION OF DEATH

I t was the year 1835, and I was an American male, a medical student studying at the École de Médecine in Paris, France. Tuition was free to Americans; you have only to pass the entrance examination. Paris was now the leader in medical technology, diagnosis, and cure. The Hotel Dieu, the largest hospital in Paris and the Archives de Médecine, a huge library of medical reference material, together with the Amphithéâtre d'Anatomie for the dissection of human cadavers sustained a medical community of the first rank. The flower of the world's brightest intellects flocked here to staff a faculty like no other.

I was twenty-seven years of age, single, acknowledged as being attractive, and not without the accompanying desires so that when I saw a very attractive young woman in her twenties seated near my bus stop with a young child asleep on her lap while she played the violin for contributions, I was overwhelmed and in a charitable mood of exuberance would often part with a portion of my lunch money. We soon became fast friends on a first-name basis. Her child, a little girl five years of age, no longer had a father, he having died in a typhoid epidemic. I had great admiration for her, because as attractive as she was, she could have had an income twenty times over had she resorted to prostitution. It must be admitted that playing the violin with the small child on her lap was most compelling and resulted in an adequate income.

A month had passed, and it soon became apparent that Paris was in the grips of a cholera epidemic. Its cause was unknown to us at this time because this was an age before knowledge of the existence of micro-organisms, although filth was a prime suspect. Future generations would learn that it was a disease of the small intestine produced by a bacterial infestation, *Vibrio cholerae*, causing severe vomiting and diarrhea. Because it was transmitted by fecal matter in impure water, Paris suffered greatly.

Unbeknownst to me, her five-year-old daughter was afflicted, children being more susceptible due to their lower stomach acidity, high acidity being a hindrance to the progression of the disease. In a matter of hours, the child became almost comatose, and the mother left the bedside to seek transportation to the hospital. In her absence, the child appearing death-like and uttering no sound was mistaken by a municipal burial detail as being dead and was laid upon a cadaver cart already laden with a dozen bodies. Upon discovering the fate of her child, the mother became hysterical. A shopkeeper identified the cart as belonging to the Amphithéâtre d'Anatomie. She knew now that her daughter was to be found in any one of a number of cadaver piles that ringed the Amphithéâtre. Instantly, she thought of me and ran the four blocks to the Amphithéâtre. Frantically, she entered the great dissection area and was greeted by the sight of some six hundred students performing dissections simultaneously. The bodies were in various stages of putrefaction, and the stench and fumes were overwhelming. Upon termination, the bodies were cremated, and small bits and pieces were fed to dogs kept in cages at the rear of the building. A nearby student escorted her to my autopsy table. I was shocked and anguished at her outpouring and immediately excused myself from the corpse.

I enlisted two of my medical friends and raced to the outside lot. There were four piles of cadavers, and in the fading daylight we lit torches. It was a gruesome search as we uncovered dozens of child cadavers and seemed almost hopeless. But when near about ready to give up, I heard the distinctly muffled cries of a child, who was not quite visible, being entangled. It required the removal of several bodies to free the child. I smiled when I realized the child seemed to have been invigorated by her brush with an unnecessary demise. She was placed on a stretcher, and we raced on foot to the Hotel Dieu, the large hospital.

In addition to the vomiting and diarrhea, she suffered stomach cramps, and by the crinkled skin on her fingers, it was evident she was severely dehydrated.

Because dehydration was the prime cause of death, it became imperative to replace lost fluids, and with that in mind, I threaded a hollow tube through a nasal opening to the stomach and administered purified water fortified with minerals and salts at a rate to match that which had been lost.

In the days to come, the child strengthened and lived to survive the ordeal. Needless to say, in the eyes of her mother, I had earned an esteem akin to "he who walked on water," and with it came her admiration and undying love. Now having tasted paradise on earth, I married her and moved to New Orleans, Louisiana, where I established a successful medical practice, and my wife became the city's violin virtuoso and a hit attraction at the several hospital canteens. Oddly enough, the mention of the disease cholera always evoked in me a perverse nostalgia. Inextricably it had been a key ingredient in the bonding process and determined to no small extent my trajectory through life.

THE MAIN GATE

It was 1961, and I was standing at the main gate of the US naval supply depot at Subic Bay, Philippine Islands, bordering the South China Sea. As sergeant of the guard, I was responsible for the orderly and lawful conduct of commerce through this gate to the town of Olongapo beyond. To this end, I had in my charge one noncommissioned officer in charge of gate and his three sentries.

All Filipinos and US servicemen were required identification and property passes, this to thwart a thriving black market. Both pedestrian and vehicular traffic contributed to the feeling of organized chaos. But make no mistake, very little escaped us.

Upon arriving at the gate, I was greeted with a raucous chorus from the gaggle of prostitutes who lined the far side of the bridge. The smell from the Olongapo River, an open sewer, did nothing to enhance their wares. But we called them our fan club and did our best to patronize the local culture.

In the midst of this tangle of red tape, accountability, and military exactitude, a Negrito family now sauntered diagonally through the pedestrian gate. The Negritos were the original inhabitants of the Philippines. Negroid and pygmy-like in stature, childlike in nature, they possessed an innocence seemingly incapable of criminal activity. The male was attired with a bow, a quiver of arrows, and a bolo knife; the female held an infant suckling at her breast; a three-year-old boy clutched the folds of her small dress; and all were in the barest attire. All business seemed to come to a stop as he gave me a peremptory salute without in the least slowing his pace. I returned his salute and smiled and looked up to see everyone smiling. This action belied all regulations, and I always found it refreshing.

It was the end of my watch, and upon being relieved, I was told to report to the administration building. Upon arriving, I turned in my sidearm to the sentry at the desk and was then escorted down a long corridor to a remote elevator. We ascended to the top floor, and I was shown into a room bereft of all furniture save for my chair in the very middle of the room. At the far end, seated behind a solitary desk was a civilian who introduced himself as Mr. Young, the head of the Office of Naval Intelligence (ONI) here at Subic Bay. Upon hearing this, my gut instinct was to genuflect, but I stifled the impulse. He said to me, "Do you know why you're here?" I said in comic relief, "Is it about those overdue library books?" He smiled. "No, nothing that serious! All kidding aside, sergeant, we need your covert assistance. Lately, ships badly in need of repairs have had to be rerouted elsewhere because of mysteriously depleted parts inventories. We're being robbed blind by a gang of Filipino civilian base employees aided and abetted by a marine NCOIC on the take, who has unfortunately succumbed to a drug habit."

At this point, we were interrupted by a knock at the door. It swung open to reveal my commanding officer, Colonel Mosely. I jumped to attention and saluted, and he responded in kind. A man of few words he shook my hand and told me to do everything Mr. Young required, "So we can put this scumbag NCOIC where he belongs. You hear me?" "I hear you, sir."

I turned to Mr. Young and learned that we will intercept a shipment at the main gate and that because I would be the senior NCO and the only one in the know, it would be up to me to ensure that the correct steps were taken and in the right sequence. The stolen equipment would arrive at the gate buried in barrels of slop from the mess hall. Supposedly on a whim, I would insist that the contents of three barrels be transferred to empty barrels for inspection. "Now, here's the hard part," said Mr. Young. "If they think that you are acting on inside information and not on curiosity, our informer who is already under suspicion is going to get castrated and only then will his throat be slashed. His life will depend on a very convincing performance on your part."

The takedown would occur the next day, and I struggled to come up with a plausible random reason for my slop inspection. To my benefit was my reputation for doing the unexpected. The ruse came to me like an epiphany. I would use Emmanuel, our main gate Negrito whom we employed out of our own pocket for odd jobs around the gate. I knew that Emmanuel had a family and a homestead with a half dozen pigs.

When the slop truck showed up, I just happened to be there making my rounds. Aroused by the smell coming from the barrels, I called to Emmanuel to bring three empty barrels from behind the office and enjoined him to pour off some of the slop for the consumption of his own pigs at home. He beamed a smile from ear to ear in stark contrast to the NCOIC who turned white as a sheet. The NCOIC stammered that the slop was paid for and would constitute theft. I overruled him, telling him it was a one-time event and wouldn't make much difference and that we owed Emmanuel a favor. After positioning the empty barrels alongside the truck bed, Emmanuel began to pour off the slop. Plop, plop, plop, followed by some very big plops accompanied by some loud gongs. I exclaimed, "Jumping Jesus, talk about lumps in the mashed potatoes." By this time, the NCOIC was sitting down and looked as though he was having heart failure. A close inspection revealed what looked like motors and generators wrapped in plastic, coated with cosmoline.

It was at this point that the driver, part of the gang, gunned the engine, toppling the barrels and Emmanuel over the side. I raised my sidearm, cocked the barrel, and fired five shots straight up into the air, it not being judicious to fire into the town.

Looking down, I saw that Emmanuel had been mortally injured, one of the barrels inflicting a grievous wound to the head. He died shortly after admittance to the hospital. The truck and its occupants were apprehended in the town of Olongapo. In less than an hour, the NCOIC turned in his weapon and confessed.

Using the carryall, accompanied by the corporal of the guard and a Philippine constable, we drove out to Emmanuel's homestead. His wife, holding an infant, with a three-year-old boy clasping her thigh, emerged from the dwelling. I held her close to me and cradled her head against my chest. The infant looked up at me as if to ask, "Who is this competitor for my mother's attention?"

I told her, and she shrieked. She must accompany me to identify the body, and because there was no one to watch over the children, they accompanied us.

She insisted on having the children with her. The sheet was pulled back. She burst into tears, and the infant followed. The boy reached up with a small hand and clutched his father's hand and soon joined his mother and tiny sister in a pitiful wail. I had never felt so low in all my life.

The marine barracks took up a collection that paid for a casket, a headstone, and a burial plot. Bowing to a great deal of pressure from Colonel Mosely, Mr. Young of ONI had a trust fund discreetly set up for the widow, dipping into funds intended to pay off informants. At the burial, we provided a volunteer honor guard of six marines who fired a twenty-one-gun salute. Viewing this, clustered around the grave, was the entire tribe numbering some 250 individuals.

I have always felt responsible, to a great extent, for Emmanuel's demise. It was like so many decisions that we make, fraught with irreversible consequences. I have never forgotten it but have learned to live with it.

HER COUSIN PADDY

It was 1964. The Cold War raged unabated. I was a US Marine sergeant stationed at the US embassy in London, England, as a security guard. A liaison with a tall Irish beauty ignited spontaneously. She worked as a telephonist in the embassy, combining a maximum of temptation with a maximum of opportunity. She was from Londonderry in Northern Ireland, twenty-six years of age (four years older than I), and was capable of cracking a walnut between her buttocks if found lodging there.

Her name was Molly Hoolihan, and I could always induce an erection simply by saying her name over and over. She lived in an apartment with a roommate, Moina, aged thirty-two, a receptionist in a legal office, and her cousin Paddy, a temporary boarder. Molly had pledged to her elderly aunt to look after Paddy. It was no mean task. Paddy who frequently stayed over was sixty years of age, habitually drunk, chronically unemployed, and lived on a diet of fish and chips. He was always with a beer can in hand—and as a consequence, his right bicep was much larger than his left—and always ready with an excuse. Molly said it was like trying to get work out of an oyster. Paddy's idea of a sporting event was to go down to the tracks and spit over the top of boxcars. The best that could be said was that Paddy was a loose peashooter.

But he was not without humor. Passing gas presented an opportunity he could not resist. Feigning arthritic problems in his lower arm, he would ask a bystander to pull his finger, synchronizing the tug with an audible breeze from his alimentary canal and pontificating that the satisfaction inherent in this act had inspired many to go on to become chiropractors. Still virile at sixty years of age, Moina said he often got out of bed like a three-legged stool and in the kitchen boasted that he knew how to make a salad dressing in his very own bed. Bathing was one of his pet peeves. He claimed there was far too much. It removed the natural oils, and for a bloke who abhorred removing oils, when it came to a cutting remark, there was nothing oily about Paddy.

Regarding Molly and I when it came to dating, we always wound up at her place, where I usually spent the night. It was a small flat consisting of a living room, a large bedroom, a tiny kitchen, and a bathroom. In winter, the sole source of heat was a radiant electric heater resembling a fireplace in the living room opposite the settee. The heater functioned only by dropping shillings into a coin box. With Moina and Paddy ensconced in the bedroom, Molly and I, bereft of all clothing, would make love on the settee, bathed in the warm glow of the heater. We were not unlike two marshmallows in front of a roaring fire. Our interlude was often broken as her roommate, clad only in a bathrobe, passed in her customary trek to the bathroom. We acknowledged her lingering smile of approval and now with renewed dedication continued melding like there was no tomorrow.

Molly could be insatiable and the thought of locking her in the broom closet, so I could sleep, crossed my mind. But eventually, we made our way to her bed. It was now 3:00 a.m., and Molly and I were nestled together like two spoons under three blankets in a frigid bedroom. The phone rang. It was a police sergeant from the local precinct. Paddy had been arrested and was being charged with purse snatching. In reality, he patronized a prostitute and then refused to pay. The purse-snatching charge was considered fair play. We dressed, went to the precinct, paid the fine, negotiated with the prostitute, and took the drunken Paddy back to the apartment.

The next morning, Paddy was all remorse and promised profusely to pay me back. I was angered mainly because of the anguish he was causing Molly. But as it turned out, there was more to Paddy than met the eye. In a daytime raid by Scotland Yard, he was shot to death in a shootout within the apartment. A search revealed three cases of dynamite along with detonators and timing devices hidden in a closet. He held the equivalent rank of colonel in the Irish Republican Army. The loose peashooter was in reality a loose cannon.

THE AMPUTEE

The rain comes down in a steady drizzle, and I am soaked to the bone. Clinging sand beneath my clothing adds to my misery. I am a landscape contractor in Punta Gorda Isles and know that I must finish cutting this lawn. There will be no time tomorrow. I have always used tenacity to overcome all adversity and this is no exception. The tractor engine drones, and I can partially hear it through my sound-attenuating headphones. The swath ahead I view through safety goggles now clouded with water droplets. Beneath my heavy work gloves my hands buzz and ache, and an old back injury begins to intrude on my consciousness.

Gradually the drone begins to convulse, and I know that the ductwork in the grass collector has clogged. Bringing the machine to a stop, the emergency brake is applied, and in a state of partial exhaustion, I lift the bonnet concealing the engine. The clog is now visible at the fan wheel discharge, and I reach into the duct with a hand clad in a heavy work glove. I am electrified by a blinding paroxysm of pain that starts at my hand and works its way up my left arm. I pull back what appears to be a shredded stump, the injury now cloaked in shredded work glove. My mind races, and I realize that I neglected to shut down the fan wheel. From this point on, I resolve not to examine the stump, rationalizing that it is not reality until seen. I look about the neighborhood, and all is still and quiet. No one comes to my aid, and I realize that even though I have lost my hand, it has gone unnoticed. I am truly alone now in my wretchedness. I bind the stump tightly in an oil-stained rag and resolve to pick up after myself. With the tractor now ensconced back on the trailer, I begin the drive to the emergency room, the rag bundle seeping blood now propped against the steering wheel.

The drive to the emergency room seems to take an eternity, and all the life changes that will now take place flash before me. I will lose all my contracts, and my business income will collapse. Being unable to make mortgage payments, I will lose my home. Unable to support my dog, he and I must part, and this alone brings tears to my eyes. My transportation will become nonexistent. I am now reduced to the lowest denominator in life. How tenuous my hold on life has been.

As the hospital parking lot looms up, I break my reverie. I lock up the truck, and I don't know why. I am greeted in the emergency room with an injection of morphine, and the long process of dressing the wound begins. I still will not look at the stump. It is not reality until I see it, but I listen intensely for clues in their comments. Strangely, no one ever comments about the actual loss of the hand, and I begin to hope that I had only my fingers shorn away. Gradually, I become emboldened by a fatalistic curiosity, but a little voice within me says, "Don't look. Don't ask. You'll be sorry. In your ignorance, there is still hope."

It is the radiologist who pierces my defenses. "I want you to see this," he says and produces my hand X-ray. I become ecstatic. There, clearly backlit, are all five digits. He indicates to me the source of the excruciating pain. At the tips of all fingers are hairline cracks. "All your nails are still there, but I'd put off getting a manicure for at least a month," he quips. My elation is on par with having risen from the dead on a Friday afternoon. When I got home, I gave my golden retriever a bear hug, and that night, we sleep soundly side by side, pain and all. I was able to juggle my contracts to achieve a four-day hiatus, and then with the injury bound up tightly, I continued my rounds and my way of life. Though it never caused any permanent physical change, it had a profound and lasting spiritual effect on my life, and I take special delight in the thought that fortune had spared me.

I AM WHO I AM

It was London, England, 1964, and I was a US Marine sergeant serving as a marine security guard at the American embassy. After having served a stint behind the iron curtain at our Moscow embassy, I now felt the exuberance of a child locked in an attic and now released into a candy shop. I was on duty in the wee hours, alone at the front desk in the huge well-marbled lobby, and as I peered out at Grosvenor Square through the massive glass doors, a tall lone figure, well heeled, with a ramrod straight bearing, clean shaven, wearing a well-tailored dark-blue overcoat with a wide-brimmed, dark-gray felt hat, barreled his way through the door. Saddled around one arm were five latest-edition London newspapers. He mounted the interior stairway, passed me with a cursory salute, walked to the elevators, and pushed a button. It was the fourth-floor button, possibly for the ambassador's suite. I briskly came from behind the desk, confronting him with "Sir, I will have to see some identification." To my astonishment, he replied, "I have none," and then to my amazement— as if being astonished once was not enough—he announced that he was George W. Ball, undersecretary of state, and produced five London newspapers, all with Ball's picture on the front page as proof of his identity. As the news photos were a little grainy, I was now in a quandary. Could this be a plot by a foreign intelligence service to gain embassy access or was it really the illustrious Mr. Ball? If I allowed him access and he proved a knave, I would be forever mentioned in the curriculum of the US Marine embassy school as an example of what not to do. On the other hand, if he was our George W. Ball, and I persisted in making a scene, I would forfeit all claim to extraordinary intuition commonly attributed to marine security guards, a trait greatly admired by our foreign service officers.

Now because one dilemma deserved another, I proceeded to ask him if he recalled the way, in 1940, the Soviet NKVD was able to identify Polish officers hiding among the Polish POW ranks. Even though the officers had surreptitiously changed into enlisted garb, they were all after being stripped, culled from the ranks because they had neglected to change their underwear, which was of a much higher quality than that of the enlisted. As a result, thousands of now-identified Polish officers were shot to death in an area called the Katyn Forest near Smolensk at the hands of the Russian NKVD bent on eradicating the Polish leadership. Perchance would Mr. Ball have on any underwear monogrammed with his initials? His eyes rolled back in his head. "No, you got me on that one," he replied.

Having decided that he was most probably George W. Ball, I escorted him to the fourth-floor ambassador's suite whereupon he produced the key. Now convinced, I leaned over and pronounced that from this day forward he will be known as George W. Ball, gave him a crisp salute, and never saw him again. The next day, all five newspapers carried a little blurb on the front page on how George Ball gained access to the US embassy by dint of showing his image on the front page of numerous newspapers. To my great relief, there was no allusion to monogrammed underwear. It was the kind of story the British public loved, and as if to validate his reputation for being gracious, he struck a letter of appreciation for due diligence and tact on my part. This letter played no small part in my being able to go to the head of the s'mores line at the embassy picnic.

In my estimation, it was a miniature contest, a test of wills between his vanity and my powers of intuition. As it turned out, we were both gratified. Although our paths never crossed again, he is remembered by countless others as the twenty-third undersecretary of state for economics and agricultural affairs, serving under presidents Kennedy and Johnson; known to Londoners in 1944–1945 as the director of the Strategic Bombing Survey; and served briefly as the UN ambassador to the United Nations.

But above all else, he will always be known as the lone dissenter in the Kennedy cabinet against an entanglement in Vietnam, telling Kennedy, "Within five years we'll have three hundred thousand men in the paddies and jungles and never find them again." Kennedy told him he was crazy, and of course, Kennedy never lived to see George vindicated. George W. Ball died on May 26, 1994, at eighty-four years of age.

INNOCENTS UPON THE SEA

T here were many children aboard this converted British passenger liner, most between the ages of five and twelve. They were evacuees from a war-torn World War II Britain, zigzagging their way to Canada across an Atlantic Ocean infested with German U-boats, the wolves of the sea. Submarine predation threatened to bring Britain to its knees. Because this was a modern liner capable of speeds in excess of twenty-four knots, three times the speed of a protective convoy and double that of a German U-boat, it would proceed on its own as a lone sprinter and hopefully much the way an antelope outruns a pack of wolves. We maintained radio silence, and every three to six minutes effect a course change of forty-five degrees, thwarting many a German torpedo calculation.

I was a US Army Air Corps major, a fighter pilot to be exact, on loan to the Royal Air Force as a volunteer. I was returning to the United States via Canada on medical leave to succor wounds both physical and mental following an air battle in which flying a Spitfire, I bested three German ME-109s. Having been awarded a Distinguished Flying Cross, in my solitude I now asked myself, "Was it worth it?" During the voyage, I lost myself by entertaining the children on deck, who were held in rapt attention by my mimicked air battles, complete with sound effects. It proved more of a tonic for me than for them. Particularly delightful was a British social worker, Kay Cummins, part of the staff charged with the guardianship of the children. A woman pleasing to the eye, with a personality to match, it was not without reason that I experienced a strong gravitational pull. Because I had become very much attached to Kay on numerous occasions, our love blossomed into a powerful bond, and with it came the realization that my trajectory through life up to this point had been essential to my future happiness. I was feted at the captain's table on numerous occasions and always requested that Kay accompany me.

For the passengers, each day began at 6:00 a.m. with lifeboat drill. Young and old were aroused from a deep slumber to don life preservers in preparation to evacuate the ship. All must be prepared to find their way to an assigned boat station under the worst of lighting conditions. In this manner, we were kept constantly aware of our vulnerability.

It was our third day at sea, the wee hours of the morning, with a stiff breeze blowing the foam from whitecaps. As the ship rose and fell in a heavy swell, I felt two teeth-jarring thuds against the side of the ship. We heaved upward and came down in a resounding crash. A large boiler explosion followed, and the ship began to list heavily in a matter of minutes. The emergency lighting failed in many passageways, and despite the many drills, chaos prevailed. Vomit on stairwells and corridors made for a treacherous and slippery escape. I arrived at the railing only to feel the deck rotate 180 degrees. This immense liner had capsized, trapping hundreds in its bowels. Eventually I was buoyed to the surface by my life preserver and gasped for air. The swells were so high that I glimpsed my surroundings in small snippets. A short distance away, I saw a rubber raft and swam to it. After I clamored aboard my view was improved, and I was at once struck by the absence of survivors. Furiously, I paddled with outstretched hands to escape the ship, which in its death throes, had risen out of the sea stern first and now slid noisily below the surface. Multiple explosions of varying intensity followed as if in final protest to its demise. I escaped its suction and spotted a large orange life raft, and after much frantic paddling, took ownership. Now riding higher, I spotted several bobbing orange life preservers nestled around small heads. They were children and one adult. All were smeared in fuel oil and barely recognizable. In the next hour, I pulled aboard six children, holding each one in turn aloft by the ankles, coughing and sputtering, the sea water drained from their little lungs. The last was an adult female. Recognizing those alabaster thighs anywhere, I knew it was Kay. We looked long and hard but could find no others.

We were most fortunate in that this fourteen-by-fourteen-foot raft was an elaborate refuge for castaways. Its storage compartments contained six gallons of water, quantities of food rations, waterproof blankets, fishing tackle, a flare gun with multiple cartridges, bright-colored water dyes, a sail, a compass, a two-way radio capable of frequency selection, and lest I incur the wrath of the children, must make special mention of the box of chocolate bars. Being a military pilot, experienced in the wiles of radio traffic, I quickly established contact with not only an American Catalina flying amphibian but also a British Sunderland flying boat, both of which were on antisubmarine patrol in mid-Atlantic. In a few hours, we were plucked from the sea to be deposited in Halifax, Nova Scotia.

Within a matter of months, Kay and I were married. It was a fusion born of high adventure and abysmal tragedy. A grafting that was an immense success but like all such unions, it remained to be seen who would be the stock and who the scion.

I'SE GWYNE TO FREEDOM

It was late 1864, and the Civil War between the states had reached a crescendo. I was a captain of Union army engineers, twenty-seven years of age, and responsible for deploying our pontoon bridge to ford obstructing waterways in our line of march. Our army of four corps consisting of sixty thousand infantry, cavalry, horse-drawn artillery, and a minimal number of supply wagons, had penetrated deep into Georgia. We were cut off from our supply line and must ravage the countryside for sustenance. It was our commanding general's intention that we make Georgia howl, and in the process we have acquired a following of black slaves, now newly liberated, who were determined to follow us northward. In reality, they were a hindrance to military maneuver, should sudden combat be required.

Our advance guard, some ten miles to our front, was obstructed by a stream, eighty feet wide and too deep for artillery limbers, caissons, and supply wagons to ford. In response, I ordered eight pontoon wagons to race ahead to the water's edge. Under sporadic Confederate sniper fire, we began to assemble our pontoons. These collapsible canvas rowboats formed connecting flotation devices to which a continuous platform of planks would be attached. These flotation bridges were strong enough to support an artillery limber drawn by an eight-horse team at an interval of twenty feet and could then be dismantled and repacked on their wagons.

The main units of our corps arrived at the water's edge as the bridge was in the final stages of completion. As unit after unit arrived, their accompanying blacks were shunted to one side of the narrow causeway leading to the foot of the bridge. It was at the behest of our corps commander, and an ominous feeling of an impending heartless turn of events began to take hold. Supervising the completion on horseback, an exceptionally beautiful and alluring mulatto woman caught my eye. Her provocative poses indicated a willingness to consummate a liaison. She was my age and was escaping a life as the mistress of a plantation owner. As proof, she proffered two toddlers, who appeared white and reminded me too much of the two I have in Michigan.

Finding her physical appeal compelling, it was with ease that I vowed to take them under my protective custody. I found a den for them in one of my supply wagons and passed her off as my laundress and cook, always accompanied by a wink of the eye that always received a wink in return. Her name was Makimba, a name much befitting her exotic nature.

The corps commander, a slave holder in civilian life but a staunch unionist, had issued orders to have all military units cross the bridge, after which I was to disconnect the pontoons on the Negro side, leaving some six hundred mostly women and children stranded on the narrow causeway bereft of protection or rations. As the pontoons pulled away to the other side, a wail of lamentation rose from the stranded, and the few black males looked back down the narrow causeway for the inevitable approach of the hounding Confederate cavalry.

The wail brought Makimba from her wagon. She was hysterical and confessed her parents were among the stranded. I was now torn between orders that I could not disobey, under threat of court-martial, and my humanity toward my ebony mistress and her like. As the last of our column rounded a bend, now out of sight, I returned to the water's edge with six engineers, who like me, were sickened by this betrayal of helpless women and children. Armed with a half-dozen razor-sharp axes, I selected two cypress trees at the water's edge, and in two-man relays, the axes began to ring out a song of deliverance. In no time at all, two 125-foot-tall cypress trees came crashing down, easily spanning the eighty-foot-wide creek. With the current not being strong enough to dislodge the trees, a mass of humanity began to grapple through the branches. The visage was not unlike a mass of ants clinging to a twig in a flood. They emerged on the far side giddy with rapture. As the last of the Negroes attained the far side, Confederate cavalry raced down the causeway, too late to intercept but bent on the infliction of mayhem. The mass of Negroes had collapsed in various stages of disarray, and the sound of coughing filled the air. I feared many would succumb to gunshot wounds, when at that instant I heard the thunder of hoofbeats on our side. It was my cousin, Lieutenant Horatio Jessup, with a platoon of Yankee dragoons in the role of rear guard. Armed with the new sixteen-shot, lever-action Henry repeating rifle, they put down a withering fusillade, and Confederate horses and riders began to tumble to earth, before beating a hasty retreat back down the causeway.

Makimba and her two toddlers stayed safely tucked away in my supply wagon for the remainder of the journey. Ever grateful for our lovemaking interlude, I saw to it that she and hers were given passage on a steamer in Savannah harbor bound for Washington, DC. There, largely through the efforts of abolitionist groups, they were placed with a Baptist congregation where she eventually married a well-educated black. I know, because at war's end, he wrote me a letter of deep appreciation and regard.

BURY THE HATCHET

It was late 1862 in the American Southwest, and the American Civil War was now raging. From the newly seceded Confederate State of Texas, heading north, you were either in the Confederacy's Territory of Arizona or the Union's Department of New Mexico, depending on where stood your allegiance.

Threatening the Union's Department of New Mexico from his vantage point at Confederate Fort Bliss, near El Paso, Texas, was a newly appointed Confederate commander, Brigadier Henry Hopkins Sibley. A former commander of several Union forts along the upper Rio Grande, he was familiar with the region and now in resigning had promised President Jefferson Davis a campaign in earnest to subdue all Union resistance in the forts along the upper Rio Grande valley. The collapse of this resistance would leave open to eventual Confederate domination, the Colorado and California gold fields whose gold and silver were essential to the Union's financing of the war against the Confederacy. For this undertaking, Davis could offer no arms or ammunition; it would be up to Sibley to recruit volunteers in Texas and to capture enemy stores from the fallen Union forts.

Physically, Sibley was an imposing figure possessing a large, stocky muscular build, of a swarthy complexion, and with a dark-black mustache that hung down below his chin to either side. Though not an artilleryman, he possessed a marked fascination for artillery pieces—the bronze cannon in particular. Because mobility in his force was paramount, his preference was the Model

1841 muzzle loading six pounder, ideally pulled by a minimum of four horses. It weighed 884 pounds, was five feet in length, had a bore diameter of 3.67 inches, and propelled an iron cannonball of like dimensions. It had a range of 1,523 yards, and the cannonball when fired down the length of an advancing enemy column, being round, had a tendency not to embed itself in the ground but to bounce on down the length of the column killing and maiming many with one stone. But aside from its military capabilities, it was the metal from which it was made that Sibley held in awe. Bronze is an alloy, typically 88 percent copper and 12 percent tin. It is harder than forged iron; only steel exceeds it in hardness. It resists even saltwater corrosion and if buried forms only a superficial layer of oxidation preventing further corrosion of underlying metal. Its metal-to-metal friction is low so that an iron ball has less tendency to stick in the barrel. Of all the weaponry at his disposal, the Model 1841s were his most prized. Some said he cherished them as he would his own children.

At his jumping-off point at Fort Bliss, Texas, he left with a brigade consisting of three regiments and what amounted to two batteries of artillery. At Valverde, in Arizona Territory, he defeated Union forces in a pitched battle and at Glorietta Pass defeated them again. But in the process, his wagon supply train was destroyed. Now without supplies, there being none to be had in the area, and without reinforcements in personnel, his fighting force began to wither. He now had no recourse but to retreat, and because his artillery ammunition had dwindled to nothing and its horses were without feed, he decided to bury his bronze cannons, all eight, in a secret location. The decision was made with a heavy heart and in much the same way as you would bury soldiers killed in combat, they were buried side by side in an excavation sixteen feet long, 6 feet wide, and 3.5 feet deep. Before the soil was pushed back in place, he descended into the pit and stroked the nearest cannon. A long silence ensued, and then he left. The retreat continued, until his long column, strung out for some fifty miles, arrived in San Antonio where it disbanded and passed into oblivion.

Years later, after the war, a US Army survey team was sent out to locate the burial site and retrieve the valuable cannons. But following Sibley's official log led nowhere, and the search was abandoned and the cannons were listed as officially lost. So it remained, until one day in 2008, on a church property in Los Lunas, New Mexico, not far from the west bank of the Rio Grande, the church gardeners in attempting to put the finishing touches on the new peace garden by planting a lately arrived small tree were astonished by the obstacles that impeded their shovels. This was a Quaker congregation, one with clergy, and the pastor offered the explanation that perhaps they were garden ornaments. Further test holes showed several more. The New Mexico Bureau of Antiquities descended on the site, and the Quaker garden created to commemorate peace and tranquility betokened anything but.

THE COMMODITY EXCHANGE

It was the siege of Vicksburg, 1863, and I was a Union soldier. As a sergeant in the Fifty-Eighth Indiana Infantry Regiment, under the overall command of General Ulysses Simpson Grant, I was not, what the South had described as, a pasty-faced mechanic. On average, we were taller, leaner, and more adept at horsemanship than our eastern counterpart and every bit the equal of the southern soldier, bred in an agrarian environment.

On this day of stalemate, we continued to subsist on hardtack, bacon, and coffee and in situations where fires could not be lit, must content ourselves with the chewing of a mouthful of coffee grounds. This army was not issued shovels so that when entrenchment was required, we resorted to the use of frying pans and mess kits. A quick rinse in a nearby stream and the pan was now ready, for of all things, the frying of bacon. To vary this diet, an occasional distribution of mule meat, which we obtained in small strips and hoarded carefully in our haversacks, was made. The strips, roasted on a bayonet over an open fire, presaged the modern-day backyard barbecue.

Barely a hundred yards to the front of my entrenchment was the Confederate earthworks, and directly opposite me was a Johnny Reb, who through a fault not entirely his own, had managed to spark a personal animosity. Over an eighteen-hour period, we took potshots at each other and interspersed these with bawdy, taunting insults. We had each blown the other's cap off and left a short-but-bloody crease in the scalp. We were, in a manner of speaking, obsessed with the other's demise, but this consuming animosity soon gave way to boredom. After a few more desultory shots, I was startled to find myself calling out, "Hey, Johnny Reb, you got any newspapers you wanna exchange?" There was a long pause, and I heard him say, "Yup. You got any coffee? I got tobacco." The thought of a couple of foot-long plugs of tobacco was too much for me to resist, and I declared an informal cease-fire, indicating I would meet him halfway. We each donned our kepis, and with the cease-fire having spread up and down the line, a general parley and item exchange took place midway between the lines.

Newspapers were highly sought after because it was usually the only way to know the significance of what was going on around you, and oftentimes the truth was to be found not in your media but in your antagonist's. As you might expect, tobacco was in short supply among Union troops, but we had an abundance of coffee. With the Confederacy, it was the reverse, and so a lively and much-needed exchange flourished in this zone of suspended hostilities.

The officers on both sides felt these exchanges dampened fighting spirit and were problematic to the resumption of hostilities, and to a great extent it was so. Men inevitably introduced themselves, stated where they were from, and there were even those who shook hands. As the exchange progressed, Yankee pipes began to belch tobacco smoke and Confederate pots began to boil coffee. Men who an hour before were trying to kill and maim one another now began to speak of their loved ones and sweethearts left back home, and in all of this a commonality of their circumstances began to manifest itself. Many men, on both sides, now knew each other by sight, so that the man you were expected to kill now had a face, and when he fell by your hand, the two children you orphaned crossed your mind.

As this exchange came to a close, the farewell refrain "May the best man win" was heard more than once. Two days later, the Fifty-Eighth Indiana Infantry began to mass along with other Union units for a massive assault on the Confederate earthworks. Our bayonets were affixed to our muskets and now glistened up and down the line. A massive barrage of Union artillery pummeled the Confederate earthworks, and on its heels we charged en masse. Men on both sides now bellowed at the top of their lungs. The Confederate cannoneers unloosed canister rounds containing some hundred musket balls per canister, and this hail of lead cut large swaths through our ranks. It was not uncommon to be splattered by the intestines of the man who was once at your side. In the thick of battle, having expended your musket ball, your only recourse was the bayonet, and many were skewered front and back. It was my turn now, and I was pierced through the liver from behind and dropped to my knees, when to my front, the Johnny Reb of my acquaintance, raised his bayonet to strike, but on recognizing me, hesitated, and in that instant, he was bayoneted from behind. We both fell against each other and slowly sank to the ground.

Hours later, we both awakened to a darkened and forsaken battlefield. The agonizing cries of the wounded filled the air. I pulled out my pipe, and he proffered his tobacco pouch. I lit a tiny fire of twigs. He filled his metal canteen cup with water, and I poured in coffee grounds. Over the next hour, we shared both pipe and cup. When we finished, a frigid drizzling rain began to fall, and in its icy grip, we both left this war-torn world for a better one.

I SAW YOU IN THE WINDOW

As I slung a large sea bag over my shoulder, it was with great anticipation that I began to ascend this gangplank. At its upper end was the US naval ship *Barrett* of the Military Sea Transport Service. It was 1961, and I was a US Marine sergeant, one of twenty-five marines being sent to various naval installations in the Philippine Islands.

We were now under way, and half of us succumbed to sea sickness, but its effects were overcome within forty-eight hours, and our voracious appetites returned. We were aged nineteen through twenty-three, and through constant physical training, our bones, sinew, and muscle were now on a biological order not unlike that occupied by titanium in the world of metallurgy. To maintain this level of physical perfection and endurance, we performed four hours of calisthenics each day on the main deck forward of the superstructure, and to ensure that our agony was shared throughout the ship, we bellowed out a loud cadence whose resonance quickly emptied the ship's antenna of all seabirds.

It was the second day of calisthenics, and I was at the front leading the cadence when I noticed a perceptible increase in speed. They were no longer following my pace, and I found myself having to speed up in order to keep up with them. As we finished the session, I was perplexed until I turned around and looked up to see a line of twelve navy nurses crowding the railing up in the superstructure, some still wearing skirts and sporting a lot of leg, or should I say promise. Even though they were officers, and we at best were noncommissioned officers, it was apparent that the distinction had been lost. As the days passed, a regular assemblage of nurses clung to the railing. Soon, marines and nurses, through the brain's ability to pinpoint direction of gaze, began to pair up at a distance, and infiltration became the topic of discussion at the evening mess table.

Being by no means immune to these machinations, I soon locked eyes with a blonde from Iowa. The eye contact flourished, and it was not unlike conjugating at a distance. As the group of marines doing calisthenics began to drift closer to the nurses clustered at the railing, and the line of sight steepened upward, the skirts began to increase, and the slacks began to diminish. Hormones had now conquered the day, and the anticipation of sexual adventure ran high.

Having decided to rendezvous with my Sue from Iowa, I slung a Clark candy bar inscribed with a time and place upward, and as if it was all meant to be, she caught it, unwrapped it, and began to devour it provocatively. I was now convinced that she was no less than my divine destiny. At the designated time of 1:00 a.m., I began to ascend the ladder rungs welded to the superstructure. As I arrived, I realized it was all so worthwhile. She was stunning in the moonlight and conjured up visions of a fertility goddess. I was awed. We embraced like two static electric particles. As she began to pull on one of my ears, I realized that she had a destination in mind. I offered no resistance and was led to an enclosed survival life raft. We gained access through a hatch and flicked on the soft battery-powered light. I found a station on the radio, and soon soft background music pervaded the tiny cabin. We divested each other of clothing in the time it took to husk a cob of corn. Our tongues wandered far and wide, and the porthole steamed up quickly. After what seemed like an eternity of conjugal bliss, the hatch popped open and we said our good-byes. I crawled the first twenty paces dragging my clothing behind me. Halfway down the rungs, I realized I had yet to don my underwear, and I heard a Filipino steward from down below exclaim, "Hey, Joe, what you doing there?" I had previously made his acquaintance so that when I told him I was trying to get a suntan, he smiled.

The only regret I had over my amorous pursuit was having run down the battery in the life raft. Even though after the voyage Sue and I never met again, unlike many other memories in life, this one would last a lifetime.

WITHDRAWAL, PLEASE

It was 1965, September to be exact, and I had recently been honorably discharged from the US Marine Corps. I was single, twenty-three years of age, and encountering patriarchal pressure from my uncle to go into the banking profession. He had considerable clout with the Consumers and Traders Trust Company, a banking house in the western New York area with numerous locations. Because I knew him to be a firm believer in nepotism and a businessman with considerable acumen, I took his advisement under serious consideration. The arrangement involved working during the day as a teller and five nights a week attending the American Institute of Banking's syllabus for advancement to bank representative. Even though the arrangement seemed fair and equitable, I was reluctant to get into a field that had so very little appeal. In time, my initial judgment would prove to be correct in that I found the work to be both tedious and smothering. To make peace in the family and to allay my mother's frantic efforts to get me to accept, I capitulated and soon found myself assigned to a suburban branch bank serving a middle-class clientele. I was introduced to my fellow employees, or should I say internees, by the branch manager, who seemed to take considerable pride in the fact that I had been awarded a letter of commendation by the Department of State for meritorious service during the Cuban Missile Crisis in Moscow, USSR. This met with applause, and from then on, I assumed that it indeed had been pertinent.

It was the age of the miniskirt, and I found that I was constantly bombarded with erotic images and struggled to focus on the mundane subject matter. The most enjoyable aspect of the job was meeting and getting to know women at the teller's window. Cashing their checks and sliding the cash through rarely failed to produce a smile of gratification. It was all so entertaining—the lingering looks, the coy smiles and innuendos, not to mention the double entendres, all providing more-than-enough inspiration. All this and at the end of the day, hopefully, not a penny out of place. It was this aspect of the business, alone, that gave it a breath of fresh air.

One of my favorite personages was a spinster by the name of Angeline Merriweather, a retired school teacher and a very cheerful and talkative lady, who seemed to take a personal interest in me, and I always found myself engaged in an amiable conversation. She now had her six-year-old niece staying with her for a few days. We parted with a smile, and I noticed that she walked with a limp. There was something intangible about her that reminded me of my mother. Little by little, almost imperceptibly, I became concerned with her well-being.

A day later, she appeared at my window requesting a withdrawal of $2,000 from her meager savings account. She insisted on cash, twenty one-hundred-dollar bills in an envelope. Her eyes were red and sunken, her voice was strained, and her hair slightly unkempt. I inquired, "Why cash?" She mentioned an electrical contractor who would accept only that. I told her my assistant manager must authorize the withdrawal. To him, though, I expressed my misgivings about the transaction and thought that she was clearly under duress. He eventually authorized the transaction, and I watched as she limped out the glass doors with envelope in hand. I instinctively closed my window and stood at the plate glass watching as she crossed the parking lot. She was met halfway by a middle-aged man who accompanied her to her car. Another man was behind the wheel, and I could see her six-year-old niece ensconced in the backseat. I sighed and the words, "Oh brother," escaped my lips. I looked over at the assistant manager, who was now busy at his typewriter and dissuaded myself from approaching him a second time. The bank closed in one hour, and I looked up her address and typed out a fictitious receipt for her $2,000 transaction. I would deliver it to her on her doorstep while surveying the situation at close hand. In reality, we were sending in the marines.

I walked up her steps and rang the doorbell. After a lengthy delay, a man opened the door and identified himself as her nephew. He told me she was napping and he would take any messages. No sooner did he speak than I heard an odd disturbance in the background, and she then appeared as what seemed like a ghostly apparition of what had formerly been a cheerful old lady. Her eyes were redder and more sunken. As she faced me, her eyes in unison, kept darting to her left. I managed an unobtrusive wink and proffered the receipt, apologizing for the bank's oversight and absentmindedly gave her a military salute. I excused myself, got back in my car, and drove directly to the police precinct. I told the police sergeant of what could only be foul play. We then conferred with a police captain who told me if what I say was true, a SWAT team was the only recourse. He added that if I was wrong, "I am not only going to see that you lose your job but that you pay for the cost of the entire operation." I told him I would agree, hoping to further spur him on.

After what seemed like an interminable delay, they raided the premises and found Ms. Merriweather tied to a chair and her six-year-old niece locked in a closet. I met her in the street as she and her niece were being loaded into an ambulance. She was ecstatic, tears of deliverance running down her cheeks. I was given a bear hug so tight that I began to think that I now needed rescuing. Her captors were two thugs who had accosted her in a parking lot. Finding out that she lived alone, they realized they could extract money and have a place to roost at the same time. Unless she cooperated, they threatened to harm her six-year-old niece.

My tenure in the banking business lasted an otherwise uneventful six months before I realized that this was not the vocation that I wanted to spend any amount of time in. As I look back on the banking phase of my life, I can think of only one redeeming reason for having been there and that was being in the right place at the right time, enabling me to come to the aid of a very helpless old woman. That was by no means a waste of anybody's time.

THE HOTHOUSE

It was 1956, and I had just turned fourteen years of age. Having an early morning paper route necessitated my getting up at 4:30 a.m., seven days a week. Although a tiring regimen, it did build discipline. My supply point for bundles of the *Buffalo Courier Express* was at Sammy's all-night delicatessen. From there, using a large wagon, I would deliver the newspapers to individual homes and businesses on foot.

One of my subscribers was a house of ill repute located on the edge of a run-down industrial area. The establishment offered a different kind of loving. The placard in the foyer announced, "A safe, sane, consensual, thoughtful controlled expression of adult sexuality, holding the promise of intense intimacy and sharing, using fantasies and role-playing, it will be the cinnamon in your potpourri." It was owned and operated by a woman I knew only as Margo, whose beauty could only be described as captivating. She had brown hypnotic eyes and glossy black shoulder-length hair, was full bosomed, and was always seductively perched on five-inch high heels. It was Margo who always paid the subscription and never failed to give me a generous tip. She was an astute businesswoman who owned and operated the business well despite a heavy drinking habit. Margo always showered a lot of attention my way and never failed to make me feel important.

The interior of the three-story establishment was palatial and was frequented by an upscale, upper-middle-class clientele, who paid substantial fees to be titillated to erotic heights using an assortment of bondage and sadomasochistic paraphernalia. As I delivered her paper one morning, I looked up to see flames belching from a third-floor window. Calling out at the top of my lungs produced no movement. Frustrated, I smashed the glass in the front door, opened the latch on the inside, entered, and began to rouse the occupants. About a dozen prostitutes, sleepy eyed and in various stages of dress, began to evacuate. I noticed that Margo was not among them and sensed that she was still inside. Groping through the smoke to her office, I found her passed out on a couch. I shook her to consciousness and braced her upright to lead her from the premises.

I remember the anguish of the prostitutes as they attempted to salvage the accoutrements of their trade. The scene was chaotic—armfuls of erotic negligees and leather outfits amid bursting bottles of Chanel N° 5; boxes of prophylactics, dildos, gags, masks, and latex outfits all burning furiously, creating toxic fumes.

The largest and most valuable of the items and in some ways the most difficult to replace were the large bondage appliances, most made of polished rosewood with solid-brass restraining points, each fitted with the softest of calfskin manacles. There was the St. Andrew's cross, popular and beloved by many; the Catherine wheel, so called because Catherine the Great was reputed to have had one in her bedroom, where many a guard's officer experienced the wheel of fortune as a carnal delight; heavy wooden bondage chairs and racks that rivaled in intensity the thrills in astronaut training; and whips and paddles of the finest leather and hardwoods. The collection had taken Margo twenty years to accumulate. In all fairness to the attending firemen, it must be admitted that they exhibited an unusual degree of involvement in the salvaging of equipment, and Margo, always with an eye toward public relations, saw to it that they each got a gift certificate. An ample fire insurance policy helped to soothe the financial wounds.

Years later, I would find out that Margo was my biological mother. She had born me out of wedlock. My father was reputed to have been a ship captain, who piloted a Great Lakes ore carrier out of Buffalo. They had had a long-term relationship, and in my best interest, I was given to a childless couple desperate for a baby. Unbeknownst to me, it was Margo who established a trust fund for my college education. When the ship captain died many years later, even though I had never met him, I was named sole beneficiary in his will.

Late at night, when alone, I frequently think back to that smoke-filled room where she lay unconscious, where I was fated to rescue, without knowing, my own mother. It has occurred to me that having had a dominatrix for a mother and a ship captain for a father, my constitution in all probability would not suffer from mediocrity. I have not been disappointed.

PIGEON POST

It was October 1918, and an American infantry battalion, made up of seven understrength rifle companies and two machine-gun companies, totaling some seven hundred men, skirmished its way through the Argonne Forest. It was the Americans' first offensive against the Germans on this World War I battleground. The forest, a tangle of dense growth situated on a plateau in northeastern France, impeded forward movement, but with dogged determination, the Americans pushed forward against light resistance. So deep was their penetration that unbeknownst to their battalion commander, they had outdistanced the French and American units guarding their flanks.

When the Germans became aware of this intrusion into their lines, they strung barbed wire across the American rear, effectively cutting it off from the rest of the American army. Now isolated, bereft of all outside contact via field phone, telegraph, or messengers, save for a portable coop of six homing pigeons maintained by a corporal from the Signal Corps, they were now on their own. The Germans reacting, now brought in reserve infantry units, attacking the Americans on three sides, together with a withering artillery barrage. Two days of relentless pounding reduced their section of forest to matchwood. Food, water, and ammunition ran low. Soldiers descending a steep ravine to fill their canteens were reduced to a bloody pulp by merciless German machine-gun fire.

Finally, the American battalion commander assigned fifty men to break out through the barbed wire to alert the American brigade of their position and to request reinforcements and artillery support. This force was ambushed just beyond the wire and only eighteen survived to regain the American lines. Now the unit's only connection to the outside world were the remaining six homing pigeons. With grave resolve, the signals corporal was summoned into the commander's presence. On a small strip of paper, now rolled into a small tight wad that would have made an executive from the Hallmark greeting card company wince, he had written the map coordinates of his position. It was inserted into a small canister on the pigeon's leg, and the corporal cast the bird upward. Quickly attaining high speed and altitude, and with a keen sense of direction, it winged its way toward its home coop from where it was taken.

At the end of its journey, upon entering its home coop, it should have passed through a wire mesh attached to a bell, alerting signal personnel at that station. The message would then have been read and passed on to higher command via field telephone, telegraph, or if need be, dispatch carrier. However, the bird did not get through, falling victim to the incessant barrage and now lay torn and still on the forest floor. Shrapnel from artillery shells were not the only danger, as the Germans employed hawks to further menace the birds. In every sense, they were soldiers on the wing.

The next day, a second bird was released, again with position coordinates, and then the next day, a third bird with not only their position coordinates but also a request for the bombardment of surrounding enemy positions. Due to an error in the calculations of Fire Direction Control, the requested artillery barrage fell on American positions, and many killed and wounded were sustained. Frantic to lift the barrage, a fourth pigeon was made ready, but before this appeal could be attached to its leg, a close burst caused the bird to take wing, and in the chaos, it was lost.

The corporal now reached for his veteran performer, a blue check hen named Chère Amie, a bird tested time and again in battle. She was awarded the French Croix de Guerre with Palm for delivering twelve important messages during the Battle of Verdun. To distinguish her from other birds, she wore a tiny headdress of red silk threads. Now in all her martial splendor, she was fitted with a plea from the American commander to lift the barrage. The little "Gunga Din with wings" now lofted her way upward and with unerring accuracy wended her way toward her home coop. On arrival, she was surrounded by her winged cohorts. She was quickly removed from the cage and found to have been pierced through the wing by shrapnel. One leg was shattered; the canister with message intact dangled from an exposed tendon. The message was passed on to brigade command, causing the barrage to be lifted, thus preventing further American casualties.

This lost American battalion was eventually relieved by advancing Allied Forces. And the French bird? Never lacking gratitude for the performance of valor, the French awarded Chère Amie additional honors. Her leg was amputated and sutured up. A prosthesis enabled her to hobble about when she wasn't perched on the shoulder of the retired French general who'd adopted her. In later years, she was often seen attending the French theater still resplendent in her red headdress.

THE SATELLITE TV DISH

I t was a time for change. I had had it with my cable company. Their inaccessibility when a problem developed and their predatory business practices had worn my patience to a frazzle. The decision was made to purchase a new thin, high-definition TV and at the same time change Internet access providers. For TV access, I decided on one of the satellite companies, having been impressed by their array of channels. It was with great anticipation that I awaited the satellite technician late one afternoon. The new fifty-inch TV had proved too large for my TV table and was now temporarily supported on a piece of plywood. I would tell the technician the style was "latter-day Depression American." When the installer's truck pulled into the driveway, it was a well-proportioned young female of Amazonian stature who emerged. She was easily six foot one. A blond ponytail threaded through the rear of the baseball cap perched squarely on her head. A halter top supported two beautifully formed orbs that promised to overflow their supports. A narrow waist was punctuated by a navel that was not unlike a hypnotic eye. Two well-formed hips complete with complementary buttocks were encased in shorts with a ragged hem. A large brass button at the top, like a sentinel at the main gate, though easily overcome, provided constriction. Two long legs, which showed no sign of ever ending, continued downward. The skin tone was that of a bronzed goddess, and as if this was not enough, two feet, lovely to behold, whose toenails, painted a luminous pink, were encased in soft leather sandals whose straps were laced halfway up her calves. For me, a card-carrying foot fetishist, the ensemble was overwhelming. I found it hard to speak and could only motion to her, pointing to the TV room.

To my exhilaration, she asked if I would hold the ladder while she installed the dish. Looking upward, at what for me was the manifestation of total seduction, she seemed to sense that I was in her thrall, so that by the time we entered the TV room, she had me transfixed with an amused gaze. As she bent over the set making the final connections, she lowered her head and looked back at me from between her legs. An unusually wide pelvis lent a cinemascopic effect.

Upon completion, she turned around and held me transfixed in her gaze. She leaned backward against the dining room table and pulled the halter top above her breasts, the pair dancing up and down for a brief instant. In a lightning-like movement, she undid the brass button on her shorts and pulled them halfway down her hips. Two insistent hands pushed my head down to her feet, a protocol providing proof of fealty. Respectfully, I undid the sandal straps with my teeth and pulled off both sandals. As my tongue slithered between her toes, she continued to fill out the form on her clipboard only with great difficulty. She paused only long enough to allow her shorts to drop down around her ankles, and with this, I rose to the occasion. My tongue, like that of an anteater, knew no bounds. The form she was filling out became largely illegible, mimicking the effect the salacious has upon literary endeavors. Now spent, I had all the demeanor of a glazed doughnut. With a coy smile of conquest on her face, she pulled her clothing together and planted a deep kiss of approval on my lips.

It was the last time I saw her, and any questions I had thereafter were routed to an overseas technician with an accent so thick you could cut it with a cake knife and a delivery that was not unlike a machine gun. The availability of channels is dazzling, but the electronic age comes with a price. I now have in my purview a half dozen different remotes and spend a disproportionate amount of my time chasing phantom problems that spring up out of nowhere, so that when all is said and done, the installation, for me, will always remain the most endearing part of the process.

COLD WEATHER PHYSICS

The place was Greenland's eastern shore during World War II. I was a physicist turned meteorologist and had been commissioned a captain in the US Army. I was one of a three-man team who had established a small-but-significant weather station here on this bleak Greenland coast. In winter, we were subjected to forty-degree-below-zero temperatures and blizzards that may exceed five days in duration, with wind gusts in excess of sixty miles per hour. We had been landed by the US Navy and had erected a Quonset hut. The meteorological data we collected, using high-altitude balloons equipped with radiosondes, were essential for analysis and forecast of weather fronts originating in the Arctic, which affected all theaters of war.

As such, the Germans had peppered the coast with their own clandestine weather stations, all supplied by U-boat with occasional air drops from large four-engined Focke-Wulf Condors. One such air drop had revealed to me the close proximity of an enemy station, just over a cluster of ridges to our south. To help with the maintenance of the station, we had employed two native women on a live-in basis, and they both contributed greatly to our creature comforts. The one named Leona I was particularly fond of and had become unduly protective of but did not admit to being in love.

On one clear day, with unusually low wind velocity, I launched a small weather balloon equipped with a radiosonde. It ascended to a thousand feet, developed a leak, and came down just beyond the ridges. Uneasy about where it had grounded, I slung a Thompson submachine gun over my shoulder and headed off on the azimuth indicated by my lensatic compass. It was in the direction of the German station, and I moved with all the swiftness and stealth that I could muster. As I came over the last ridge, I could see a lone figure bending over the collapsed balloon, the radiosonde in his hand. Unaware of my approach, he stiffened when he heard the click of the safety latch on my submachine gun and instinctively dropped the sonde, raising both hands into the air. Intuition told me he was not from Brooklyn, and I asked him if he spoke English. He answered affirmatively in so heavy a German accent that I could not contain my smile; he, in turn, smiled back and lowered his hands. He identified himself as a captain in the German Wehrmacht. He was, like me, the commanding officer of his weather station. We fell into a long conversation, one scientist conversing with another. He, like me, had been caught up in a conflict not to his liking, and finding common ground, we began to discuss the difficulties of collecting data in the Arctic. They had only one advantage over us in that their team of four included a medical technician who was capable of minor surgery and administering anesthesia.

As this outpouring of commonality between two frustrated physicists reached its conclusion, and I needed a prisoner like I needed a small hole in my forehead, to his astonishment, I saluted him, took my balloon and sonde in hand, and marched back over the ridge. I told no one and therefore answered to no one. Months passed without further contact, and the event faded from consciousness until my dear Leona began to show the unmistakable signs of an attack of appendicitis. Our area of coast was isolated by a severe weather front, and the US Army Air Corps could not parachute drop a medic. In desperation, I set out over the ridge following that same azimuth. To my immediate front now loomed the German station. I banged on the door. It opened to reveal two technicians who brandished a submachine gun and a Luger. The German captain came to the fore, and I explained the situation. In a remarkable display of trust, he asked no assurances and quickly instructed his medic to prepare for possible surgery. The three of us—the German captain, his medic, and I—set out immediately. We arrived not a moment too soon and in so doing, saved Leona's life.

Afterward, we all sat around a table, and using a cache of Scotch kept for special occasions, we proposed one toast after another. We spoke of the promise technology held for the future of humankind, devoid of all politics. We all agreed that our collaboration would best remain a secret to avoid any possible accusations of indiscretion. And so it has, until now.

THE TOMB BUSINESS

It was Egypt, the year 1866, and I was the nineteen-year-old son of an astute and highly successful Egyptian businessman engaged in the acquirement and sale of Egyptian antiquities. The lore of ancient Egypt was all the rage in Europe, and with that curiosity came great numbers of European tourists by rail and steamship in quest of the many artifacts, taken from tombs, mummy caves, and pits. The bazaars were choked with the genuine and articles of recent manufacture, made to fool even the most discriminating collector.

Egypt was part of the Ottoman Empire and was poorly governed. Even though regulations were in place to protect archaeological sites, they were largely ignored, and tomb robbers and tourists plundered shoulder to shoulder. The large government-subsidized museums of Europe sponsored expeditions and shipped to Europe the more heavy and cumbersome antiquities in return for political favors to the Ottomans. The mummy pits and caves were used for the burial of mummified commoners and typically the mummies, wrapped in coarse linen, had little ornamentation or papyruses. These my father would pulverize, and after passing the remains through a wire sieve, would pack into jars to be sold to the European pharmacological trade as medication for ailments and diseases. My father would always say that what we washed from our hands, the Europeans ingested. The more wealthy ancients were mummified and wrapped in tightly bandaged fine linen. The body within might be adorned with rings, bracelets, armlets, pectoral ornaments, and the ubiquitous scarab—the

Egyptian symbol of eternal life—all of precious metal. Within the folds of the linen could usually be found papyruses, inscribed with hieroglyphs depicting the name of the deceased and any incantations. This tightly bound corpse was encased in a finely painted wooden mummy case made of sycamore. The whole was varnished, giving a soft-but-lustrous sheen. This procedure was the exact process followed within the warehouse of woodworkers my father employed to manufacture counterfeit cases. It was not for nothing he was called the Antonio Stradivari of mummy cases.

A whole culture of tomb robbing developed among modern Egyptians and this was very many more times profitable than farming along the Nile Valley. But along with the occupation came the eternal stench of the mummy, the stale, musty, malodorous smell of desiccated flesh now airborne as a fine dust. Within a minute it would produce a taste in the mouth, but because it was always there, it would fade from the senses and become part of the ambience. The environment was a contrast to the immaculate and well-aired warehouses my father maintained where skimpily clad, well-endowed, former belly dancers, with feather dusters in hand, circulated among wealthy Victorian gentleman buyers. On display were genuine and counterfeit statuettes, stone slabs inscribed with hieroglyphs called stelles, scarabs of precious metal, escutcheons inscribed with the names of the nobility called cartouche, carvings of wood and stone, small obelisks, and stone sarcophagus of red granite, quartzite, or translucent alabaster. Also available were sections of fresco mounted on hardwood backing.

For the ancients, the papyrus sedges growing along the Nile banks provided ample writing material, the strips of pith from each reed being pressed together and allowed to dry. Some papyruses came in rolls more than a hundred feet in length inscribed with hieroglyphs—characters that may be symbolic as well as phonetic to describe a single word, these attracting a buyer of a higher intellectual bent. It was in this milieu that I took Naomi, one of our feather dusters, a girl I held dear to my heart, on an excursion to the Valley of the Kings to explore the tombs of the pharaohs long since discovered and picked over. My father had always admonished that it was his belief that these great masses of pyramidal stone still contained hidden chambers and passageways yet to be discovered. Indeed, in evidence were jagged apertures where early tomb robbers had punched through false walls to gain access to hidden wealth. It was with this vision in mind that

I lovingly patted Naomi's posterior for good luck. The expression on her face indicated that luck would be in abundance, and so we passed through our first entryway. I carried a small pick ax, a heavy pry bar, and a fifty-foot length of palm fiber rope; she brought two candle lanterns, water, flat bread, goat cheese, and a stalk of dates for the sweet tooth. The passageway was strewn with stone chippings and shards of wooden mummy cases. Human skulls, foot and hand bones littered the floor, no doubt the servants of the noble personage. These unfortunates were buried alive. Farther down the sloping floor, we came to a drainage pit. It is twenty-five feet deep but still straddled by timbers placed there by early plunderers. The logs were still sound, and we passed safely across and entered a large chamber strewn with debris. There was a small keg to one side, and lifting the lid and making an assumption peculiar only to youth, I pronounced it to be mummy dust. We left a lantern atop the keg and moved on to the next chamber. Within a minute, a tremendous blast reverberated from the chamber we had just left—proof positive that the keg contained gunpowder. In our chamber, we were both alive, temporarily deaf, and bleeding from the nose and ears. When the dust had settled, with our one remaining lantern, we made our way back to the blast chamber. The wall at the point of the blast now had a jagged hole through a thickness of thirty inches. It was anything but a false wall. The climb through the aperture revealed a burial chamber in pristine condition. Varnished mummy cases of the nobility stood along the walls, and in the center of the chamber, sunk into the floor, was a polished pink quartzite sarcophagus in which we would later find out contained no less than a queen. On her person was found pectoral ornaments, rings, bracelets, armlets, anklets, a massive scarab in her hair, and a necklace of large emeralds, totaling more than five pounds of gold. She came complete with an alabaster jar containing her embalmed intestines, ensuring that in the next world she would be ready to resume her obligations. In the sarcophagus with her was a seventy-five-foot-long scroll of papyrus listing all her particulars.

Because my father had all the machinery in place to absorb this newly discovered wealth, he was immensely pleased, so that at the tender age of nineteen, I received an increase in my allowance. The reward was something of a letdown, and it was only the great distraction and solace in Naomi's charms that eased my wounded pride.

THE STOPOVER

It was July 1942, North Africa, Libya to be exact, and an officer of the German Wehrmacht piloted an observation plane over searing desert sands some fifteen miles west of Bir Hachiem, an outcropping of rock, now heavily fortified by the British Eighth Army. The aircraft, a Fiesler Storch, was light, single engine, and used for observation, liaison, and evacuation. It cruised at one hundred miles per hour, could take off in 210 feet, could land in sixty feet, and had a range 631 miles so that checking out the keys to the Storch had become the high point of this German officer's day. But on this occasion, far from base, he was confronted with a sputtering engine. Knowing he must set down, he transmitted his estimated position to German headquarters using a low-level code. The British intercepted the message and had no difficulty in its deciphering. As he glided down, he began to discern what appeared to be a small oasis with a grove of date palms and a few buildings. His landing was uneventful and the forward impetus of the plane carried it within the shelter of the date palms. He quickly enveloped the craft in dead palm fronds and detritus matter to keep it from prying British eyes. On foot, he cautiously approached what appeared to be the home. Passing a few deserted buildings, he was unaware of the beautiful pair of eyes that had been watching his entire descent. The owner of these eyes now emerged from the house, a very attractive middle-aged woman—their ages were not far removed. In her hand, she clutched a revolver. Strangely, he took no notice of her gun, as though from such beauty could come no harm, and kept his Luger in his holster. She was French by origin, and because he understood French, they soon conversed in that language. She found him to be attractive, of a solid wholesomeness and integrity, and soon found that she was falling under his spell. She was intrigued by the Knight's Cross, an appendage to the Iron Cross, that hung from his neck. Without noticing, her firearm now hung down loosely at her side.

She beckoned' him into the house, and he noticed her face taking on a deep sadness. She pointed to a large room, and on entering, he saw the body of her husband, now laid out in mourning on the dining table, the victim of a heart attack the day before. So distraught had she now become that she fell into his arms without thinking. As she sobbed, he embraced her. At that point, he too forgot himself and kissed her deeply on the lips. At the moment of realization, they both parted in mild embarrassment. With eyes riveted upon each other, he spoke words of condolence, and as if by magnetic attraction, they again found a deep satisfaction in each other's arms. She threw her head back, and he found her neck irresistible. Coming to his senses, the pragmatic German officer now manifested himself. He told her that she must get him buried now, because the heat produced rapid decomposition. He dug a deep grave nearby, going to a depth of nearly six feet. A Christian prayer was intoned, a cross was planted, and they reentered the house and showered together, the water provided by a large well and gravity from an overhead water tank. With a Teutonic thorough-ness, he dried her with a towel, paying careful attention to every little nook and cranny, and she him. During the next hour, their love knew no bounds, and then he sat bolt upright, the German officer returning. He told her that she could not stay here alone, that both the British and the Germans were now looking for him. She told him that she had a father and sister in Tripoli, which was under German occupation. He told her he thought he could arrange her transportation to that city.

No sooner had they dressed than a convoy of British armored cars sur-rounded the compound. She hid him and his paraphernalia in a secret closet between walls and to British queries, denied seeing anyone. Through an over-sight, that corner of the grove containing the Storch was omitted from the search, and tire tracks were obliterated by the wind. The British left, but within an hour, they heard the martial strains of his favorite German marching song blaring from loudspeakers. He looked at her, shook his head, and laughed. "They are my Africaners," he explained, and indeed they were: two tiger tanks, three armored cars, a platoon of Panzer Grenadiers, and a flatbed trailer to retrieve the Storch. He completed his military attire, clicked his heels, and to the strains of the German equivalent of the "Colonel Bogey March" blaring from loud-speakers, opened the door. He found his adjutant Colonel Schmundt standing there to whom he asked, "What took you so long, Schmundt?" Schmundt, smiling ear to ear, replied with the German equivalent of "Better late than never."

The drone of incoming engines now took center stage. Two British Blenheim fighter bombers began their attack run. A German 88 mm high-velocity, flat-trajectory antiaircraft gun was unhitched and manned by three highly skilled gunners. Both Blenheims were set on fire in short order and crashed into the desert. In a loud voice, Schmundt addressed him as Herr Field Marshal Rommel. She, on hearing, this was indignant and pulled up her décolletage. "A field mar-shal?" she protested. "Why didn't you tell me? I would have brought out my best china." With a lame smile on his face, he replied that he wanted to surprise her. "I should say, you'll be able to arrange my transportation."

In time, her frown was transformed into a smile of wonderment, and because he had long ago told her he was married to a Lucy and had a teenage son, Manfred, in Wiener Neustadt, Austria, the ultimate outcome was no sur-prise. In the end, the ultimate frustration was that her sister was never going to believe her.

THE SERENDIPITY

I was twenty-three years of age and had just been honorably discharged from the US Marine Corps. On my way back to my hometown by bus, I had the good fortune to sit next to a very attractive young lady. Her name was Laurie, and she was on her way to manage the household of her near-invalid grandmother. Our attraction for each other was instantaneous. In dire need of assistance with her task, she thought that I was the answer to her prayer, but in reality, she was also the answer to mine. Caught up in this powerful magnetic field, I volunteered my services, room and board being my only compensation, so to speak.

The residence was a large house on a hill in Ithaca, New York. We found the house in disarray and immediately begin to clean and eliminate the clutter. Our attraction for each other grew as we worked closely together by day and in close proximity by night. The grandmother was a woman of distinguished charm and bearing with a distinct resemblance to Laurie. She was gracious and much appreciated my help in her hour of need. It was apparent that she approved of our match and seemed to encourage our intimacy. She was eighty-seven years of age, and her mobility was greatly reduced, though she was still possessed of an agile mind.

The house, mounted high on a hill, was a large Victorian clapboard, not without considerable charm. The upper floors were accessed by three separate stairwells, though these floors were seldom used. Laurie and I inhabited separate bedrooms on the second floor for the sake of appearances. Although most nights were spent in amorous delight, there were many sounds that I could not account for, and we were then left in wide-eyed apprehension.

On one night, at 2:30 a.m., we were awakened by the sound of the television on the first floor, now at full volume. I rose, threw on the lights, and descended the stairs. The grandmother was at her bedroom door and judging by the bewildering look on her face, I knew she was not the cause. I turned off the television, scoured that area of the house but found nothing, returned to my bed, and lay awake for an hour.

On another night, at about 3:00 a.m., as Laurie and I lay nestled together like two spoons in a silverware drawer, I was awakened by a vase as it shattered upon impacting the floor. I bolted upright as did Laurie. In the dim moonlit room, I scanned the dark shadowy world before flicking on the bedside lamp. My eyes were drawn to the shards arrayed on the hardwood floor at the base of a knickknack table. With the absence of wind or vibration, I could not conceive of a plausible reason for its demise and determined there had been someone in the room. And because we had the door bolted from our side, the little hairs on the back of my neck began to stand on end. But with Laurie initiating another round of recreational activities, the sensation was confused. I traveled around the world and upon returning, whispered in her ear that she was to leave the shards. "Don't walk in that area of the room," I admonished.

In the morning, on all fours, I lowered my head close to the floor and with the rays of the sun glinting off dust particles, discerned a distinct pattern of footprints. They led to a mahogany panel, tall enough to accommodate the stature of a man. I armed myself with a twelve-inch bowie knife and began to probe the panel for leverage to gain access. A small piece of trim swiveled aside, revealing a latch. Although Laurie was outside in the yard, curiosity overwhelming, I decided to enter on my own and unbuckled the strap on my scabbard. With a flashlight in one hand, I found myself on a stairwell. Two rats in quick succession scurried past. My attention focused on a path of footprints in the dust. They led down to the first floor. As I moved along, I saw light streaming from a peephole in the wall. I put my eye to the hole and saw Laurie's double bed, the scene of so many carnal delights. We had provided sexual gratification for an unseen individual. I had been the star in many a tawdry peep show. Chilled to the bone, I moved on in dreaded anticipation. Arriving at the first-floor landing where the footprints terminated at a tall panel, I discovered the latch and ever so slowly swung the panel. Now slightly cracked, I determine it was the grandmother's bedroom. In slow motion, I continued the swing and the grandmother's double bed came into the field of view. I was astounded. On it clothed only in black net stockings and her wig was the "grandmother." With a leering smile on her face, she clutched what was clearly a large penis between her legs. She maintained a powerful rhythmic up-and-down stroke not unlike the piston in a reciprocating engine. I lingered long enough to convince myself I was not hallucinating and closed the panel securely.

I conferred with Laurie out in the yard. She was shocked and speechless. She must obtain a court order to have this person physically examined and his true identity established to determine what had happened to her real grandmother. Being convinced of my sanity and in conjunction with my sworn testimony, she obtained that court order. After being chased around the bedroom and being subdued by two matrons, the hen was pronounced a rooster. In a long drawn-out confession, he admitted to being a female impersonator who murdered the real grandmother and took possession of her home, wealth, and identity. He had welcomed Laurie's letter offering assistance as an opportunity for an erotic adventure.

Laurie and I eventually married and settled into her newly inherited house. She always considered our confluence as serendipitous, having saved her from a ghastly fate. And wouldn't you know it? Our first remodeling project was filling in the peepholes.

HOME SWEET HOME

I had recently married and was in the process of purchasing our first home. It was a bargain. The price had been greatly reduced because of a past history involving infestations of rats and roaches. I would learn later that the list also included garter snakes and blackflies. My wife was worried, and I assured her a thorough treatment by a pesticide applicator would put an end to the problem. The house was sealed off, fumigated, and then aired out for several days. To further assure my wife, I followed it up with a Russian Orthodox house blessing conducted by Father James, whom I had gone to high school with. He was now the pastor of her family's Russian Orthodox church.

Tonight, the house was to be blessed, following which we would sleep in for the first time. Father James was assisted by an altar boy. A brush was dipped into a bucket of holy water and slung at the walls and ceiling. The altar boy carried an incense burner. The priest chanted as he moveds from room to room. The incense began to accumulate, and it was not unlike fumigation in its own right. At last, the ritual was completed, and the priest assured us that all would be well, his function was now analogous to that of a pesticide applicator. It was eleven o'clock at night, we bolted the doors to the outside world and retired to the master bedroom to shower in the adjoining bathroom. There was an extraordinary beauty about Tania as she emerged naked from the shower. Her long glossy black hair hung down almost to her waist. It was the way she dried every little nook and cranny; the way she bent over to dry her toes proffering a beautifully proportioned fanny that would be the envy of a cherub; and the way she dried her hair with one hypnotic eye staring through the folds of her towel. My arms now enveloped her with all the intent of a forklift. She became limp and trance-like, and I soon became her sole support. I asked, "What's it going to be tonight?" And she answered in a husky voice, "Attila the Hun." "That guy," I retorted, "was just here last night." Her face blossomed into a lascivious smile, and I allowed my natural inclinations free rein. But in all fairness, Attila the Hun would have taken notes had he been there. What seemed like ten minutes was in actuality one hour of unbridled passion. We were now spent, limp, and drained of all tension and drifted off into a deep sleep.

In the wee hours of the morning, I felt something slithering over my wrist and yet again a slithering across my inner thigh. The sensation was so unlike Tania. Simultaneously, scores of blackflies began biting. I heard a muffled scream and instinctively, I groped for the light. The room became lit, revealing a floor crawling with garter snakes, each about eighteen inches in length. Tania shrieked and sprang from the mattress. In one bound, she leaped onto my shoulders. We were both naked, and I was standing at the side of the bed. She lost her grip, and her body slipped upside down, her thighs clasping the sides of my neck. I peered out from between her legs to see myriad numbers of cockroaches competing with the garter snakes for floor space. I was bitten on the foot and looked down to see a dozen rats that had just scurried from beneath the bed. In an instant, the house lost power, and with no moon, we were plunged into darkness. Tania, perched as she was around my neck, was traveling first class by comparison, as each step I took entailed stepping on a snake and being bitten on the foot in quick succession. Tania, with both arms free dragged two blankets from the bed, and I groped my way through a hallway to an outside door. We escaped onto the front lawn and made our way to Mrs. Mulhaney, a widow who lived next door. We phoned Tania's sister, who had her own apartment not far from our location, and we spent the night with her.

The next morning, together with the pesticide applicator and a denizen from the board of health, we inspected the house. The vermin were greatly reduced and had evidently returned to where they'd come from. It was the consensus that there had to be a large subterranean cavern where these things were breeding. Only a ground radar unit could detect its location, and with that as my only resort, I hired an operator. It was a hot, humid morning when he began to scan the ground surrounding the house with a machine the size of a push mower. Having piqued their curiosities, both the pesticide company and the board of health were at the site. About halfway through the scan, he found what he believed was a man-made structure of either concrete, stone, or masonry whose dimensions precluded it from being a septic tank. The roof was five feet below ground and its dimensions formed a rectangle eight foot by twelve foot. The radar contractor brought in a back hoe, and the pesticide contractor lined up a dozen CO_2 fire extinguishers, some large heavy-duty plastic bags, and several leaf rakes.

As the operator got down to the structure and began to gingerly trace its outline, the skin on my neck began to crawl. The ground suddenly came alive with scores of snakes, rats, and roaches fleeing the structure. We sprang into action, spraying the CO_2 and freezing the snakes and roaches in place. Volunteers raked up the immobilized vermin and using work gloves scooped them into plastic bags. The digging had revealed a structure of interlocking massive stones. The roof itself was a simple Roman arch that was now a solid mass due to precipitate from dissolved minerals in the soil. Removal of the entry stone caused a fresh wave of vermin activity. We were awed. This was no root cellar; it was a burial crypt. After the arrival of an archaeologist and a police forensic expert, we learned that it was from the late eighteenth century. There were two adults and one child lying amid what had once been pine coffins. Weeks went by as the site was photographed, surveyed, and cataloged.

But in time, our lovemaking continued in the very same bedroom, with not even so much as a fly swatter as a precaution. Ah, such is the magnitude of enthrallment with the human body—to all distraction.

I CAN SEE EVERYTHING

At twenty-three years of age and having just been honorably discharged from the US Marine Corps, I had to decide how I wanted to make my living. Having attended an engineering preparatory high school in the Buffalo, New York, area, I leaned heavily in that direction, and the New York state employment service, using a government subsidy program for veterans, was able to secure me a drafting position at Haber and Williams consulting engineers.

Initially, it was a most humble position in that it fell to me to purchase the doughnuts for the morning's coffee break, and in no time at all, I could recognize a jelly doughnut from an éclair and a croissant from a Danish. But there were challenges on the drafting board. It was the age of slide rules, the electronic calculator being the stuff of imagination, and in a few years' time, I would accumulate a collection of six of the best quality. My boss, Frank, one of the partners, would describe me as a quick study, and indeed I quickly immersed myself in a world of drafting boards, T squares, plexiglass angles, and a plethora of mechanical drafting pencils. The calculations involved for sizing heating, ventilating, and air-conditioning systems for architectural buildings I mastered in short order. Frank would decide the type of system he wanted on each floor, and I in turn would do the load calculations to size the equipment, pick the actual units out of the manufacturer's catalog, and draw them on the floor plan to actual scale. There were revisions to be made in consultation with our client architects, but eventually a design would solidify.

Making renovations to existing buildings was a more complicated process and always involved on-site inspections with a clipboard, measuring tape, and existing floor plans in hand. Meeting the managerial people who worked in these buildings was a prelude to scaling ladders and sliding into crawl spaces. One morning, I was given a new project involving complicated renovations to an old turn-of-the-century men's club, a very exclusive facility, long a temple of the white, Anglo-Saxon, Protestant establishment. The residents were all well-connected professionals and carried considerable political clout in the area.

At the first on-site inspection, I met with Miss Beverly Hobart, the head manager, an attractive woman in her midforties sporting an inordinate amount of décolletage and wearing a pleated skirt cut high above the knee. She proffered an unusual amount of eye contact, and I assured myself that I had established a good rapport. I had an existing set of floor plans with me, but she insisted on accompanying me, disappeared into her private lavatory, and then quickly emerged. I was interested primarily in the large attic area beneath the roof where most of the heavy ductwork was located. She took me to a ladderway on the top floor, and I was surprised when she preceded me, taking hold of the metal rungs. Following directly behind, I was mesmerized when I looked up her skirt to see a total absence of undergarments. She stopped at the hatchway in the ceiling and knowingly looked back down at me, studying the expression on my face. She seemed gratified by what could only have been my look of awe and wonderment and coyly bent one leg backward at the knee, affording a more panoramic view in more detail, simultaneously lifting the hatch. It gave way, and she disappeared within. I followed her like a piece of lint drawn up by an electrostatic charge. Even though I was holding a clipboard and measuring tape, I was unhinged and began to take her waist measurement. Sensing that I was beyond the point of no return, she hiked up her skirt and in what seemed like well-practiced choreography unhinged my belt and leaned backward against a railing. I assumed dominance and the onset of fusion soon followed. The epilogue was a long, deep kiss.

As she descended back down the ladderway, she said, "Now, then, I think you can carry on for yourself." "Indeed I can," I said. That I was now distracted was an understatement, but I managed to take what measurements I needed. Although I never related the experience to anyone, it was from that point on that I became an ardent supporter of women's liberation.

THE RAGTAG ARMY

It was the early 1950s—1953 to be exact—and a newly installed leftist government of a banana republic struggled with its populist program of land reform. It had wrested power from a small oligarchy that had ownership of most of the land, with its political power closely associated with the United Fruit Company, an American entity, that retained control of the process through bribes and payoffs. It was the largest employer in the country, and relations with them were now prickly. Their ability to select political leaders from the military was now at an end, and in derision they were called "El Pulpo," the octopus, by the people.

Initially, as many as a hundred thousand landless families would be given parcels of land averaging twelve acres. Because it would come from expropriated United Fruit Company property, a hew and cry was raised in Washington, and the CIA, sensitive to communist incursions in the Western Hemisphere, lowered its antlers.

President Eisenhower, then in power, seeing communism as a monolithic threat, felt it had to be combated and authorized the CIA to begin plans for a coup. Because Washington had cut off arms shipments, the leftist government turned to the communist bloc, and when a ship loaded with arms arrived from communist Poland, the CIA was given the final green light. A training camp for several hundred exiles and mercenaries was established in neighboring

Honduras and in south Florida, and a military man was selected as leader. This army would call itself the National Liberation Force.

The coup called Operation Success was launched on June 18, 1954, and for all its training and preparation, it proved to be very ineffectual. But because the CIA had barred the American press from the area, this condition went unreported. Its military leader refused to leave the safety of the border—not an auspicious beginning. Within days, the pathetic effort appeared near collapse, and the CIA, always generous, assigned two more antiquated aircraft to the invasion. The air force of the leftist government was totally unprepared, both physically and psychologically, and could not loft a single plane airborne, so that ineptitude was matched with equal ineptness on the other side.

One CIA pilot, flying low, dropped hand grenades from an open cockpit door, to which teenage boys, on the ground, retaliated by throwing tomatoes. Two hits in quick succession on his windshield prompted the American pilot to sing aloud over his radio the refrain "Devil or angel, I can't get you off my mind." A failure to take things seriously seemed to pervade efforts on both sides.

Another CIA pilot, so caught up in the confusion, neglected to watch his gas gauge and was forced to land on a street in Guatemala City to the irritation of vendors, whose enchilada stands lined the street. It was clear this was not to be a day of business as usual.

The governing leftist radio station was jammed by the CIA, and in its place, a clandestine radio station outside the country began to broadcast a blow-by-blow description of the fighting, one that was an entirely fictional account that bore no resemblance to the actual struggle on the ground. One column of leftist forces, at a critical point in a skirmish, was described as having broken ranks in order to pick wild bananas by the roadside, suggesting the defenders were in no way dedicated.

Two huge columns of the CIA's National Liberation Force were depicted as converging on the capital, a total fabrication, but as a result, in a fit of self-imposed desperation, the leftist president declared a cease-fire and effectively surrendered. It was an almost-bloodless revolution but for one CIA Guatemalan soldier who suffered a fractured skull when he was hit over the head with a wooden oven spatula by the three-hundred-pound lady of the house as he attempted to pilfer a loaf of hot bread. To say the casualty rate was far from ghastly was no exaggeration.

It was a revolution brought to a successful conclusion almost entirely by a fictional account scripted by a radio station. President Eisenhower was duly impressed, not to mention the United Fruit Company, and the operation became a model for several future attempts at the imposition of American-friendly regimes, some successful and some not. Even though the West felt it had scored a victory against monolithic communism, the real loser was not the Eastern bloc but the Guatemalan people as land reform came to a bone-jarring halt and with it all chances at social mobility and economic improvement.

GARDEN OF SWEETS

The Garden of Sweets was a renowned ice-cream parlor on Buffalo's eastside during the 1950s. For a few dollars you could experience the Pig's Trough. It was a wooden serving receptacle fourteen inches long, four inches wide, and four inches deep into which was mounded, side by side, five different flavors of ice cream, and these in turn smothered with five fruit sauces and the whole showered with chopped nuts. The entire contents had to be consumed on the premises, supposedly without the help of friends or relatives. Those who succeeded in this gastrointestinal feat of endurance were awarded a golden medallion, worn around the neck, emblazoned with the words *I'm a Pig*, and it was generally agreed that they were more than entitled to this distinction. People came from all over the city, and there were many professionals who claimed their credentials would not be complete without the medallion. Having met some of them, I had to agree.

I was about fourteen years of age at the time, a male, and in this age of the sex change, I will add that I still am. Though above average in intelligence, I am lame, the result of a car accident as a small boy. Though I ambulate well, it is with a limp. The owner, an astute Swiss American businessman, had stipulated that I would be paid less. Because jobs for the lame were scarce to nonexistent, I acquiesced. If not moving fast enough or performing a task to his satisfaction, I was slapped in the back of the head, frequently in front of Karen, an eighteen-year-old waitress, a lovely girl with long blond hair done up in a bun and deep-blue eyes, the quintessential long-legged beauty. Though she did not know it, I had a crush on her and was often betrayed by my fleeting glances. When being humiliated by the owner, it was not so much my degradation that wounded but her witnessing of it. Because my small income was essential to my grandparents, who were raising me, both my parents having been killed in a car accident, I resigned myself to this indignity.

Karen at first took little issue of my lowly status, but as time passed she began to express concern. She was not without her trials and found herself increasingly fending off his crude sexual advances. For me, it was a mental torture, and I tried when able to thwart his advances by my mere presence. Though I was often slapped and rebuked, I succeeded in frustrating many an attempt.

It was on a Tuesday night shortly after closing time. The old man, who was both the dishwasher and the ice-cream maker, had left, leaving the one large ice-cream mixer still churning. The owner would see to its final completion. The machine had acquired the nickname "The Beast," as an untimely embrace could be your last. Still, he preferred to have the safety guards removed. It was more facilitating that way. He took special pride in the making of ice cream and used only the best ingredients.

Thinking that I had left and that he was now alone with Karen in the kitchen, he lunged at her and in a viselike grip began to ever so carefully unbutton her blouse. Her screams, which seemed to excite him all the more, did not carry beyond the walls. Now naked above the waist, he began to devour her. She struggled as she had never struggled before. Faintly hearing the commotion, I pushed open the swinging doors. He was distracted and reeled around. As he did so, he placed his arm within the bounds of the revolving blades. He was instantly pulled in, and in seconds, his arm, head, and neck were mangled, terminating only when the motor burned out. Karen was shaking uncontrollably. She hugged me, and I was shocked and in seventh heaven all in the same instance.

I telephoned the police and requested an ambulance, though it was apparent that he was dead. After the police investigation, when all was said and done, the district attorney gave Karen a choice. She could file no charges, eliminating a trial with her being dragged through the mud and at the same time magnanimously preserving the owner's reputation. Because it was in the best interests of all concerned, it was legally deemed an industrial accident and left at that. Having been a lifelong ice-cream lover, it had occurred to me that his final demise was not without compensation. You see, the vat did contain butter pecan, his very favorite.

MON CHÉRI POTLUCK

There was a time when I thought that subscribing to a matchmaking service was beneath me, but the more I thought about it, the more convinced I became that it was indeed an intelligent option. Even if I gave them my specifications, and they were met, I could still always back out. It was that all-too-elusive electricity that for me was essential in a sexual liaison.

It was 1980, and I had just divorced. I was supporting two daughters, aged four and ten, who lived with my ex-wife. Because computers were not yet commonplace, the upscale dating services employed skilled sales personnel, who during an in-home interview would quote you a fee for an annual contract. The fee was far from standard and was actually based on what in their estimate you were capable of paying. To the first quote I received, I queried whether this was an annual fee or a ransom for her release. He seemed intent on the amount, and so I informed him that I would not pay that even if she were delivered in a jade crate by a UPS truck. Now in sympathy with me, he reduced the fee by a third, and I, in fear of being sent a pig in a poke if I went any lower, accepted.

The initial selection was made from a photograph, and as you might expect, the selection process could abruptly end here, going no further so that the initial stimuli may be likened to that experienced by someone in a butcher shop looking at various cuts of meat. Having selected a female who was physically enticing, I now hoped she would possess the more substantive personality traits so essential to a long-term relationship and fulfillment.

My first introduction took place in a Thai restaurant. My prospect was a Russian émigré by the name of Maria Propenskaya, a ballerina, who now past her dancing prime, had become a ballet instructor. She had blond hair in a bouffant hairdo, catlike eyes, and a stature, were she an automobile, not unlike a Lamborghini. Having served as a marine guard at the American embassy in Moscow, her accent seemed both alluring and familiar. I was enthralled, and in my most sultry voice, I leaned over and whispered in her ear, "Do you have any diseases?" As luck would have it, she took no offense at this, assuming I was a physician and a complete medical history followed. Dating began in earnest, and the sexual escapades that followed seemed choreographed to the very moment of ejaculation. It was a demanding discipline hitherto unknown to me. For me, the distinction between sex slave and boyfriend began to blur, and as incredible as it may seem, I began to envision an early death from physical exhaustion. Because the relationship suffered from a dearth of spirituality, I broke it off.

But such are the inherent advantages of a dating service that a list of a half dozen prospects awaited my perusal, greatly reducing the stress of separation. Next in line on my sexual odyssey was a femme fatale who traveled through life under the name of Natalie Lambrusco, a captivating creature with a ravenous sexual appetite, marbled with a homicidal streak. I was always careful to hide my kitchen knives and other sharp objects. She, for years, had been married to an abusive air force officer, who, when she wasn't chained to an exercise machine, kept her locked in a closet. With Herculean efforts at patience and tolerance, I was able to exert a calming effect, but the realization that I was getting too old for this kind of effort caused me to disengage gradually, so that the breakup manifested very little pain.

The spirituality in these encounters did not improve, so that my third introduction, to a female instructor at a teenage boy's detention center, was without a doubt the most hard boiled. Had she aspired to be a professional dominatrix, it would have required very little adjustment on her part. And so it went from one introduction to the next so that I couldn't help surmising that there was a fateful flaw in my preferences, a flaw that spurned the proverbial librarian, pure as the driven snow, preferring the dangerous and alluring vixen. But over the years, the problem has resolved itself, and in my old age, I have transferred my emotional attachments to a long line of pedigree German shepherds of the canine variety.

MY DOG CHILD

Having barely recovered from the sudden loss of a beautiful golden retriever, my beloved Flag, I resolved to rescue another dog from our local pound. I arrived there to see only an assortment of pit bulls and soon despaired. As I began to leave, a five-month-old male, of German shepherd mix, caught my eye in a distant cage. He was a new arrival, was still being processed, and was to be put up for adoption tomorrow. Clearly, a German shepherd in appearance, he was half chow, rendering him a long beautiful coat whose two-tone color I could only describe as root beer. He was extraordinarily energetic and playful and being five months of age had an insatiable curiosity. I signed the necessary paper work and picked him up the next day. We spent many hours at the dog park, where he was more often than not the life of the pack—running at breakneck speed, diving into sand holes, landing on his back with all four paws clawing the air, and then racing out with the pack in hot pursuit.

As he matured, he developed a wolflike regal bearing together with large brown eyes and a formidable set of canine teeth that always reminded me of small tusks of ivory. I named him Tony. He was an intensely personal dog, tending to respond to me alone and would always lock eyes with me until I averted my gaze. He obeyed most of my commands and the rest belatedly. But there was a gradual and subtle change that took place in Tony's demeanor as time passed. He was no longer tolerant of people, and other dogs sent him into a rage of barking and snarling. I had to chain him in the garage when repairmen entered the house. Taking him for a walk during the day was always a challenge as any response on the part of passers-by sent him into a fury. By necessity we were alone most of the time. Tony was very responsive to my affections and would allow me all liberties with the exception of muzzling him. Here, there was a distinct danger of losing my hand, posing a problem for the veterinarian attempting to administer injections.

A visit to the veterinarian produced a prescription for canine tranquilizer pills, having just missed the criteria for the tranquilizer gun. His diagnosis was that he felt there was something organic going on, possibly a recessive gene had kicked in producing atavistic traits in what was previously a normal animal. He spoke despondently and suggested euthanasia as a practical option, at which point I looked over at the dog and said, "Tony, let's leave." I thanked the vet but told him I was going to stick it out. He said he had expected as much.

When I got Tony home, I said to him, "Aha, so that's it. You're a wolf in dog's clothing." Tony spoke not a word but nestled up beside me, and in response I crinkled up my nose and told him, "Now I know what little Red Riding Hood felt like." Now that I had his attention, I told him in all earnestness that if I abandoned him, they would in all probability kill him, so that our bond was now much stronger than ever. We are now committed, both man and beast, to for better or worse till death do us part.

GO TO THE HEAD OF THE LINE

In the US Marine Corps, embassy duty had a definite mystique no matter what your occupational specialty, and for most of us, it held an allure far out of proportion to its mission of providing security guards for US embassies worldwide. Being highly coveted and with relatively few positions, the prospect of being accepted for embassy school always seemed an unlikely possibility, so that when an agent of the Office of Naval Intelligence (ONI) asked if I knew what it was, I was both surprised and intrigued. Here at the US naval supply depot, Subic Bay, Philippine Islands, I had on numerous occasions worked with ONI in covert operations as a uniformed marine who just happened to be in the right place at the right time to make an arrest. As a token of their appreciation for past services rendered, I was offered a chance to go to the head of the line, as he put it.

Having decided to accept their offer, I reported to the administration building the next morning. The paper work was already completed. I signed on the dotted lines and was shown into the colonel's office. As my commanding officer, he shook my hand and wished me "God speed." During the day, I packed, and that night, I descended on our Filipino haunt, the Choked Chicken, for a boisterous farewell party. Two days later, I grabbed a flight out of Clark Air Force Base for mainland United States, and after a succession of flight connections arrived at the marine security guard school in Arlington, Virginia, part of that great complex that is the Washington, DC, area.

We were assigned four men to a cubicle and were immediately given a haircut that rivaled the one we received in boot camp, and many as a sign of being fully committed, shaved their heads with an electric razor. It is a twelve-week course packed with subject matter and arduous training. We were each issued a new semiautomatic .45 caliber pistol that would remain in our possession until the end of the tour. One hour of pistol marksmanship was given daily in the indoor range. From there to the gymnasium for judo instruction on floor mats. Classes on bomb-making materials and timing devices soon followed, and we became surprisingly expert in bomb construction. Several hours a week were devoted to the history and rudiments of cryptanalysis, and my love letters to the girls back home began to take on a new dimension. Classes in State Department etiquette ensured that my table manners would never be the same. The entire curriculum seemed orthodox until we began a subject designed to weed out the ranks. The class titled whimsically "The Psychology of Torture and Interrogation" was conducted by six of the largest marines in existence. These, I was convinced, were the descendants of Dominican monks employed in the Inquisition. The class's intended purpose was to familiarize you with the various methods of extracting information and the psychological methods by which your predicament may be mitigated. We were each given an ultra-light breakfast. We were judged on our ability to absorb punishment. Each trial lasted for twenty minutes—no more and no less. If at any time you found that you could not stand it, you had only to call out, "I want out," and indeed you would be mustered from the program, and this decision on your part would not appear in your military service record. These sessions were conducted over a five-day period, and the building in which they were conducted was referred to as the "spa."

First on the agenda was the wet submarine. I was strapped to a chair. A towel was placed over my head and face, pulled back taut, and water was poured from a pitcher onto the towel. I coughed and choked, and in attempting to breathe, drew water into my lungs. On successive days, I was introduced to more torment. Strapped to a table, the bottoms of my bare feet were belted mercilessly and were now so badly swollen that I could not don my boots. I was garroted from behind and strangled until I lost consciousness. I was lowered into a hole in the floor upside down. It was twenty-four inches in diameter and eight foot deep, and I battled claustrophobia. I was hosed down with ice water and locked in a refrigerated compartment and shivered like never before. Sensory deprivation took the form of being strapped down on a table with multiple leather straps across the length of my body. I was blindfolded, my ear canals were plugged, and my hands were enclosed in large mittens to minimize the sensation of touch. I was confined in a dank, hot, humid cell for two days without water with a table laden with a pitcher of ice water in plain sight beyond my reach. And last, I was subjected to two days and nights of sleep deprivation under bright spotlights. They were constantly slapping my face so that it was impossible to doze. Halfway through, I remembered thinking, ""This embassy duty is devoid of any fun at all," and I began to laugh. From that point on, I knew I was going to make it.

The spa reduced our ranks by 30 percent, but those who survived were deemed worthy of graduation and forthwith bused over to Stein & Company, tailors, where we were measured for three tailor-made suits and a complete complementary civilian wardrobe. The marine corps provided two new dress blue ensembles.

It was now graduation day and tension ran high. Some would be assigned to flea-bitten rat holes that must be endured for the next twenty-four months. The old chestnut about the marine who was assigned to Mogadishu, who got drunk, stuck his head into a toilet bowl, and attempted to drown himself by pulling the flush valve made its rounds. But most were simply glad it was over.

The school commandant, in strident tones from the podium, called out the assignments. When I heard my name and Moscow, USSR, intoned in the same breath, I was stunned. Had I known the Cuban Missile Crisis would take place one month after my arrival, I would have been even more stunned. Fortunately, my training at the spa never came in handy.

WE'RE GOING HOME, JOHN

It was early morning as I emerged from the shower room clad only in a towel. It was 1961, and I was a US Marine sergeant serving at the US naval base, Subic Bay, Philippine Islands. I was met by Master Sergeant Gulliver in the hallway, who was not unlike a casting director on a movie set. A man of few words, he was brief and to the point. "We got a hot spot in the northeast quadrant. Take four men, no radios, travel light. This is strictly reconnaissance. You will not engage but gather all information possible. We have reason to believe you will find an encampment of timber thieves. You leave in one hour and twenty minutes." I took it all in and gave him the obligatory nod. I grabbed Corporal John Wilder, and we descended on the captain's office where we hovered over classified maps of the naval reservation.

Corporal Wilder would be my second in command. He was a highly skilled tracker and because he too was a noncommissioned officer, our close friendship was permitted. John was so skilled a tracker that it was widely acknowledged that he was part bloodhound. He and I usually went on liberty together, and it was not uncommon for us to discuss old girlfriends and our current Filipina flames. There was only one area where our interests diverged and that was in the usage of drugs. John imbibed a variety of substances, but to me, it was always a fantasy world devoid of reality and therefore never became one of my pursuits.

There were five of us, and we descended on the property NCO. We were each armed with an M-1 Garand rifle, a Colt .45 caliber handgun, and a twenty-four-inch length of bolo knife whose visage always reminded me of the gladius, the short double-edged Roman sword used for in-fighting, suitable for hacking as well as thrusting.

We were on foot, and using a series of well-worn trails, we approached our jumping-off point and were soon swallowed up by dense vegetation. From here on, sunlight would be a rarity. By early afternoon, it is determined that we were approaching our objective. I halted the patrol, and four of us hunkered down while John continued on alone; it was our best chance to remain undetected. Two hours passed, and John's return was now overdue. His absence was ominous, and I directed the remaining three marines to stay in place while I continued on ahead following in John's wake. In the event I did not return in three hours, they were to return to base, where without doubt, a large marine strike force would be deployed the next day to seek answers and mete out justice, a euphemism for the wrath of the Lord. Upon parting, we each clasped a hand with the forearms coming together, the marine sign for farewell and good luck. Its equivalent was the sign of the cross. I took the safety off my rifle and handgun and unclasped the strap on my long knife. Slowly, I parted the thick foliage, soon finding the faint markings of John's passage. It was anything but quiet, a cacophony of tropical bird shrieks created a steady din. It helped to mask my passage. The heat was unbearable, and sweat ran down my back in torrents. Wet hands made for a precarious grip on weaponry, and the slightest exertion was done with the greatest difficulty.

Suddenly, I froze in place. Not twelve feet to my front lay what could only be a human form prostrate on the jungle floor. I inched closer. It was clothed in marine garb. I call out softly, "John, John." There was no reply. I turned slowly 360 degrees, scouring the foliage for imminent danger. Inching forward, I hovered over what I saw to be John. His eyes were wide open. I blew on an eyeball, but there was no movement. My ear to his chest revealed no beat. There was no pulse at the neck. Tears were now added to the droplets of sweat running down my face. I saw no wounds or blood nor garroting marks about the neck. I could think only of heat stroke having caused his demise. I was jolted out of my reverie by the sound of a steel ax biting into wood. I looked at John and whispered, "You found 'em, John. You found 'em." I crawled another hundred feet to observe their encampment at the edge of a man-made clearing and made mental notes of everything I saw. Satisfied, I crawled back to where John lay.

It is a standing precept that US Marine dead are never to be left behind and whenever possible are to be brought out. I brushed the ants away who have already staked out a claim on his body. Given their voracious foraging abilities, he would be a skeleton in three days. I buried all weaponry and carried only my handgun and long knife. I brushed a tear away from my eye and exclaim, "We're going home, John." I heard nothing from him and assumed we were in agreement. As I draped his 175-pound frame over my shoulder, I staggered and wondered if this was at all possible given the heat, conditions, and the terrain, but he was my closest friend and I could not leave him. I staggered on looking for the tree markings I had left behind. Bracing myself occasionally against trees helped me to cope as I stumbled onward. At one point, I was halted in my tracks by the hissing of a large Philippine cobra directly to my front. I braced myself motionless against a tree, and it slithered off. True to life, John was not bothered in the least. Eventually, I was confused and found myself asking him for advice. But not wanting to interfere, he allowed me to reason it out for myself. Not long after, I sank to the ground under both our weights and concluded that this was the end. I was too weak to even unburden myself. But as I settled into this deathlike stupor, I was suddenly jolted awake by vigorous slaps to the face. It is the marine corps; my three marines left in the rear. After a period of rest, water, and high-energy bars, I was ready to walk out. John, still the center of attention, now rode on a litter fashioned from saplings. Though he spoke not a word, I knew he was glad to be going home.

A week later, a naval autopsy revealed that John had died of an overdose of amphetamine aggravated by heat prostration. Like so many young lions before him, his life was sacrificed to the god of high-energy, high-performance, and superhuman expectations.

THE CHERRY PICKERS

Having received a letter notifying me of my ineligibility for enrollment in a medical insurance plan simply because I had contracted hepatitis A while serving as a marine in the Philippine Islands, I sat down and indignantly wrote the following letter to my insurance agency who was handling the plan. At the time, hepatitis A was a not-so-uncommon disease and was as rampant and contracted in a similar manner as food poisoning. I was laid up in the naval hospital at Cubi Point for one month, bed rest being the only treatment. The illness had occurred some thirty years prior to my present application.

Dear Sirs and to whomever:

It is with amazement and indignation that I received your letter of rejection. At the time of occurrence, I was approximately nineteen years of age, and being a US Marine, I felt a certain amount of indestructibility. On jungle patrols, when pinned down by sniper fire from timber thieves, a gurgling stream of clear water can be irresistible in the stress, heat, and humidity. In my case, it became rife with consequence.

It is with stark contrast that I compare the ramifications in the aftermath with your present attitude. After being released from the hospital, though still a little jaundiced, no one seemed a bit concerned when they sent me to embassy school, more anxious that I be enrolled in that particular class than anything else.

Upon graduation and being assigned to our embassy in Moscow, USSR, just in time for the Cuban Missile Crisis, no one dared ask whether I had ever been afflicted by the disease. After being honorably discharged, I received a Western Union telegram from the Department of State offering me a position as a courier behind the iron curtain—again, my prior affliction being of no consequence whatsoever to these "harebrained fools."

The above letter I then mailed to my insurance agency. A week passed before I was informed by phone that I had been reevaluated and was now accepted, and in what seemed to be nothing less than a wave of patriotic fervor, the phone was handed to four different insurance agents who proceeded to congratulate and thank me for my military service. Later, I learned that the letter had so impressed the head of the agency that he read it aloud at the podium of a regional insurance conference. So much for the power of a ballpoint pen. I miss not my revolver one iota.

THE COLLECTOR

It was a spring day in the city of Moscow. This was Khrushchev's Soviet Union, and the year was 1962. I was a US Marine sergeant serving in the capacity of a security guard at our embassy on Tchaikovsky Ulitsa. It was my day off, and I made ready for a leisurely shopping trip on foot, fortifying myself with a breakfast that would choke a sumo wrestler. Being alone on foot affords a maximum opportunity for mischief on both sides, and each trip became a small adventure.

I breezed through one of two front gates. Its ramparts were bounded by two gargantuan Soviet militiamen, each a superb specimen of anabolic steroids. I paused abreast of one, made a fist, and pummel his shoulder in what was a mock show of affection. He balled up a fist the size of a ham and returned the blow. This act of solidarity among warriors now completed, we exchanged warm verbal "good mornings" as I strode out onto the street. The Tchaikovsky Ulitsa thoroughfare was many things, but quaint it was not, being twelve-lanes wide, six one way and six the other.

I walked half a block and turned my head abruptly, making eye contact with my shadow, sometimes referred to as my alter ego. He was almost always a low-level militiaman on temporary additional duty to the KGB, easily identified as the one who jumped behind the lamppost on making eye contact. They were rotated daily, and it was never the same individual. I cut through the interior of the city. My destination was Red Square. As I walked, I passed through a veritable forest of sturdy, young blond women, whose bosoms were all amply endowed. It was a genetic predisposition, and I marveled at the scale of its recurrence.

An outdoor café loomed up ahead, and I was drawn to a well-sighted empty table. I ordered the equivalent of a submarine sandwich and directed the waitress to wrap one up and deliver it to the man at the lamppost. Upon receiving it, he was at first embarrassed, but after receiving a salute from me, he resigned himself to his good fortune and began to devour it with gusto. When he had finished eating, I continued on and soon arrived at the GUM State Department Store. It faced Red Square, opposite the Kremlin, and was a single building the size of a typical American mall of later years. I gravitated to the counter that stocked a complete inventory of Soviet military uniform paraphernalia. I intended to mount eventually in a glass case backed by green velvet an entire collection of Soviet military insignia—both metal and cloth badges, chevrons, pins, shoulder straps, and various insignia of all branches of the Soviet military. But on this occasion, the usual salesgirls were not in attendance. Instead, I found a very attractive tall, blond woman, who spoke impeccable English with an encyclopedic knowledge of military insignia. She was very engaging and hung on to my every word. Clearly, she was in the employ of the KGB and had a sexual agenda. Not being as dumb as they had hoped, I turned down the invitation to her small apartment for a drink, pleading that I had a tight schedule. I filed this in my memory as a "what-if experience" and left Red Square in a state of arousal. My shadow, none the worse for her rebuff, assumed his position in my train.

The next stop on my way back to the embassy was the Soviet post office, where being an avid collector, I purchased new-issue stamps in blocks of four to be kept in mint condition for future resale, an investment of sorts. I had in my collection stamps commemorating Yuri Gagarin, the first human into space, and Valentina Tereshkova, the first woman. How did I make out with my choice of investments? Not very well at all. Fifty-two years later, military insignia from that era can be had for a small nominal sum per bushel basket, and the stamps have accrued very little in value.

However, there is one thing from that era that has accrued in value with time. It is the memory of that attractive tall blonde at the insignia counter, who, as a measure of her patriotic fervor, was willing to do anything in the service of her country. It's enough to make the toughest stalwart at the American Legion cry.

FOLLOW ME

It was one of those events in life, though momentous, was more worth forgetting than remembering, let alone writing about. But I confess it here in pursuit of honest revelation.

It was 1989, and I was seized by the urge to hunt in dangerous surroundings. Together with my younger brother Gary, my backup, it being suicidal to enter Big Cypress Swamp alone, we obtained the necessary hunting permits. I was armed with a Remington .270 high-powered rifle with scope, a .44 magnum revolver served as a poisonous snake decapitator and emergency backup weapon, and a bowie knife. I was clad in knee-high rubber boots overlaid with hard plastic stovepipe-like snake guards. The guards were fang resistant, but with regard to alligators, the most that could be hoped for was imparting a slight case of indigestion to the alligator in retribution, a small consolation. My head was encased in a soft, floppy wide-brim hat with attached mosquito net. Long-sleeve shirts and canvas leggings completed the ensemble. In my haversack, I carried an extra canteen of water and energy rations. Gary was similarly attired. A lensatic compass was my only means of navigation, my only thread back to civilization, the loss of which could entail a watery, wandering death.

Having been a marine corps jungle patrol leader in the Philippine Islands, navigating with a lensatic compass was not new to me. What was new was the apparition of hundreds of mosquitos alighting on insect-resistant sleeves and pant legs. Our quarry in these hunting excursions was the Florida deer, about the size of a Great Dane, and the wild boar, extremely dangerous, whose sharp tusks enable it to inflict mortal wounds on its tormentors.

To alleviate boredom, we had in our midst the powerful jaws of the alligator and a variety of insidious snake venoms, both neurotoxin and hematoxin. Between these two toxins, we had the unique opportunity to either hemorrhage to death or suffocate. Neither of us ever expressed a preference.

The years passed, and almost without fail, Gary and I trudged through the swamp in pursuit of wild boar especially, of which we did eventually bag two. As a team, we became especially adept at dealing with a variety of dangerous situations, and our confidence level rose accordingly.

It was at this point that I had the brainstorm. "Hey, let's take little Louie along with us next time," I said to Gary. Louie was my nephew, Gary's ten-year-old son. Gary had custody of Louie for one or two days a week as a divorced father. "Think of the opportunity for this kid at show-and-tell in school. What other kid has two jackasses for an uncle and father wandering around in the swamp up to their rear ends in water?" "Probably none," Gary said. "That's what I mean. It would be a very unique experience. He'd remember it for the rest of his life." "Yeah, but it's why he would remember it that I'm worried about," said Gary.

After a lot of pondering, Gary reluctantly consented and told his ex-wife that we were going to take Louie to, of all places, Disneyland. We went through great pains to make sure Louie was well sequestered especially so because he was the perfect bite-size morsel for an alligator snack. Louie was kept blissfully ignorant of this size preference. As a benevolent uncle, I was determined to pass on all my jungle lore, gloating that any future Boy Scout hikes would pale by comparison.

The day arrived, and we slid into that watery world with Louie perched high on my shoulders with his legs wrapped around my neck, resembling a mahout on his elephant. After a while, I began to feel like his elephant because he'd jab his feet into my ribs whenever he wanted to go forward. He was without a doubt thrilled, his eyes as wide as saucers.

Finding a suitable clearing, we began to make a small campsite as part of Louie's training, the highlight of which was the building of a campfire. I took my rifle and sidearm and began to explore in ever-widening circles around the camp to discover any danger before it discovered us. Upon returning, I could hear Gary shouting. He had turned his back on Louie for about a minute, and in the interim, Louie had put an excess of dried plant material on the fire. The wind now kicked up and spread the burning plant material to the surrounding brush. An ever-expanding circle of fire now proved impossible to beat out.

It soon became apparent that we would have to flee for our lives, and I mean run, such was the speed of ignition, the wax in the cabbage palm fronds acting as an accelerant. Scooping up our weapons and with Louie clasped around my neck like a small boa constrictor, we barely kept ahead of the smoke and flames. At one point with the wind gusting, the issue of our survival seemed in doubt.

I struck an azimuth on the compass enabling us to intersect a wide jungle trail. Once on the trail, our speed of egress increased considerably. Overhead, we could see and hear a ranger helicopter whose persistent buzzing indicated his concern for our welfare. We eventually made it to the administration building. Expecting to be crucified, I was surprised when they told me it was not a serious thing, the area having already been scheduled for a controlled burn. They even encouraged us to continue our hunt, but Gary had had enough excitement for a year, and Louie had to be pried from my neck with a spatula.

The next day, Gary's ex-wife phoned. "What's this about a forest fire?" she said. "One of the trash cans in the pavilion caught fire. It's his imagination," Gary said. When it came time for Louie's show-and-tell at school, I told Gary I had just the item and rushed over to present him with a large piece of charcoal. Gary took one long look at the charred remains and said, "That's it in a nutshell," and we both broke out into a deep belly laugh.

LOOK DEEPER

Now, I like to think that my dog Tony was about as smart as they come. Being an alert German shepherd mix, he didn't look stupid by any means, but there was one behavior of his that gave me pause for thought. When he did it, I alternated between fascination and compulsive laughter.

When in the house, on the carpet, with a six-foot leash attached to his collar trailing loosely behind him, and I call him from the other side of the room, he would take one or two small reluctant steps. He would look back at the trailing leash and then at me, attempt one or two more hesitant steps, and then promptly become immobilized. I would break out in laughter and appropriately but gently admonish, "Tony, you dumb son of a bitch, come here." He would look back at the trailing leash and then at me and think to himself, "Has this jerk lost his mind? Doesn't he see the leash? Doesn't he know that signifies restraint? For me to move freely under these circumstances would violate the spirit of intent." Being the dummy that I am, I would continue to laugh. I would remove the leash, and I could almost see a sense of relief on his part, brought on by a release from this moral dilemma.

However, this morality did not apply outdoors as my good friend Peg Stunford found out, especially if Tony spied a female dog. Peg, with leash in hand, described her ground-dragging experience as similar to a derailed caboose being dragged along by a locomotive. Peg's flight path across the sod created a furrow that is still there today and serves as a dog-made birdbath for the neighborhood chirpers.

I conclude that Tony can wax philosophically when it suits him and denude himself of all restraint at an opportune moment, which leads me to further conclude that dogs do imitate their owners.

FOR WHAT ΛILS YΛ

It was another hot, sweltering day at the US naval base at Subic Bay, Philippine Islands. It was 1961, and I was a US Marine sergeant serving in its guard detachment. As I emerged from the shower room, clad only in a towel, I saw two of our houseboys wrestling a large cardboard box into my cubicle. It was a package from my parents back home in Buffalo, New York. I asked the houseboys to stay and opened it in their presence. It was loaded with a cornucopia of taste treats. "Call the other two houseboys here," I told them. There were four of them: Tony, Ramon, Pepe, and Lupo. To Tony, the head houseboy in his thirties, I gave the bottle of Johnny Walker Scotch. My father, with a magic marker, had scrawled on its label, "For what ails ya." In alternating succession, I gave to each of them processed cheeses, jars of olives, artichokes in olive oil, an assortment of canned hams, smoked baby clams, oysters, lobster, kippered herring, bars of halvah, dried figs, dried cherries, several boxes of gourmet cookies, and last chicken liver pâté in brandy sauce. They were flabbergasted and dewy eyed and had no small difficulty getting back out the door. I peered into the empty box and thought to myself, "Bread cast upon the water" and began to dress for evening chow.

Two weeks later, naval intelligence received information concerning illegal timber removal activity from the US naval reservation. The felling and removal of mahogany trees using carabao, a Philippine water buffalo, was perpetrated by timber thieves who in many instances were renegades of the defeated Communist

Huk Rebellion, who met their final defeat after an infusion of advanced military hardware from the United States in 1954. It had been seven years since their defeat, and those who remained would stop at nothing. Now a murderous lot practiced in the use of the punji stake, a booby trap consisting of a sharpened bamboo stake smeared with human excrement, an abundant biological agent, and then implanted point up in the bottom of a hole. The surface of the hole was covered over with detritus matter, and woe to him whose leg collapsed into the hole. The pain as the leg and foot are pierced was excruciating, and massive infection with eventual loss of the leg or death was common. The first soldier of a Western army ever to be skewered by a punji stake was a British Army officer in India fighting the Kachins of northeast Burma in the 1870s. The term *punji* is taken from the Kachin language.

In concert with naval intelligence, a patrol was quickly organized. I drew patrol leader. My second in command was a corporal, and with six privates first class and a Philippine constable, we approached the property NCO. I was issued an M-1 carbine caliber .30 and a .45 caliber Colt M1911 handgun. My carbine had a thirty-round magazine, and marines liked to say, "You can shoot all day with it." The corporal also had a handgun, but his rifle was a 30-06 M-1 Garand semiautomatic; all others also had this rifle. Although it had only an eight-round clip, it was offset by the marines' deadly accurate fire. We had no radio or helicopter support, and as we entered the jungle at the perimeter, we knew that we were truly on our own. Unbeknownst to us at the time, the property NCO had neglected to pack the first-aid kit in the knapsack, and I had neglected to discover it.

After two hours of trekking, part of the way on trails and part slicing our way through dense jungle, we arrived at a clearing where it was apparent that logging was under way. Rifle fire rang out, dirt was kicked up at our feet, and bark splintered overhead. We dived for cover, and I signaled to spread out and now began a slow, arduous advance in a semicrouch. The tension was almost unbearable, and the sweating was not unlike someone having stuck a garden hose down your shirt and left it running. Two separate marine rifle shots rang out, followed in quick succession by two falling bodies crashing through branches and landing with an audible thud on the jungle floor. We were three quarters of the way across the clearing. Having to scan the treetops, I was distracted, and in a split second, my leg was swallowed into a punji hole. The fecal-smeared stake pierced the side of my foot, and the tip continued up, imbedding itself in my calf. I emitted an involuntary yelp, and I cursed myself more for giving away my position than stepping on the stake. The remainder of our foes scattered into the jungle, and three marines come to my assistance. My foot was threaded back up the length of the stake. Much of our precious drinking water was used to cleanse the wound, and we now dug into the knapsack for the first-aid kit. Its absence was devastating. The hydrogen peroxide was my one salvation. Time was now of the essence. The leg was wrapped, and with the use of a crutch, we began our trek to civilization. At the first village, we asked for antiseptic, alcohol, and even whiskey and offered to pay black-market prices. The wound was already showing signs of festering. An old man approached from the group, took a long hard look at the wound, and very reluctantly told us to wait. He disappeared into a dwelling and returned holding an unopened bottle of Johnny Walker Scotch. He handed it to me, and there on the label was magic marked "For what ails ya." I looked at it in disbelief. "Where did you get this?" I asked. He replied that his son worked at the naval base and had given it to him for safe-keeping. A marine gave it to him as a gift. "I am that marine," I replied. His eyes grew as wide as saucers, the coincidence seeming to him to have great import. I remembered being held down as the Scotch was drizzled over the wound and was soon engulfed in blinding, searing pain. Could my fellow marines really be my friends? On arriving at the base perimeter, I was whisked to the hospital by jeep. It was the doctor's opinion that the Scotch greatly retarded the onset of infection, and now with the addition of antibiotics, I would be well on my way to recovery.

Contemplating my plight afterward, I couldn't help but marvel at my ultimate convergence with that bottle of whiskey, deep in the jungle, so far from the liquor store where my father had thought, "This will be good for whatever ails him."

FOLLOW THE LEADER

It was June 25, 1959, and having enlisted for four years in the US Marine Corps, I sensed that I had cast my fate to the wind. For me, a Herculean challenge, both physically and psychologically, now awaited me. The train ride southward through rural and urban America, past clotheslines and back alleys, took me ever closer to the rim of the crucible.

We arrived at Yemassee, South Carolina, in the wee hours of the morning. It was the end of the line but the beginning of a new life. Still in civilian garb, we were accosted by the marine receiving detail, and the reception of Jews, upon exiting boxcars at Buchenwald, became less difficult to imagine. It was clear at this point that we were not considered homo sapiens, and the brutal process of reduction to the lowest common denominator began. It was unrelenting and seemed without mercy. Our bus ride took us past miles of alligator- and snake-infested swamps, and any thoughts of flight were quickly disabused. It was June here at Parris Island, South Carolina, and this marine corps recruit depot was sweltering. Upon exiting the bus, we were herded, still carrying our duffel bags, in a tight formation, so tight that we were tripping on the marine to our front. It was a mile to our barracks, and many unaccustomed to the heat began to collapse and were in turn trampled by following marines. Two ambulances following in our wake picked up the fallen, leaving no trace. But because none of us were bayoneted, it fell far short of the Bataan Death March. Now convinced that we were thoroughly worthless, a gradual process designed to produce a "lean, mean, fighting machine" began.

We received the regulation haircut and were issued our uniforms and combat paraphernalia. The equipment was thrown at you, to be caught in midair. A rifle, specific to you, was issued and received in much the same way as your newborn child. Failure to achieve marksmanship on the rifle range was the equivalent of sexual impotence. A grueling regimen of physical training began each morning within ten minutes of being roused from sleep with a three-mile run and culminated at the mess hall for an unlimited breakfast. Marines must qualify as swimmers, and the ability to retrieve a nine and one half pound M1 Garand rifle from the bottom of a twelve-foot swimming pool was challenged for good measure. In addition, we were well grounded in bayonet tactics and the martial arts so that hand-to-hand fighting would come not as an unknown terror.

All this prowess would find demonstration in the ability to conquer the Confidence Course, a series of obstacles constructed of logs, some of which were four stories high. It was the equivalent of completing your thesis in academia and was the fruition of the entire effort. At a point where we were well along in our training and displayed no small degree of cockiness, we were confronted at two o'clock in the morning by our inebriated chief drill instructor, Master Sergeant Cadwallader. We were placed on full-combat alert and must be ready to move in thirty minutes. Each of us would assemble a giant seventy-two-pound field transport pack in fifteen minutes. Now laden with this pack, a rifle, and a steel helmet, we assembled outside on a moonless night. Sergeant Cadwallader marched us to the edge of the great swamp that bordered our barracks, and we descended into an inky blackness. At first, the water was shallow, and contact with the marine ahead was easily maintained. But as the water grew deeper and the obstacles more difficult, maintaining contact became all but impossible.

And then it began—the spastic splashing, yells and shrieks, coughing, and then an eerie silence. I counted six of these cataclysmic events before the air was filled with a cacophony of confusing commands. Eventually, as we froze in place, the grim reaper ceased his harvest, and now with the aid of lanterns, we slowly made our way back. Six marines at their peak of fighting perfection, drowned that night.

Sergeant Cadwallader was duly court-martialed, but because his road to hell was paved with good intentions, he was demoted to the rank of private and served one year in a military stockade before voluntarily leaving the service—a relatively light sentence befitting a lightheaded noncommissioned officer.

THE SEAT BELT

There was a time when I would ask myself why was it that I kept going to the laundromat. I could easily have afforded my own washer and dryer. Perhaps it was a sense of loneliness, a desire to commune with the rest of humanity, however humble?

Pulling up in front of the laundromat on the night of December 4, 2000, nothing seemed out of the ordinary as I carried the hampers of soiled laundry and a box of laundry powder in from the truck. I was greeted by the typical sight—a young Hispanic housewife with three small children running amok; four Hispanic men, most probably pickers; and a fat elderly woman glued to the television set. The drone of machinery drowned out most conversations. Quarters were the coin of the realm here, and I left lighter than I came.

I was finished, the truck was loaded, the box of laundry powder placed on the floor of the cab, and in a very unlikely reflex action I buckled on my seat belt. Now, I almost never restrain myself with a seat belt, but for some reason unknown to me at the time and to this day, I did.

Pulling out onto Highway 41, I attained cruise speed in the extreme left lane and droned homeward. All was well, when in the next instant an SUV on the other side of Highway 41, traveling in the opposite direction, pulled into a pass-through in the center median and exited across the path of oncoming traffic. I was the oncomer. I had two seconds before impact. In those two seconds, I steeled myself for the thud of my life. In the instant before impact, I was able to reason that I would not apply the brake or attempt to swerve fearing this would precipitate my rollover. I welded both hands to the steering wheel and braced for what I foresaw to be an impact that in all probability I would not survive. My truck T-boned him squarely on his passenger side. I felt the shock of the impact on my seat belt. It traveled from my hands through my arms and into my shoulders. My neck experienced a tremendous lurch, and I sensed my brain sliding forward and impacting at the front of my skull like a mass of Jell-O. I lost consciousness for fifteen seconds. All vision faded away into a gray nothing; my ears sensed only a steady static. Gradually, my consciousness came back. I realized that I was still on the front seat, my hands were still welded to the steering wheel, and I was still alive. My truck had freed itself from the other vehicle and with its front end entirely bashed in was now chugging out of control across three lanes of oncoming traffic. Braking and shutting off the ignition switch had no effect. It came to rest in the grass on the far side of Highway 41. Much of oncoming traffic had veered to a stop to avoid my passage. Fearing flaming death, I attempted to exit the cab but could open the door only slightly. It was jammed. At this point, I realized that everything, including me, was bathed in a whitish cast. It was due to the box of laundry powder exploding on impact. I slid across the seat to the other door and it opened. I tumbled out into the cool night air, and it reassured me that I was indeed alive. I had not a scratch or a trace of blood anywhere, and were it not for the white patina of the laundry powder, it would have been difficult for anyone to believe that I had indeed emerged from the inside of that cab. Because my neck was extremely sore, I was placed in a neck brace by EMS and checked out at the emergency room. The other driver had been drinking and was not hurt but was charged accordingly. After being released from the hospital at about 1:00 a.m., I chose to walk home alone in the cool night air.

I had a lot to contemplate. There was no getting around it. If I hadn't buckled up, I would have gone through the windshield like a torpedo. I would now be dead. But what haunted me was why, in that instance, I had chosen to buckle up, an unlikely occurrence. Was I part of some cosmic script that prevented my exiting life at this point? Was I somehow part of a grand design? Was I then really master of my own fate? It was difficult to imagine that I was that important in the scheme of things to warrant a cosmic rewrite of events. Was there something vital that remained to be done that would require altering this sequence? Perhaps having to put a new roll on the toilet paper dispenser? Surely that couldn't be it.

I have never been able to fathom this scenario, but I do believe that on December 4, 2000, at the age of fifty-eight, I began my second life for reasons forever unknown.

THE SECURITY BLANKET

It was 1864 on a homestead thirty miles east of Denver. The parcel of about 150 acres, only half of which was cultivated, was farmed by a settler, his wife, and four children: a twelve-year-old boy, two daughters aged nine and seven, and a four-year-old boy who was ill and bedridden.

In the gathering dawn, a war party of Cheyenne Indians began to stir amid the trees surrounding the cabin. Shrill war whoops rent the air, and six arrows impaled themselves on the front door in quick succession. The mother opened the door and was mortified. The father pulled her back and slammed the heavy wooden door shut, barring it. The father distributed three Colt Model 1851 six-shot revolvers. He strapped one on, gave one to the twelve-year-old boy who stuffed it into his belt, and the other to his wife who lodged it in her apron pocket. These were augmented by two Springfield 1855 rifled muskets. The rifles were fifty-six inches in length and must be loaded from the muzzle end with black powder and a .58 caliber lead Minnie ball, the whole being rammed down the barrel with a rod. The father, firing through apertures in the walls, handed the expended rifle back to the boy who laboriously reloaded it again. The twelve-year-old, known affectionately as String Bean, mustered all his strength to cope with the nine-pound rifles. The braves, who were forty-eight in number, battered in the front door using a heavy log. The mother, with both nine- and seven-year-old daughters, huddled at the far end of the cabin. As Indians raced through the front door in a torrent, the mother expended the last of six shots from her revolver. In quick succession, they were slashed and clubbed to death. The father and twelve-year-old could only watch helplessly as they themselves were overwhelmed. Both were slashed to death in a knife-wielding frenzy.

Having disposed of the parents and siblings, the savages now turned on the four-year-old boy. The boy, who was ill and now the lone family member among the living, had curled into the prenatal positon. As the brave approached, the boy sprang upward in terror. On his person were to be found no revolver, no long rifle, nor bowie knife. In his little fist he clutched a small blanket and thrust it upward. It was his final defense in an uncaring universe. The brave snatched the blanket from the boy's hand and simultaneously began to bludgeon the boy to death with a tomahawk. A few squeals of terror escaped the boy before, mercifully, death intervened. The brave left the cabin, and as he approached his horse, he looked down to see the small blanket in his left hand. He folded it and tucked it into his saddlebag.

Before the cabin was fired, the bodies were dragged to the well, where they were scalped. The father was skinned from the waist down. The skin would be cured and used as boot leggings. At the edge of the well, the bodies of the husband and wife were trussed tightly together with the rope extended to each of the children's legs. The bundled bodies of husband and wife were then heaved into the well, and the rope dragged all four children down in turn—together in death as they were in life.

It was dawn now. The war party had ridden all night and was approaching the outskirts of their encampment. They were greeted by jubilant children and barking dogs. The brave, his tomahawk now seasoned with a child's dried blood, embraced his wife and his own small boy. Remembering the blanket, he pulled it from his saddlebag as though pulling a rabbit from a hat, and the boy's eyes lit up and grew wide. It was a colorful blanket like none he had ever seen. He was the envy of his playmates, and many came to see and touch. But in a week's time, the boy developed a fever, as did many others.

The day of his bludgeoning, the four-year-old boy had been, in fact, infected and in the early stages of smallpox. Unbeknownst, the blanket was now laced with a contagious, systemic viral disease manifesting itself in erupting pustules. The few who did survive were severely disfigured. It is doubtful if the brave ever made the connection between the blanket and the plague that decimated his entire tribe, but what is certain is that the four-year-old held in his hand something far more lethal than blade or projectile, and in the end, extracted a frightful vengeance on his executioners.

UNDER THE TABLE

It was 1962, and here at the American embassy in Moscow, USSR, I headed the Internal Political Unit. I was a US Foreign Service officer, an FSO, with some twenty years of experience. This was my first iron curtain posting to Moscow, and I was fascinated by its intrigues. With dozens of Soviet cavity resonators long since implanted in the walls, all conversations were considered compromised. The resonators were bombarded by microwaves emanating from outside the embassy and served as acute listening devices. Without microwave activation, they lay dormant and could not be detected. We have had windows and cocktail glasses in their cabinets shattered.

To combat this loss of confidentiality, we had devised a room within a room made entirely of plexiglass. A plexiglass conference table and chairs made up its furnishings, the whole being entirely transparent. Outside the room, a radio receiver was turned up to a loud hiss. This was also the world of the "honey trap," a term used for sexual entrapment, and to this end, the Soviets had stocked the embassy with local female employees whose voluptuousness any nation would be hard pressed to match. We had to accept whomever the foreign ministry sent. As our maids, hairdressers, laundresses, and minor administrative employees, they would report to the KGB once a week and respond to any queries they may have. It was a foregone conclusion, on our part, that they would be key to the implantation of any future listening devices.

In this world, the standard secrecy designation of Top Secret was not enough, and a more-stringent designation of Sensitive Compartmented Information was used. Here, every copy of its distribution was worded differently, so that in the event of its compromise, it could be traced back to an individual. Currently, the head of mission here was the ambassador, and serving beneath him was the counselor, who in military terms would be the executive officer. The various departments were headed and staffed by first, second, and third secretaries, all of whom were FSOs. Occupying an importance all his own was the regional security officer, or RSO, whose sole responsibility was security. The marine security guard detachment, a strong-arm force, served beneath him, and he was often in jest referred to by more-conventional FSOs as Al Capone.

All military intelligence gathering was performed by attachés from the army, navy, and air force with marines serving in supporting roles as required. As head of the Internal Political Unit at this mission, it was taken for granted that I would develop what was referred to as back-channel communications. To that end, I had latched on to an acquaintance by the name of Anatoliy Semenov, who passed himself off as an appointee to the State Committee of Science and Technology. In reality, I knew him to be a colonel in the First Directorate of the KGB and as such he was privy to a wealth of information. We cultivated each other in hotel restaurants, coffee shops, and even on park benches. At first, the information passed was innocuous but clarifying. As time passed, this insider's view began to enhance our acumen in each of our departments. But a transition gradually took place, and the information began to transcend beyond administrative clarification to sensitive confidential information. Over time, we both received promotions and increased status within our spheres of influence as a result of our enlightenment, but there came a point where self-realization took hold. I could only describe it as a cold fist clutching at the heart followed by emptiness. I was due for rotation in a week, and it was at that point that I decided to unburden myself.

In Washington, DC, at a court of inquiry attended by State Department Security and CIA officers, it was determined in the exchange that I had received the more valuable information. It was deemed a case of quid pro quo—something given for something else in return. Having now had this experience, contrary to what you might expect, I was thereafter considered a very experienced and battle-hardened cold warrior.